W9-AOA-283

Once a Scoundrel

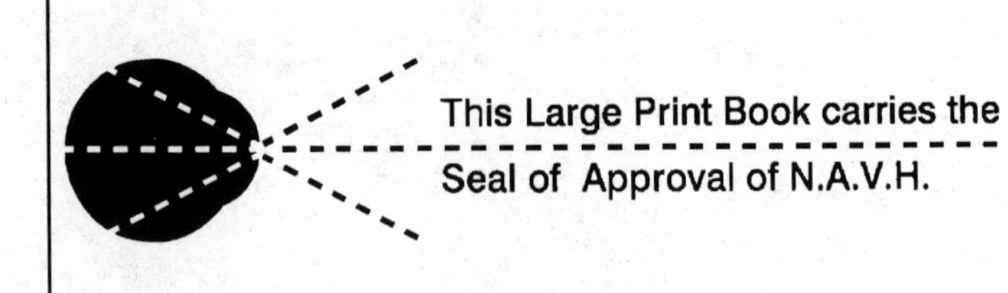
This Large Print Book carries the
Seal of Approval of N.A.V.H.

ROGUES REDEEMED, BOOK 3

Once a Scoundrel

Mary Jo Putney

THORNDIKE PRESS
A part of Gale, a Cengage Company

Farmington Hills, Mich • San Francisco • New York • Waterville, Maine
Meriden, Conn • Mason, Ohio • Chicago

Rogues Redeemed.
Thorndike Press, a part of Gale, a Cengage Company.

Thorndike Press® Large Print Romance.
The text of this Large Print edition is unabridged.
Other aspects of the book may vary from the original edition.
Set in 16 pt. Plantin.

**LIBRARY OF CONGRESS CIP DATA ON FILE.
CATALOGUING IN PUBLICATION FOR THIS BOOK
IS AVAILABLE FROM THE LIBRARY OF CONGRESS**

ISBN-13: 978-1-4328-5770-7 (hardcover)

Published in 2018 by arrangement with Zebra Books, an imprint of Kensington Publishing Corp.

Printed in Mexico
1 2 3 4 5 6 7 22 21 20 19 18

To my ever patient and ever cuddly
Mayhem Consultant:
Hugs to you and the cats!

And to the Real Spook,
who is certainly a Real Cat.

PROLOGUE

Gabriel Hawkins Vance stood in front of the massive door and tried to control his shaking. He'd entered the Royal Navy at the age of twelve and had not been the youngest in his group of midshipmen. In the six years since, he'd faced cannonballs and lethal diseases, helped put down a mutiny, and, at age sixteen, commanded a captured French prize ship that had to be sailed to Portsmouth.

But nothing had terrified him as much as having to face the man on the other side of this door.

Accepting his fate, he took a deep breath and gave a brisk double rap before opening the door and entering his grandfather's study. Admiral Vance was sitting at his desk with a frown, but he rose when he saw his grandson, his frown deepening.

Tall, white-haired, as inflexible as weathered oak, he wasted no time on pleasantries.

"You are a disgrace to your name! Generations of Vances have served and died in the Royal Navy with no stain on our honor. Until *you*!"

Gabriel tried to control his flinch. "I'm sorry to have disappointed you, sir."

"You were doing well. I was proud of you. And then you threw it all away." The old man's face twisted. "It would have been better if you'd died in battle!"

Gabriel thought of the bodies of his fellow sailors after they had been torn into bloody shreds by French cannonballs. That was usually a quick way to die and it would have satisfied the old admiral, but Gabriel couldn't bring himself to wish that he was dead.

"I am sorry to have disobliged you," he said, trying to keep his voice steady. "But you are aware of the circumstances that led to my dismissal."

"Those circumstances, your youth, and your family name saved you from a court martial and being hanged," his grandfather spat out. "Even though you deserved that."

With a sudden, urgent need for honesty, Gabriel said, "I would do the same thing again in those circumstances."

"You unrepentant scoundrel! Get out of my sight!" his grandfather snarled. "Don't come back unless you have restored honor to your name!"

The words were ice in Gabriel's veins. "As you wish, sir," he said stiffly. He gave his grandfather a perfect salute, pivoted on his heel, and marched from the room, knowing he'd never see the old man again. Never . . .

He was heading blindly toward the front door when his grandmother intercepted him. "Oh, my darling boy!" She enveloped him in a warm embrace as if he were a child rather than half a head taller than she was. "It was bad?"

"He doesn't ever want to see me again." Gabriel hugged his grandmother, choking back a shameful urge to cry. "Not unless I've restored honor to my name, which means never, because to him, honor means only the Royal Navy. Now that I've been forced out, that can't happen. Not ever."

"Oh, Gabriel, my dear." She released him, her face sad. "He is only so harsh because he cares so much for you."

Was it caring, or had the admiral looked on him as a vehicle for family tradition rather than as a man in his own right? Gabriel thought he knew the answer. "He won't miss me. He has other grandsons."

"Yes, but you've always been his favorite." Her voice softened. "For what it's worth, I think you did the right thing. I'm proud of you."

The knowledge helped a little. "Thank you." He kissed her soft cheek.

"What will you do now?"

He hesitated because he'd been unable to think beyond the inevitable, brutal confrontation with his grandfather. "I'm not sure. Find a berth on a merchant ship, I suppose."

She studied his face with shrewd eyes. "Would you have chosen the navy as a boy if you'd had a choice?" Her words struck to the heart of his life.

He thought of the sea in all its changing moods. Beauty and terror, exhilaration and endless boredom. "I don't know. Perhaps not," he said honestly. "But it's the only trade I know." And now the sea would provide solace.

"Whatever path you choose, walk it well," she said firmly. "And please! Write me. You can send letters to your Aunt Jane."

"I will," he promised, unable to bear the thought of losing the one person whose love he'd never doubted. "And I'll take a different name so Grandfather won't be further embarrassed by me."

"Use Hawkins," she said with wry humor. "It's your middle name and Jack Hawkins was one of England's great seafaring heroes."

His grandmother had always shared his sense of humor. "I'll do that. From now on, I'm Gabriel Hawkins." He gave her a last hug, then walked out the door into a future he couldn't imagine.

Chapter 1

London
Autumn 1814

Lord and Lady Lawrence were enjoying a pleasant afternoon in the library when the letter arrived. The butler himself delivered it to the earl. Sylvia Lawrence glanced up and saw that the missive was wrapped in stained oilcloth and must have traveled a great distance. "Is that a letter from Rory?" she asked eagerly. "We haven't heard from her in so long! Is she coming home?"

Her husband unwrapped the letter and read it with a deepening frown. Then he swore with the vibrant profanity that only one person ever invoked. "Your daughter, Lady Aurora Octavia Lawrence, has gone and done it this time!"

"She's your daughter, too," Sylvia pointed out as she began to worry. "What's wrong?"

The earl snarled, "The letter is from the British consul in Algiers. Your damned daughter was captured by Barbary pirates and they're demanding an outrageous ransom to return her!"

Sylvia gasped as levity was replaced by horror. "How is that possible? I thought the Barbary pirates had given up their thieving ways after the Americans fought them and forced a treaty."

"The pirates of Barbary are not great believers in treaties," her husband said bitterly. "The consul says she's unhurt, but she's locked in a harem and will be sold into slavery unless she's ransomed." His voice rose. "Fifty thousand pounds! *Fifty thousand pounds!*"

He slapped the letter onto the desk, sending a fine goose quill pen flying. "Well, they can damned well keep her! I'm not paying a ha'penny to get the girl back."

"Geoffrey, you can't possibly mean that!" Sylvia gasped. "Our youngest daughter! Rory was the delight of your life."

"Until she grew up, and she's been nothing but trouble ever since." He scowled at Sylvia. "She won't make a proper marriage and she's spent her inheritance from her great uncle on her travels. She's a clever minx. Let her get out of this scrape on her own. I can't afford her anymore."

"She's our *daughter*!"

"You think I don't know that?" His initial rage was cooling and there was pain in his eyes. "I may be an earl, but I can't afford a sum that large. It took me years to pay off debts left by my father, and you know the amount of the mortgages we've had to take out to establish the rest of those eight children you had."

"You had something to do with all those children," she pointed out dryly. "We've been blessed with eight healthy, charming, intelligent offspring. Which of them would you give up?"

He sighed. "None, but giving them the futures they deserve has exhausted the family resources. There simply isn't the money available to pay such an enormous ransom. Not even for Rory."

Sylvia bit her lip because she knew how difficult it had been to raise the money to establish the older offspring. "But slavery in Barbary, Geoffrey! That's not a scrape — it's disaster! Just think of the horrors she might suffer!"

His mouth tightened. "She's pretty enough to avoid the worst atrocities. She'll probably end up as chief concubine of the dey of Algiers. I'm sorry, Sylvia. Rory has made her bed." His voice broke and his pain showed. "Now she must lie in it with whatever man is willing to pay her price."

The countess cringed. Geoffrey had decided that the ransom was impossible and he wouldn't lift a finger to help Rory. She closed her eyes, shuddering as images of her youngest filled her mind. She loved all her children deeply, but Rory had been such a golden, happy baby. That was why Sylvia had named her Aurora, for the dawn.

Aurora had quickly become Rory as her daughter had grown into laughter and mischief. Yes, she sometimes got into trouble, but that was because of her appetite for life. There was no malice in her.

Sylvia knew her husband. Now that Geoffrey had analyzed the situation and decided there was nothing he could do, he would close the door on Rory and concentrate on problems closer to home that he could solve. He'd bury the fate of his daughter so deeply that he wouldn't feel the pain, except in his nightmares.

But that didn't mean that Sylvia must do the same. She'd heard of a man who was good at dealing with difficult situations. An aristocrat with connections to people in all walks of life. She'd call on him in the morning. Perhaps — pray God! — he knew someone who could bring her daughter home.

The schooner Zephyr
Pool of London, England

As a boy, Gabriel had dreamed of being the bold captain of a sailing ship, a privateer like Drake and his own legendary namesake, Sir Jack Hawkins. Imagination did not include long, boring weeks at sea or weevilly ship biscuits or granite-textured hardtack.

Nor accounting. His was casual because he was owner as well as captain, but some figuring was required to keep the *Zephyr* running properly. Luckily, his last mission to America to rescue a stranded English widow had been very profitable, thanks to the lady's generous family. As a bonus, he'd even avoided being blown up by the Royal Navy warships that had been thundering up and down the Chesapeake Bay.

He was glad to set aside his account book when Landers, his auburn-headed American first mate, rapped on the frame of the open door and entered his cabin. "Morning, Captain. We'll be through with the provisioning by tomorrow or the day after." He handed over a list. "These are the supplies we're waiting for."

Gabriel scanned the list, then nodded. "Even if it takes longer, it's worth waiting for Halford sails. One should never skimp on good sails."

As he handed the list back, Landers asked, "Where will we be heading next?"

"That's an excellent question." Gabriel leaned back in the chair that was secured to the solid oak floor and absently scratched the head of the white and gray ship's cat that was snoozing on his desk. "I'm not sure. With Napoleon in exile and the British and Americans in peace negotiations, there aren't many blockades to run. I'll have to rustle up some regular cargo. Safer but less profitable."

"I'm getting old," Landers said with a sigh, being all of twenty-six years of age. "We've dodged enough cannonballs that safe is sounding good."

"Even without cannonballs, the sea can kill us quickly enough if she chooses," Gabriel said dryly. Being past thirty himself, he'd seen enough danger to agree with his mate, but a man must do something to keep himself busy, and he was well experienced with the sea. "I'm considering the China tea trade."

"The *Zephyr's* speed would be an advantage there, but the voyages are very long." Landers hesitated before continuing. "I wouldn't sign on for that. My father is halfway done building a first-rate coastal trading vessel. It will be ready in the spring.

I've been thinking that it's time to go home to Maryland and find me a wife before all the pretty girls marry someone else."

"I'd miss you," Gabriel said with real regret, "but the China trade isn't a good fit for a man who wants a home and family. It's time you had a ship of your own."

Speaking with the zeal of a happy romantic, Landers asked, "Have you thought about settling down and finding a pretty wife of your own?"

Gabriel's brows arched. "I wouldn't know which side of the Atlantic to settle on, and in my business, I meet very few pretty ladies, so the answer is no."

"If you settle in St. Michaels, I guarantee you'd find no shortage of attractive females interested in furthering your acquaintance," Landers said with a grin.

"A first mate has many important duties on shipboard," Gabriel said acerbically. "Matchmaking isn't one of them."

"I have a very fine cousin named Nell," his mate volunteered. "Pretty as a picture, and can bake a cherry pie that would make angels beg!"

Gabriel gave his best ferocious captain glare. "Go!"

The glare must not have been working because Landers was laughing as he withdrew. When his mate was gone, Gabriel returned to his accounts, but his mind wandered.

He'd seen more than his share of dire times, but in recent years, he'd done rather well. In fact, he had reached the point where he had choices. But what the devil did he want for his future?

Since he had no idea how to answer that question, he was relieved when Landers stuck his head in the door again. "There's a Mr. Kirkland here to see you, and he looks like someone you might want to talk to." Landers vanished again.

Kirkland? Coming to sharp awareness, Gabriel got to his feet. He knew the name, but why on earth . . . ?

The tall, dark-haired man who entered the cabin ducked to avoid hitting his head with the ease of someone accustomed to sailing ships. At first glance, he appeared to be merely a well-tailored gentleman, not a spymaster who worked magic behind the scenes. A second glance revealed rather more. "I assume you're not Mr. Kirkland, but the legendary Lord Kirkland?"

His guest smiled. "If our mutual friend called me legendary, surely it was with sarcasm."

"A bit, perhaps," Gabriel allowed as he

offered his hand. But there had also been respect in that description. "Welcome to the *Zephyr,* Lord Kirkland."

The other man returned a firm handshake. "Kirkland will do. Do you have a few minutes? I have a proposal I'd like to discuss with you."

What could a spymaster want with Gabriel? Intrigued, he said, "I have the time." As he gestured his visitor to a chair, a gray and white streak darted from Gabriel's desk and out the door.

Kirkland blinked. "That was a cat?"

"The ship's cat. He's a very good mouser, but shy. He doesn't like to be noticed so pretend you didn't see him." Gabriel crossed the cabin and closed the door. "Speaking of our mutual friend, have you seen Gordon and the intrepid Callie since their return to London?"

"Yes, and they're flourishing." Kirkland settled in the other chair. "It was during our discussion of Gordon's mission that he suggested I should make your acquaintance because you're well suited for certain kinds of work."

"Work that involves sailing ships, I presume," Gabriel said as he took his own seat. "But what can my ship offer that you can't find in your own merchant fleet?"

"Experience of the Barbary states," Kirkland said succinctly.

The back of Gabriel's neck prickled. "Where did you get that idea?"

"Gordon said that one night when you were transporting him to America, the two of you shared brandy and stories," Kirkland explained, an amused glint in his eyes. "Apparently you told him that you'd spent time in Algiers and had also visited some of the other Barbary states."

Gabriel had talked about that? He must have had more brandy than he'd realized. But he and Gordon shared a bond formed in mutual danger, and it was easy to talk to him. Plus, Gordon had more than his share of amazing stories. It had been quite a night. "What did he say?"

"That you'd been a slave," Kirkland said steadily. "That you managed to escape with a mixed crew of American and European sailors by capturing this very fine ship from the corsairs who had originally taken it from the Americans. Those are impressive qualifications, Captain."

He had *definitely* had too much brandy that night. "The escape was a joint effort that involved a number of men, providentially dreadful weather, and a good bit of luck."

"After I heard the story, I did some investigation. The consensus was that without your sailing skills and your fluency in the local Arabic dialect, there would have been no escape."

That was true, so Gabriel didn't try to deny it. "Why does this interest you?" he asked bluntly.

Equally blunt, Kirkland said, "A young woman, Lady Aurora Lawrence, was taken prisoner when her ship was captured by an Algerian corsair. When her captor learned that she's the daughter of an earl, he demanded a ransom of fifty thousand pounds. Her father can't pay that."

Hawkins whistled softly. "That's a king's ransom! But refusing is a harsh thing for a father to do. Did he consider negotiation?"

"There are a number of other children and the family doesn't have limitless wealth, and of course negotiating is difficult from so far away. But yes, it's harsh." Kirkland's gaze was steady. "And a situation you might have some sympathy with."

The spymaster had obviously done research into Gabriel's past. His mouth tightened. "I do, but I still don't see what this has to do with me."

"Lady Aurora's mother doesn't agree with her husband's refusal, and she's pawned her jewels and other personal property and borrowed every penny she can in hopes of obtaining her daughter's release."

"Has she managed to raise the fifty thousand pounds? If so, it shouldn't be too difficult to arrange the ransom and retrieve the girl."

"She could only find about half the amount, which is why she needs a shrewd and knowledgeable agent. She'd heard of my reputation and approached me, hoping I knew a man who was brave, honorable, familiar with Barbary, and a really good negotiator." Kirkland smiled a little. "With half the experienced diplomats of Europe dancing around each other at the Congress in Vienna, the list of possibilities was very short. Is this a job you'd be willing to undertake?"

Even though Gabriel had guessed where the conversation was leading, Kirkland's words were like a kick in the belly. The Barbary Coast. Scene of the worst hells of his life, and also the beginning of his resurrection.

Gabriel didn't even realize that he'd risen from his chair and started pacing until he found himself automatically dodging the two cannons that shared his cabin. He stopped and stared out a porthole at the busy Thames, where boats of all sizes skimmed back and forth in happy turmoil, a quintessential London scene. So very different from the sun-scorched shores of the Mediterranean.

Kirkland said quietly, "I gather that is a question not lightly answered."

"You gather correctly."

"Since our countries aren't at war and you'd be carrying legitimate credentials, you shouldn't be in any danger if you return," Kirkland said in a neutral voice.

"True, and I'm not likely to be recognized anyhow. I had a shaggy beard in those days and I'm not particularly distinctive looking."

"Would the *Zephyr* be recognized? She was captured by Algerian corsairs and spent time in the harbor there."

Gabriel shook his head. "Because of storm damage and repairs, there have been modifications over the years, including changes to the rigging. She might be identified as of the same American schooner type, but not as the same ship. Yet even if the ship and I aren't recognized, the Barbary shores are volatile. I've avoided the area ever since I left."

"It's currently even more volatile than usual," Kirkland agreed. "With Europe busily rebuilding after Napoleon's defeat, it must be like sharing a bed with a restless elephant for the countries on the south shore of the Mediterranean."

Amused by the other man's vivid description, Gabriel turned to Kirkland. "Tell me more about the suggested arrangements and about the young damsel in distress."

"You'll be paid a reasonable charter fee for your efforts, though it won't be as profitable as your journey to America with Gordon," Kirkland replied. "I can get you letters of introduction from high-level government officials, and I think I can get you a temporary rank of consul."

"Those things could be useful, unless some corsair captain attacks for no good reason and blows holes in my ship."

Kirkland nodded with rueful acknowledgment. "That's not impossible. I'll personally reimburse any repairs that might be necessary for such a reason."

"That's generous, assuming my ship isn't captured or sunk," Gabriel said with desert dryness. "What of the girl? Do you know her? Is she worth all this effort?"

"Her mother thinks so. I've never met Lady Aurora, but her nickname is Roaring Rory Lawrence and she has a reputation for being intelligent, charming, and dismayingly independent." Kirkland reached into an inside pocket and pulled out an engraved gold locket. Snapping it open, he said, "Her mother lent me this miniature in the hope it would help me recruit a champion for the girl's freedom."

Gabriel opened the locket, and felt a strange, painful shock as if lightning had savaged his heart. Lady Aurora was a golden blonde, very pretty, but what made her irresistibly engaging was her laughter. She looked like a young woman who deserved to be free and happy, not imprisoned for life in a foreign harem, a possession rather than the vibrant woman he saw in the miniature.

In an odd way, she reminded him of all the ways his life might have been different. He couldn't change his past, but perhaps he could help this golden girl regain the freedom and laughter she deserved.

His mouth twisted as he realized that he'd been wondering what he should do next, and fate had decided to whack him with a rescue mission to a place he thought he'd left for good. He snapped the locket shut. "Her English rose coloring must make her valuable, though they prefer them younger."

Kirkland nodded agreement as he tucked the locket away. "Usually when ransom is demanded for a captive, time is allowed for the demand to be sent to the family and for money to be gathered and a response returned. But there's always the danger that a captor might tire of waiting and auction her off. Are you willing to undertake this rescue and leave almost immediately?"

"I'll surely regret it," Gabriel said dourly, "but yes. I'll have to ask my crew if any of them choose not to go on this voyage." Seeing the lift of Kirkland's brows, he said, "This isn't the Royal Navy. A man should have a choice about what risks he is willing to take."

"That's reasonable. Do you think many of your crewmen will choose not to go into such uncertain territory?"

Gabriel smiled a little. "They've all run blockades with me so I doubt the Barbary Coast will disturb them. But as I said, they get to choose."

"If you need replacements, I can supply you with seasoned sailors," Kirkland said.

"I'll bear that in mind." Gabriel cocked his head. "Why are you so sure I'm the best man for the job?"

"Gordon said that besides being a first-rate seaman, you went above and beyond the terms of your employment when you took him to America, into a war zone no less. A mission like this needs a man who will do whatever is necessary."

Which was true. Remembering that golden, laughing girl, Gabriel knew that he would do whatever was in his power to bring her safely home to her family.

But he couldn't help but think of the last time he'd seen Algiers, in a raging gale with scattered Algerian warships trying to shoot holes in the *Zephyr's* hull as he escaped captivity in the city. Having been mad enough to agree to return there, he was glad that he would be doing so as the captain of a well-armed ship. Credentials to make him a temporary British consul would also be useful.

The times had changed and in theory, there was peace between Algeria and the nations of Europe and the United States. Which didn't stop corsairs from sometimes taking captives and demanding ransoms.

Old customs died hard.

CHAPTER 2

A shattering impact rocked the ship violently, jolting Rory from sleep. Shouts and gunshots drowned out the soft night sounds of waves and creaking rigging. Dear God, a pirate attack? The *Devon Lady* should be safe in the mid-Mediterranean, but that gunfire was very real.

She slid from her narrow upper bunk, heart pounding. Her companion, cousin, and friend, Constance Hollings, stirred in the lower bunk, coming awake more slowly. "What's happening, Rory?"

She peered out the porthole, squinting to decipher what she saw. Her stomach clenched when she saw that a long, low galley had rammed into the *Devon Lady,* its battering ram crashing over the top deck and locking the two ships together. Rope and grappling hooks had been up hurled into the deck of the schooner, and pirates were swarming aboard. "A corsair attack!"

Feeling sick, she continued, "Remember the conversation we had with Captain Roberts over dinner the night we sailed from Athens? You asked what we should do if pirates captured the ship. He laughed and said that wouldn't happen, but if it did, we should dress in our most expensive clothing and look as if we're worth being ransomed."

Grimly, she opened her small chest and located a silk gown by touch, then yanked it down over her shift. Constance rose and fastened the back, then dug into her own chest for clothing.

Rory added her best jewelry, then sat on Constance's bunk and tugged on sturdy half boots in case she ended up having to march across desert sands in whatever she was wearing tonight. As she rose to help her friend dress, she said, "I'm going to take a few things like my notebooks and pencils in case we aren't allowed to come back to our cabin."

Having been raised in a doctor's household, Constance said, "I'll pack my medical kit. There may be men wounded in the fight."

Besides her notebooks, Rory tossed her jewelry box into her canvas knapsack, hoping it would be interesting enough that the pirates would ignore the notebooks. Then a wide-brimmed hat and long cotton scarf to protect her eyes and face from the ferocious Mediterranean sunshine.

She was slinging the bag over her shoulder when the door to their cabin was wrenched open and a richly garbed and turbaned pirate stormed in, others behind him. He barked brusque words and made harsh gestures that were clearly orders to go with him and his companions.

She followed quietly, her heart pounding as she was marched through the dark, narrow passage, then climbed the ladder to the main deck. Face set, Constance followed. Moonlight revealed the aftermath of battle. The crew of the *Devon Lady* was gathered in a tight knot ahead of her, and some were wounded. Merchant ships like this one had crews of only a couple of dozen men, and she knew them all, from Captain Roberts to the young cabin boy.

Constance swore under her breath and moved toward the wounded crewmen. When a corsair tried to stop her, she glared at him and brandished the roll of bandages she carried. He stepped back and allowed her to continue. She dropped beside an injured sailor and went to work.

Rory was led to a heavily armed man who wore richly colored layers of clothing, topped with a turban and a lavish, fur-trimmed burgundy red robe. This must be the reis, the captain of the pirate galley. He was broad and intimidating and had a scar curving down his left cheek into his beard. His eyes looked surprisingly light, though she couldn't tell the color in the darkness.

His gaze moved over her, coldly evaluating clothing, jewels, her ringless left hand, and the body beneath her silk gown. "I am Malek Reis, the master of the Middle Seas," he barked in accented French. "Who are you? A great lady or a rich whore?"

She raised her chin, refusing to look cowed. "I am Lady Aurora Lawrence, daughter of a great English lord, Earl Lawrence," she said in her most aristocratic voice. "He will pay a good ransom for me, but only if the ransom includes my cousin, Lady Constance Hollings, and the crew of this ship." She gestured at the knot of sailors.

The reis's eyes narrowed. "Why would he care for such common men?"

"My father is known for his sense of justice. These men have become my friends, and I insist they be freed with me."

"You insist . . . !" He laughed nastily and reached out to her. . . .

Rory jerked awake, heart pounding as fiercely as when they'd been captured. She'd had nightmares about the attack ever since. If she was lucky, she woke before the reis grabbed her. She hadn't suffered a fate worse than death, but Malek Reis had held her jaw in a ruthless grip as he'd studied her with chilling practicality, as if she were a *thing.*

She'd stared back, struggling to hide her fear. He'd reluctantly agreed that if the ransom was sufficiently large, he'd release the captive crewmen as well as Rory and Constance. She'd been grateful for his agreement, but it was a temporary victory at best.

She uncurled from her narrow bed and walked barefoot across the cool tile, not wanting to wake Constance. Her light robe flowed around her as she opened the door and stepped into the small courtyard. At this late hour, the air had cooled pleasantly. Moonlight leached color from the flowering shrubs and silvered the fountain whose gentle splashing soothed her to sleep every night.

Their quarters were comfortable and the courtyard lovely, but it was still a prison and the walls seemed to crush closer every day. She crossed the courtyard and settled on the rim of the fountain, trailing her fingers through the water. The moon was a slender crescent in the sky, reminding her of how many weeks had passed since the capture of the *Devon Lady.*

It took weeks or months for Barbary ransom demands to reach a captive's family. Then time to collect money, more weeks for the response. Malek Reis was waiting with increasing impatience for a fortune to be delivered, and Rory doubted it would happen.

She'd been appalled when Malek had told her how much he was demanding for the release of Rory, Constance, and the ship's crew. Fifty thousand pounds was a staggering sum, enough to support a gentry household for decades. It was far more money than her family could afford, even if her father was inclined to ransom her from captivity, and she wasn't at all sure he would.

Like many aristocratic families, the Lawrences were rich in lands and other holdings, but poor in terms of available cash. Her father wouldn't beggar the family to save one wayward daughter whom he loved, but found infuriating. He'd never understood her restlessness, and she suspected that he would see her captivity as trouble of her own making.

He wouldn't be wrong. If she'd been willing to marry one of her well-bred English suitors like a proper young lady, she'd have caused her family no trouble at all, apart from going quietly mad. She liked men very well, but the thought of marrying one made her feel suffocated. She simply wasn't suited to marriage.

Though she accepted that her father wouldn't bankrupt the family for her sake, she did not want to spend the rest of her life as a harem slave in Barbary. From the way Malek Reis treated her, she sometimes wondered if he'd demanded such a high price because he didn't really want his ransom demands to be met. He regularly summoned her to the gardens or his private menagerie, talking to her and studying her intently, perhaps wondering whether it would be worth foregoing a fortune in order to keep her as one of his concubines.

If that happened, she wondered how long it would take to find a way to kill him.

In a soft voice that couldn't be heard over the sound of falling water, she murmured, "If I ever get back to England, I'm going to publish an exposé about life in a harem. There's nothing romantic and glamorous about this — it's just *boring*!"

The sky was lightening in the east when Constance joined her at the fountain. Though she was softer and rounder, and her hair was dark blond rather than golden, she resembled Rory enough to prove they were related.

Though Constance was a first cousin, they hadn't known each other growing up, but when Rory had learned that Constance had been widowed and left virtually penniless, she'd asked her cousin if she would be willing to become Rory's travel companion.

Constance had immediately said yes, and not only because she was impoverished. She shared with Rory a longing to see distant lands. They traveled well together and had become close friends in the process. But Rory had never thought that her actions would bring her friend into slavery in Barbary.

Constance perched on the bench by the fountain and joined Rory in watching the sky turn pink. "I think our quarters would be improved by having a few pets. A cat or two, or a dog. Which would you like?"

"Either. Both." Rory smiled. "Or some of the miniature animals that Malek keeps in his menagerie since they're near at hand. A pair of the adorable little goats, perhaps. Do you think he'd let us keep a pair here if I asked him?"

"Despite your legendary ability to charm men, I doubt it," Constance said, her brief humor fading. "We may be privileged captives, but we're still captives."

Rory made herself ask a question she'd avoided before now. "Are you sorry you accepted my offer of employment? If you hadn't, you'd be safely back in England now."

"Up until the corsairs came, the answer was easy. If I were in England, I'd probably be living a horrid, constricted life as a teacher or governess, shivering in an unheated attic room. I've seen wonderful things traveling with you." Constance sighed. "Do you think we'll ever get out of this comfortable yet damnable cage?"

"I haven't wanted to think about that too much because I might not like the answer. But I don't believe we'll be kept here forever," Rory said slowly. "Even though the time in captivity seems to have dragged on forever, it's only been a few short months. Something will change, and being a foolish optimist, I'm hoping it will be for the better."

"Your optimism has carried us through challenging times before." Constance bleakly regarded the high walls surrounding the women's quarters. "I keep thinking how we might get out, but it always come back to the knowledge that it's impossible to escape on our own. Even if we could scale these walls, we'd be captured before we could leave the city, and we'd never be able to escape by ship or through the desert."

"Ransom is our best hope, but Malek's price is extortionate. We'll have to hope he'll accept less," Rory said. "I wouldn't mind being cheap merchandise if it got me out of here!"

They both laughed, but Rory's secret fear was that her father wouldn't even make a counter offer. They would stay here in purgatory until Malek Reis's patience ran out. Then she and Constance would be sold, probably into separate harems of rich men. Though they'd never see each other again, they'd be relatively safe. But the crew of the *Devon Lady* would be sent to the mines or the galleys. Such slaves did not have long life expectancies.

She didn't want to think about that, so it was a relief when their breakfast arrived. They were almost finished with their bread and fruit and Turkish coffee when Abla, the matron in charge of Malek's harem, entered their quarters.

The bread turned to sawdust in Rory's mouth. The older woman said brusquely, "There is a viewing this morning. Prepare yourself."

Rory had endured this humiliation several times and learned to control her expression. "I'll be ready soon."

Abla settled down and spread honey on a piece of bread as Rory and Constance withdrew into their sleeping chamber. Her friend's expression was wretched as she opened their storage chest. They were fortunate that they'd been allowed to keep most of their belongings, apart from jewels and weapons.

Resting on top of their European gowns were folded squares of virtually transparent silk veils. They took very little space.

Rory stripped off her regular opaque robe, then stood still as Constance wound layers of translucent silk around her. She felt like a piece of marzipan being wrapped. Then she pulled a long blue scarf around her head and lower face so that only her eyes showed. Last of all, she donned a dark mantle that concealed every inch of her.

As she tweaked the mantle around Rory, Constance said, "Surely the ransom will arrive soon and we will be free. Then you'll no longer have to endure such humiliations."

Rory wished the same, but she'd learned to accept what she couldn't change. "I should be back soon. These things don't usually last very long."

Her mouth a thin line behind her scarf, Rory returned to the courtyard, where Abla was waiting. Outside the women's quarters, they were met by two muscular guards whose interested gazes flicked over Rory. The interest suggested that they weren't eunuchs, but they could see nothing of her under the voluminous robe, which was rather the point of such garments.

She was escorted to the expansive menagerie, which was Malek's favorite place for these viewings. The reis kept exotic animals in spacious high-walled compounds, and the distinctive musky odor of lions drifted across the tree-lined alley. Like Rory and Constance, the animals seemed to have adjusted to captivity, but they didn't look particularly happy about it.

In the center of the menagerie was a wide pavilion with cushioned seats and patterned Turkish carpets. Two musicians played softly, their music blending in with the splashing of a three-tiered fountain. Half a dozen richly dressed and bearded men were drinking cool beverages from goblets, but their casual talk stopped when Rory appeared.

"Ah, my golden desert flower!" Malek said genially in French as she approached. Surely he saw the fury in her eyes, but it only amused him. "My friends wish to see if your beauty is as great as I have said. Come and prove my promise."

The first time Malek had forced her to display herself, she'd resisted furiously. Unperturbed, he'd produced a vicious whip and said he'd use it on her cousin if she didn't cooperate. Feeling ill, Rory had agreed to put on lascivious shows on demand.

Wishing she could feed all these leering men to the lions, she slowly opened the mantle, sliding gracefully away as the heavy fabric folded to the ground. There was a gasp of shock from the assembled men when they saw that she wore only layers of translucent silk that did little to conceal her body. Rory survived these humiliations by imagining she was someone else, a fictional and powerful temptress named Sheba who could drive men mad. She was no longer well-brought-up Lady Aurora Lawrence, and that distance made these horrid performances possible.

The musicians changed tempo to a dance rhythm. Rory glided away from the men and released the outermost veil, letting it float to the tiled floor of the pavilion as she modestly cast her gaze downward. What would her mother think if she saw Rory's dancing? The teacher Malek provided taught sensuous moves nothing like what her childhood Italian dance master had taught the Lawrence offspring.

As the second veil drifted to the ground, one of the viewers said in a thickened voice, "The blue eyes are interesting, but I want to see her face and hair."

Usually that came later, but when Malek nodded to Rory, she started unwinding the head scarf, taking her time and undulating a little under the silk veils. When her golden-blond hair spilled free, there was a strange sound like a sucking in of breath.

She tossed her hair seductively and pulled the scarf from her face. One of the watching man began rubbing his genitals as he stared at her hungrily. She almost gagged at his vulgarity.

Another man said, "She's old and too thin," in a tone that suggested not disapproval, but that he was trying to bargain her price down.

"Not so very old, a virgin, and with all the feminine delights a man would expect," Malek said lazily. Clearly he enjoyed showing off his valuable captive.

"She doesn't look very docile," another man said thoughtfully.

"Docile women are boring," Malek responded as he gestured to Rory. "This one will never be boring."

Rory was tempted to leap at Malek and pull his dagger from its sheath so she could prove just how un-docile she was, but the short-term pleasure of knifing him wouldn't be worth the cost to her and her fellow captives. She contented herself with baring her teeth in a threatening smile. Several of the men looked taken aback. The others looking annoyingly intrigued.

Rory caught a movement out of the corner of her eye and turned to see a European man being escorted to the pavilion by two of Malek's guards. Tall and broad-shouldered, he had sun-touched brown hair and an air of calm, unshakeable competence. This man would be a safe haven in any storm, she sensed.

He didn't look at Rory, who was off to one side, but at Malek. Both of the men's expressions changed with what she realized was recognition as they exchanged words. These men had a history, and if she was any judge, it wasn't a comfortable one.

Then the newcomer's gaze shifted to her and she felt a snap of something she didn't recognize. *This one,* a voice deep in her mind whispered.

This man. Now.

CHAPTER 3

Gabriel could see that the corsair who'd captured Lady Aurora Lawrence had done well from his piracy; his home was not a mere house, but a sprawling palace. Did he demand an exorbitant ransom to maintain this splendor, or was he so wealthy he no longer understood what money meant to lesser folk? Gabriel could only pray that the fellow would be willing to negotiate the price for his captive's freedom.

Gabriel's command of the local dialect was still fluent enough to startle the servants, and perhaps that was why the majordomo offered to take him to the master right away. They passed from house to gardens to the impressive menagerie. There was the distinct musky scent of lions on the right, and above the opposite wall of the walkway a giraffe could be seen peacefully grazing on a tree.

Thoughts of exotic beasts vanished when

his escort brought him to an open-sided pavilion where half a dozen richly dressed Algerian men were gathered. The broad, powerful figure in the middle turned to see who was coming, and the sight of his face stunned Gabriel to near paralysis. The name Malek wasn't uncommon, and he hadn't expected to see a man he knew, and had never thought he would see again.

The moment of shock was swift and mutual. Using all his hard-won discipline to control his expression, Gabriel gave a courteous nod. "Malek Reis. It is my honor to be received by you. I have come all the way from England to discuss the freedom of a lady in your custody."

Malek's expression was as guarded as his own. In Arabic, he said to his fellows, "The viewing is over, my friends. I thank you for coming today."

A man said with annoyance, "Does this mean the merchandise is not for sale?"

"That remains to be seen." Malek ushered his guests down the steps and onto the walkway that led out of the menagerie.

While the small knot of men left, talking intently, Gabriel scanned the pavilion, and for the second time in a matter of minutes, he was lightning-shocked to his core, this time by the sight of a profoundly naked young woman.

No, she wasn't quite naked, for layers of transparent silk veils floated around her flawless body. They had the paradoxical effect of emphasizing how very bare she was. The golden hair and delicate features confirmed this was Lady Aurora, but she wasn't laughing as she'd been in the miniature portrait inside her mother's locket. Her blue eyes were stark as hot, humiliated color rose in her face. She looked ready to faint. Even so, she was shatteringly beautiful.

A dark pile of fabric lay crumpled on the ground. He scooped the material up and handed it to her at arm's length, forcing himself to keep his gaze on her face. Speaking in a low voice so as not to be overheard by Malek, he said, "Lady Aurora. I'm Gabriel Hawkins, captain of a ship from England. I've come to negotiate your freedom."

She grabbed the garment, a voluminous cloak, and wrapped it around herself so thoroughly she looked like a nun. That didn't diminish the impact she had on him. She'd been stunning in her portrait, and was even more so now.

Lady Aurora's face reflected a tumult of emotions: shame, fury, and humiliation, but also courage and determination. The face of a woman who was as admirable as she was beautiful.

Having composed herself to apparent serenity, she spoke as if that shocking scene hadn't taken place. "I'm very glad to see you, Captain Hawkins. My father sent you?"

"Not your father. Your mother."

She bit her lip. "My father couldn't pay Malek Reis's exorbitant demands, so my mother collected what she could and sent you here with hopes and prayers?"

"You know your parents well." After a moment's hesitation, he added, "Though I did not meet your father, I'm told he was deeply concerned for your welfare. But he couldn't meet the price."

She smiled ruefully. "I don't know how much money my mother could raise, but I'm sure it was much less than fifty thousand pounds. I hope you're a good negotiator."

"Reasonably so, but my principal qualification is having some knowledge of the Barbary Coast. How are you? Have you been treated well?"

"Apart from having to appear naked before men who would show more respect if I was a horse?" she said bitterly.

He winced. "Apart from that."

"There was a very unpleasant examination to certify my 'purity' since that affects my price, but otherwise I've been treated well. Comfortable quarters, good food, and a language tutor to help us learn Turkish and the local version of Arabic." She smiled a little. "A dance instructor to learn shameless exotic dances. Those are rather fun. Some women would consider it a wonderful life, I imagine."

"Some songbirds might not mind their cages," he said quietly. "But others beat against the bars till their hearts burst for a chance to be free."

She drew a shaky breath. "Exactly."

"I will do whatever I can to free you," he said tautly.

Their gazes locked. "I believe you will do your best. I pray that will be enough. I do not underestimate the difficulties," she said softly. "I hate that there is so little I can do for myself!"

He wished he could take her hand to offer comfort, but that might annoy Malek, who could see them even though he was out of earshot. The reis's good will was required if Lady Aurora was to be released. "The fact that you are calm and clear sighted about your situation is more help than you realize."

"I hope so. It's all I've had." She smiled. "But now I have you."

Her smile was enough to melt a man's

bones. Before he could think what to say, Malek returned. They'd been speaking in English, and Malek spoke in the same language, saying, "So we meet again, Hawkins."

"You speak English?" Lady Aurora asked, startled.

"I am a man of many talents," the reis said blandly. "What brings you to Algiers, Hawkins? Courage or stupidity?"

"A quest to save a damsel in distress." Gabriel gestured at the estate surrounding them. "You have prospered, Malek Reis."

"Indeed I have." A touch of malice in his voice, Malek continued. "Are you still merely the master of one small ship?"

So they were going to fence with words. "Great possessions are a great burden," Gabriel replied. "A man is very free when he sails a single ship, and my *Zephyr* is a free wind blowing."

Malek gave a snort of acknowledgment. "So with your freedom, Hawkins, you have become Lord Lawrence's errand boy to retrieve his careless daughter."

Gabriel smiled, unperturbed. "Exactly so. Lady Aurora's family cherishes her and wishes for her return home."

"You have the fifty thousand pounds to

purchase her freedom?" Malek asked sharply.

"Not so much as that," Hawkins replied. "As a wise man once told me, all transactions are subject to barter."

Malek gave a bark of laughter as he recognized words of his own from the past. "Your friend is indeed wise. How close are you to my ransom demand?"

"Not as close as you would like, I'm sure, but nonetheless, I am authorized to offer you an enormous sum of money."

Malek frowned, and Gabriel wondered if the other man needed the full ransom amount in order to achieve a particular goal. "I must consider whether there is room for negotiation in this case." He made a dismissive gesture toward Lady Aurora. "The wench must leave so we can discuss business."

"Wench?" Lady Aurora said in a dangerous voice.

Gabriel said, "Why should the lady leave when she has the greatest stake in our negotiations?"

Malek hesitated, then shrugged. "As you wish. But females greatly complicate business discussions. Have a seat and I will order refreshments brought." He made a gesture to a servant outside the pavilion.

They settled on cushioned seats, watching each other like points on a triangle. Lady Aurora kept her cloak wrapped protectively around her, though a glimpse of bare ankle was visible under the folds. Her face was still as carved marble.

"Where shall we begin the negotiations, Hawkins?" Malek asked bluntly. "You've already admitted that you don't have the full amount of the ransom."

"A ransom which was absurdly high," Gabriel retorted. "A mere starting bid. Though Lady Aurora is beautiful and beloved by her family and friends, fifty thousand pounds was surely just a way of saying that you expect a high price. I'm not aware of current market prices of beautiful European slave girls, but even in Constantinople such an amount would be ridiculous."

Malek's dark brows arched. "You didn't know that the lady insisted the ransom must include not only her cousin, Lady Constance, but the captain and all the crew of the *Devon Lady,* the ship I captured?"

Startled, Gabriel looked at Lady Aurora. "As a sailor myself, I appreciate your generosity toward the crew, but I can understand why that raises the ransom price."

She lifted her chin. "Should I go free and the others spend the rest of their lives in slavery because of the lucky accident of my birth?"

"In the eyes of God, no, but it's the way of the world in which we live." He thought a moment. "Your cousin, Lady Constance. Will her family contribute toward the ransom?"

Lady Aurora looked a little shifty. "Though Constance is wellborn, she has no close family or resources of her own."

In other words, no money there. Gabriel's brows furrowed. "I'm trying to calculate the fair market price of two wellborn young Englishwomen and a couple of dozen sailors. My best guess is that the value would still be under twenty thousand pounds. Furthermore, you already have the value of the captured ship. I think that twenty thousand pounds would be a very good price, don't you, Malek Reis?"

"The price is whatever I want it to be!" Malek snapped.

"Of course, it's your right to set whatever price pleases you," Gabriel agreed in a mild voice. "But an item that is priced too high will remain on the shelf. There's no profit in that."

The conversation paused when servants appeared with trays of food and drink. Though Lady Aurora refused everything except a goblet of chilled mint tea, Gabriel was hungry. The *bourek,* triangular pastries stuffed with spiced meat or eggs or vegetables, were delicious, as were the olives, flatbread, almonds, dates, and soft goat cheese.

"If you keep eating like that, I'll have to raise the ransom price further," Malek said dryly.

Gabriel grinned. "Surely this comes under the category of hospitality to the weary traveler."

Lady Aurora had been silent, but now she said abruptly, "Malek Reis, virginity is greatly prized here. Could you auction mine off and earn enough to bridge the gap between the ransom Captain Hawkins has brought and the amount you consider acceptable?"

CHAPTER 4

Lady Aurora's shocking words fell into stunned silence. Malek recovered first, asking incredulously, "Are all Englishwomen so mad?"

"I've often been told I am one of a kind," Lady Aurora said wryly. "It's not usually a compliment. Virginity means much less to me than freedom."

Malek pursed his lips, calculating. "If you're serious, Lady Aurora, such a sale might raise as much as five thousand pounds."

"This is absurd!" Gabriel burst out. "If the lady's virginity is worth five thousand pounds, I'll buy it to keep her safe!"

"Can you afford that much?" Malek asked with interest.

Gabriel did a swift inventory of his savings and assets. "Yes, but you'd have to accept a draft on my London bank. Would you trust me for that?"

Malek considered, then nodded. "I would."

Lady Aurora stared at Gabriel, startled. "Would you spend that much so you could have me? Or would you do so and then honorably refuse to touch me?"

He gazed at her, his brain paralyzed by erotic images of kissing her. Pulling away those gossamer veils so he could run his hands over warm, soft skin, sinking into her . . .

Five thousand pounds might buy passive acceptance, but would it buy passionate desire? Knowing that passive acceptance would never be enough with this woman, he said brusquely, "You'd be safe from me. I'm not in the habit of buying bedmates." Feeling as if he could read the thoughts behind those misleadingly innocent blue eyes, he added, "And don't think you could sell your damned virginity twice if I didn't demand full value for my money!"

"I did wonder if that would work," she admitted with a self-mocking smile. "But it would be very unsporting on my part."

"As entertaining as it is to observe the mad English, none of this it to the point," Malek said sharply. "I need at least forty thousand pounds and you have not come close to that amount even with the lady's foolish suggestion."

"If I had sufficient funds, I would be happy to give them to you," Gabriel said. "But I don't. Could I perform some service that would make up the difference? The *Zephyr* is larger, faster, and better suited to long voyages than your corsair galleys. Would you like me to take you to England and back? To America? Some other destination?" He spread his hands. "There is little else I can offer."

Malek started to snap a reply. Then he stopped as a thought struck him. Abruptly he stood and began pacing around the perimeter of the pavilion, frowning.

Taking advantage of his distraction, Lady Aurora slid along her cushioned bench so that she was close enough to touch Gabriel. Leaning forward, she said in a low voice, "Malek speaks English so well. Is he a European renegade who was captured by corsairs and turned Muslim to win his freedom?"

Grateful for how well her cloak covered her, Gabriel replied, "No, he's Algerian born and bred, but his mother was English. I believe she found the harem to be a better life than she had in England and settled into it comfortably."

"Perhaps that's why he doesn't understand

why some English women don't want to embrace the life," Lady Aurora said tartly. "But your suggestion seems to have given him an idea."

"Yes, and I wonder what it might be." Gabriel's gaze moved to the other man. "I won't let him have the *Zephyr.* If he tries to capture it, my crew and I will fight to the death. That won't help you, so I hope it doesn't come down to that."

"So do I," she said starkly.

For the first time, Lady Aurora's confident façade cracked to show fear and vulnerability. Gabriel took her hand, intending comfort but feeling a snap of startling awareness. Knowing it wasn't wise to be so attracted to a woman he had come to ransom from captivity, he masked his reaction and said quietly, "There are no guarantees in life, Lady Aurora. But your situation is far from impossible."

"My mother was fortunate to find you." She cocked her head. "But since she could only find about half the ransom amount, I imagine you aren't being paid a fabulous sum. So why are you taking such a risk for a stranger?"

"Life is a risk and ultimately fatal." Realizing that he was still holding her slim fingers, he made himself release her. "Freeing a captive countrywoman seems like a risk worth taking, Lady Aurora."

"I hope you don't come to regret that belief!" Her smile would have warmed him to his toes even on the North Atlantic. "Call me Rory. My friends do, and I hope we are going to be friends. Calling me Lady Aurora reminds me of all the bad poetry written in my name during my London seasons."

He chuckled. "Along the lines of 'golden-haired Aurora, goddess of the dawn, bright sprite ascending'?"

She shuddered elaborately. "Exactly! I do hope you aren't a poet, Captain. Though if you are, I imagine you're good. You seem too competent to write bad poetry."

"Don't worry, I'm no kind of poet, good, bad, or indifferent." Caught by the intimacy of the conversation, he continued, "If we're moving to a first-name basis, my name is Gabriel."

"So we're both in semi-divine territory!" Rory said with pleasure. "You an archangel and me a minor Roman goddess. I think you outrank me since there are only a few archangels, but many minor Roman divinities."

"If we're looking at worldly rank, you're the daughter of an earl while I'm a disinherited son," he said bluntly, wanting to reveal something important about himself. "Better not to look at rank."

Before either of them could say more, Malek pivoted on his heel and stalked back to his guests. "I have an idea, Hawkins." His mouth curved in a dangerous smile. "But you won't like it."

Warily, Gabriel asked, "What do you need done that I won't like?"

"Since your ship is larger and better suited to carrying passengers and cargoes than any I command, I want you to transport me and a number of my men to Constantinople. And then, Allah willing, home to Algiers."

That would be about six weeks round trip, plus whatever time was spent in Constantinople. But if that would do the job, Gabriel was willing to offer ferry service. Wanting to be sure he understood the bargain, he asked, "That and twenty thousand pounds will be enough for you to free all your prisoners?"

Malek's teeth showed again. "Besides me and my men, you must also transport a number of the animals from my collection."

So his lovely *Zephyr* would be turned into a floating menagerie. Knowing how complicated it might be to carry wild animals the length of the Mediterranean, he said, "As you wish, though the number will be limited by the amount of food and bedding and other supplies the ship can hold."

"Many are miniature animals, perhaps the finest collection of such in the world." Malek's expression turned calculating. "Your Lady Aurora is very popular with them, so she must accompany us."

When Gabriel looked at Lady Aurora, she said, "It's true. He has a collection of the most delightful small creatures. I'd love to travel with them and do what I could to keep them calm."

So a ship full of corsairs, animals, and one beautiful captive lady. It would be a memorable voyage. But there must be more than one lady. "It isn't right that Lady Aurora should be the only female on board. At the least, she should have her cousin, Lady Constance, as a companion."

Malek considered, then said, "You're right." His gaze moved to Rory. "But the crew of the *Devon Lady* will remain here as my hostages." He bared his teeth in an unnerving grin. "How soon can we leave?"

"It depends on how many animals you propose to take, and what kind of stabling and cages will be required. Transporting horses is straightforward and I've done it before," Gabriel said. "And we routinely carry pigs and chickens on longer voyages so we can have fresh meat. But rare wild animals will require experienced keepers."

"Experienced grooms will travel with them," Malek said. "But you first must dispose of your pigs. They are forbidden to good Muslims, and I will not travel on a ship that carries them."

There were other European ships in the harbor whose captains would be happy to buy the pigs. "Very well. What other kinds of animals do you want me to transport?"

"Come and see. Lady Aurora will accompany us."

Rory rose, looking pleased. "You will enjoy this, Captain."

Malek led them down the main walkway, then left into a lane that ran between animal enclosures. In the heat of the afternoon, most animals were drowsing under their trees, but when Malek stopped by one spacious pen and gave a sharp whistle, there was a sudden rumble of hooves. Small hooves.

Gabriel blinked as a dozen miniature horses, only about three feet tall at the withers, galloped toward the fence. He'd seen ponies almost as small, but ponies were sturdy little fellows. These lovely creatures had the sleek conformation of horses.

"Oh, my darlings!" Rory cooed as she

opened the gate and stepped into the enclosure. "I haven't seen you in too long!" She began petting and sweet-talking the horses as they churned around her.

Malek entered after her and gestured for Gabriel to follow. "They are bred of Arabian stock. The most beautiful horses in the world."

As he closed the gate behind him, Gabriel asked, "Do you want the whole herd transported to Constantinople?"

"Only those four geldings." Malek indicated several silvery grays with dark muzzles and stockings. "They're trained to work together as a team, and they pull a small, boy-sized chariot I had made. There is not another team like them anywhere."

Geldings so the next owner would be unable to breed them, Gabriel guessed. Smiling, he knelt so that his face was on a level with the miniature horses. One of his chief regrets when he was sent to sea was that horses were no longer a daily part of his life. When one of the silvery geldings trotted over to him, he said apologetically, "I'm sorry I have no sugar or carrot for you."

The horse shoved his head into Gabriel's chest, almost knocking him over. Gabriel laughed and caressed the long, flowing dark mane. "Do you have a buyer in Constantinople?"

"Not a buyer. A villain who must be bribed." Malek's tight voice held barely suppressed fury. "Because I haven't sufficient gold, I must offer him something rare and wonderful to make up the difference."

Wondering what could be worth such a huge bribe, Gabriel stood and the silvery gelding twined around him like a dog. "Certainly these horses are rare and wonderful. Are you sending other animals as well?"

"Yes, come and see." Malek led the way back to the gate.

"I'll be back to visit again soon," Rory promised her equine entourage as they followed her to the exit.

Gabriel had to block two of the horses to prevent them from surging outside with her. "Frisky little fellows!" he said as he shoved them back inside and secured the gate.

"They're adorable," Rory said fondly. Intent on the horses, she didn't notice when her cloak parted to reveal one bare, perfect breast.

The sight temporarily stopped Gabriel's breathing. Rory was even more beautiful than the miniature horses.

She saw his expression and hastily tugged

the cloak around her again, blushing. He probably blushed as well. Turning and pretending that moment hadn't happened, he followed Malek to the next enclosure, which held miniature gray donkeys with dark masks and mischievous eyes. Unlike the small horses, which had the conformation of full-sized adult horses, the donkeys had the soft, irresistible features of young foals.

The donkeys greeted Rory with as much enthusiasm as the miniature horses. As she scratched the fuzzy gray head of the most insistent one, she said, "They're mischievous and rather dangerously clever. Not to mention stubborn!"

"But charming," Gabriel said as he made friends with a darker donkey. "How many do you wish to transport to Constantinople?"

Malek frowned. "Only two, I think. They're appealing but not so unusual." He moved along to the next enclosure, which contained pigmy goats.

Tiny but intrepid, the goats scampered around their visitors. One tried to climb Gabriel, and another started chewing the braid off his uniform. Laughing, he said, "You should start a children's menagerie, Malek. They would go mad for these little fellows."

Malek made an odd sound, and Gabriel saw that the other man had a strange expression. Vulnerability, perhaps. Gabriel wondered if Malek had had a child or children who had died and that was why he had this extraordinary collection. It was not the sort of question one could ask, but it made Gabriel wonder if Malek had a wife. Or wives. A family. In the years since the two men had met, anything could have happened.

"Come along," Malek said gruffly. He'd gone only a few steps when a servant approached Malek and bowed deeply before starting a conversation with his master. Malek led him out of earshot, but kept his watchful gaze on Gabriel and Rory. Maintaining a discreet distance between them, Gabriel and Rory leaned against the fence and watched the antics of the goats, which were being fed by a keeper who'd emerged from a stable at the back of the large enclosure.

Already lively, the little goats went berserk with excitement. One leaped on the keeper's shoulders. The man laughed and fed it tidbits. "All of the animals are delightful," Rory said. "I don't know which are my favorites."

"Whichever ones you're looking at?" Gabriel suggested.

"You're probably right. Look at that little fellow who is jumping over the others like a steeplechaser!" She chuckled. "I suggested to Malek that the miniature hogs I saw in India would fit into his collection nicely since they weigh only about a stone. But he rejected the idea of any kind of pigs."

Gabriel had been told Lady Aurora had been in India, but not why, so he asked, "What took you to India?"

"A desire to see the temples and ancient ruins." She smiled mischievously. "It was also a good way to avoid more seasons in London. My parents thought I needed the steadying influence of a husband so they pushed me into the marriage mart. That was not a success for any of us."

Very aware of her lovely face and vibrant charm, he said, "You must have had your share of offers. Are you opposed to marriage in general, or was it that you didn't meet anyone you wanted to marry?"

"Some of both," she said thoughtfully. "Most people seem to find marriage a good thing. I can see the appeal. My parents are still very fond of each other even after decades together and eight children."

Her gaze followed the cavorting pygmy goats. "But at eighteen, I didn't feel at all ready to marry and settle into staid domesticity forever. Perhaps the right man would have changed my mind, but I didn't meet anyone I liked that much. My mother was horrified when I refused a most flattering offer from a duke."

He supposed he shouldn't be startled. As the daughter of an earl, she was a suitable bride for a man of such high rank. "You didn't want to be a duchess?"

"He was portly, old, and deadly boring," she said tartly. "And he had snuff stains on his clothing."

"Those are good reasons to decline an offer," he agreed. "But surely there were younger, more interesting candidates for your hand."

"Yes, but I didn't want any of them, either," she said ruefully. "If I'd married one of those eligible wellborn men, he'd expect me to live like a wellborn wife. I would need to dress well, entertain well, raise wellborn children. The idea was — suffocating."

"Perhaps there was no right man because you weren't the right woman at that time," he suggested. "Eighteen is very young to decide one's future, which marriage usually does, especially for a woman."

"Very true," she agreed. "No man looks like a husband when one isn't in the market for a mate. Or maybe I'm cold natured. My older sisters were always swooning over handsome stable lads and dancing masters. I might admire a handsome young man, but I had no interest in pursuing him."

"I have trouble believing a cold-natured woman would reduce the chances of regaining her freedom by insisting on the release of her ship's sailors," he observed. "Since you weren't passionate about finding a husband, what were you passionate about?"

"Learning," she said promptly. "Travel. Seeing places very different from my homeland. I adore maps and globes. The best present I ever received was a globe two feet across and beautifully detailed. It's still in my bedroom back home."

"Who knew you well enough to give you such a gift?"

"My aunt, Lady Diana Lawrence. She's my godmother and my parents say I'm far too much like her. She's a happy spinster who has traveled widely and seen wonderful things. She's currently living in India, which is half the reason I wished to visit."

He chuckled. "The other half being the temples and ruins?"

She nodded. "Exactly. The three of us, Aunt Diana, Constance, and I, had a marvelous time seeing the great sights of Northern India. So much grandeur and history! But I wish I hadn't convinced Constance we needed to visit Greece."

"I'm told Greece is one of the world's grandest destinations."

"Oh, it was! With the wars over, it seemed like a good time to visit. But if we'd sailed home from India to England, around the Cape of Good Hope, Constance and I wouldn't be here." She made an eloquent gesture that encompassed Algiers, her captivity, and the whole Barbary Coast. "We also thought it would be interesting to take the overland route up the Red Sea, across Egypt, and then across the Mediterranean to Greece. We were captured on the voyage from Athens to London."

"No one could have predicted that. British shipping in the Mediterranean is usually safe from the Barbary pirates."

"Usually, but not always." She sighed, her gaze on two goats who were playfully butting their heads together. "And now I'm facing a possible lifetime in a harem, which is surely the most constricting prison of all."

"Most women live constrained lives," he said quietly. "It takes courage and imagination to break free of the shackles as you've done, and you surely will again."

"It's easier to avoid constraint if one

comes from a family with money," she said. "Though the Lawrence exchequer isn't sufficient to pay an extortionate ransom for me, there has been enough for me to live independently and to travel."

"When you are freed, will you continue your travels?"

"Thank you for saying *when,* not *if.* As for the traveling . . ." She hesitated. "I love the places I've seen, the people I've met, but it's rather tiring to always have to be figuring out how to do things in a strange land and a strange language. The thought of living in England sounds peaceful and appealing now."

"As long as you're not constrained," he said with a smile.

"Precisely. If and when I'm free again, I might be a little more cautious, but I'll still be Roaring Rory, the most eccentric twig on the Lawrence family tree. I don't think I have it in me to be staid."

"Traveling as you have done is unusual, but are you truly outrageous? Do you sometimes scandalously wear men's clothing?" he asked curiously.

"That's not outrageous, merely practical when doing things that require agility." She hesitated, then gazed up at him with a mixture of shyness and teasing. “Can you keep a secret?”

Chapter 5

"I'm quite good at keeping secrets," Gabriel said, amusement in his eyes. "But if you've been madam of a house of ill repute in Bombay, someone else will surely carry the news back to London."

She laughed as she hadn't for . . . far too long. Gabriel radiated a quiet strength and protection that let her relax enough to laugh again. "Nothing that outrageous! My guilty secret is that I've always loved reading and writing. When I started to travel, I found I wanted to tell stories set in the places we visited. So I began writing the kind of Gothic adventure romances that are scorned by all folk of education and refinement."

He grinned. "That might horrify high sticklers, but it sounds like great fun."

"It is! Constance and I work together because we've found that it's an excellent way of passing time on long sea voyages. I do most of the actual writing, but we discuss ideas together and she edits me, pointing out when I become too outrageous even by our standards. She also writes out the finished copy in her beautiful handwriting, and because she's a fine artist, she draws illustrations. Her pictures of the people and the exotic settings really enrich the stories."

Looking genuinely interested, he said, "I'd buy such a book. Have you had any published?"

"I don't think they're publishable because my heroines are not beautiful, simpering maidens who need rescue," she explained. "This is where I become truly outrageous. My heroines are bold adventurers. One is a lady privateer who wears breeches and carries a cutlass. Another is a warrior queen in a desert kingdom, leading her people to defend their freedom. One is a thief, though for a noble cause." She grinned as she thought fondly of her heroines. "They aren't at all ladylike. Sometimes they rescue the hero. Sometimes hero and heroine rescue each other."

"They sound like women I'd like to know," he said thoughtfully. "What are your heroes like?"

"Oh, shockingly handsome, of course! Possibly a great lord in disguise, though not a duke, because my experience of them is not romantic."

"Portly, boring, and snuff-stained," Gabriel said gravely.

"Exactly. My characters invariably meet when she is being outrageously unladylike. He is intrigued and attracted, and he's so confident that he is never upset by a woman's strength. He can be dangerous, but also kind. And most importantly, he has a flexible enough mind to accept her differences as the reason he's so attracted." After a pause, she added, "Sometimes it takes him a while to become that tolerant."

Gabriel smiled, his eyes warm. "That's understandable. I'm sure such stories aren't for everyone, but I don't know that they're unpublishable."

She caught her breath as she fell into that warmth. It occurred to her that Captain Gabriel Hawkins was rather like one of her romantic heroes. He was strong, he was kind, he seemed very tolerant of her outrageousness, and she suspected that he could be very dangerous. And though not shockingly handsome, he was a very fine-looking man. She studied his broad, powerful shoulders. Very fine looking indeed.

Pulling her distracted thoughts together, she said, "That's what my Aunt Diana said after she read one of our stories when we were in India. She liked it so much that she asked to read the rest. Constance and I were flattered, of course. She said they were well written and entirely worthy of publication and said she'd send the stories to a publisher she knows in London. We listed the author as 'Countess Alexander' rather than our own names. If the publisher is mad enough to want to put our work out to the world, that might spare the family some embarrassment."

"Because the stories combine romance, travelogue, and adventure, they could appeal to a broad audience," he said seriously.

"Do you think so?" she asked, wanting to believe that. Then she noticed how Malek was watching them, even as he talked to his servant, to make sure they weren't doing anything unacceptable like plotting escape. Brought back to reality, she said with an edge of bitterness, "If we don't escape from Barbary, we might never know even if the books are published."

"You will be free," he said firmly. "Perhaps you'll return to England and find your books the talk of London."

"That's a lovely fantasy." She bit her lip. "Constance and I have needed our fantasies in order not to be driven mad with fear about what might happen. A much more modest dream is to escape and find a nice cottage where we can write stories together, though I'd have to make them less outrageous if I ever want to sell any."

"We all need dreams to survive," he said quietly. "Since it's a dream, don't tame your heroines. They inspire hope."

"I agree," she said regretfully. "But if — when — I am free again, I must be practical if I mean to support myself."

"Rather than change the existing books, you could write new ones," he suggested. "A pair of beautiful ladies captured by Barbary pirates would be a good subject for a story and it might be easier to start afresh than to change a story you've finished."

"You might be right. If I change the heroine in an existing story, I also have to change the hero and other characters, and the plot as well." She made a face. "Easier to start anew. Actually, we've been working on a Barbary captive story since we were taken. I'll see if I can make my heroine better behaved. The hero is *not* a corsair! There is nothing romantic about being captured!"

"I couldn't agree with you more," he said grimly.

Hearing darkness in his voice, she said, "You know my story now. What is yours?"

His relaxation vanished, and his gaze went to the goats. Rory remembered that her heroes tended to be mysterious about their past, and information had to be dragged out of them. Though it could be intriguing in a fictional hero, it was somewhat annoying in real life. Not that she had any right to delve into his past.

He broke a long silence by saying, "I suppose that's only fair. I come from a Royal Navy family and followed in those footsteps with never a second thought. I started very young and was considered promising until I did something that disgraced my family and led to my being forced out of the service."

When he halted, she said encouragingly, "You were outrageous?"

"I didn't think so at the time. I still don't. But I broke one of the rules of war. If I were older and came from a less distinguished naval family, it could have led to my being hanged." He shrugged. "Instead, I was merely disgraced and disowned."

She winced. Her family might be exasperated by her, but there had never been any question of being disowned. "So you became a merchant seaman."

He shrugged again. "I knew nothing else. I'm comfortably situated now with a good ship and crew, and I've enjoyed greater variety than I would as an officer in the Royal Navy. Carrying cargo. Other less respectable things."

"Smuggling?" she asked with interest.

"Occasionally, but only once or twice when it seemed necessary. There have been odd missions like coming here. Recently I transported a man to America to rescue a woman, then had to get them both safely back to England." He smiled. "I've done quite a bit of blockade running, but now that peace is in sight, there will be no more blockades for me to run."

"Blockade running!" she said with delight. "A hero to the people who desperately need the supplies you bring, a scoundrel to those who set up the blockade!"

"Do I see a story forming?" he asked, amused.

"Exactly! The heroine is a blockade runner, the hero is captain of a naval ship that is maintaining the blockade." Her voice became low and dramatic. "She swings up into the rigging of her ship with her cutlass in hand, defying fate and danger. He sees her through his spyglass and is stunned by her wild, free beauty."

"It's a start," Gabriel said a little doubtfully. "How do you get them together and overcome the inherent conflict between a blockade runner and the man who is pledged to catch her or blow her ship out of the water?"

"Conflict is what makes a story interesting. I'll think of something," she said confidently. "Developing a plot and making it at least slightly plausible takes time."

His idea was a good one, but she realized the story of his past wasn't very detailed. A little hesitantly, she said, "You and Malek Reis seem to know each other."

"We do. It's a long story."

Before Gabriel could continue, Malek finished speaking with his servant and called, "Hawkins! Lady Aurora! Come!"

Gabriel pushed away from the fence. "A long story for another day. Shall we see what other creatures Malek wishes transported to Constantinople?"

When they caught up with Malek, he said brusquely, "This way," and led them down another lane to the right. The next enclosure they approached contained amazingly tall, leggy birds with dramatic plumage. "Ostriches?" Gabriel said. "I've seen the feathers, but never the actual creature."

Malek gestured at the half dozen giant birds, who were ambling around their enclosure. "I'm thinking of sending a pair.

Would their height cause difficulties?"

Gabriel frowned as he calculated. "A section of the hold is high enough to accommodate them, though the male won't have much head room. I don't think I could safely transport giraffes, though."

"Ostriches will suffice." Malek pivoted and strode off along the alley. The next enclosure on the opposite side of the walkway announced its inhabitants by both musky scent and a bone-shivering roar. Lions.

This enclosure they didn't enter. Gabriel studied the tawny beasts with fascination. He'd seen lions once or twice before, but not from so close. A massive, heavily maned male sprawled in the shade of a vine-covered shelter, his family around him. The adult lions were also drowsing, though several playful cubs tumbled together in the sunshine, tawny balls of fur with claws.

"So beautiful," Rory breathed. Gabriel glance at her rapt expression, thinking she was rather like a golden lioness herself. Sleek, beautiful, brave — and quite possibly deadly in the right circumstances.

His musing was interrupted when a young male suddenly leaped onto the back of the lounging lord of the pride. The leader erupted from the ground with a shattering baritone roar and the two males tore into a vicious version of the playful cubs' wrestling.

As the lions crashed across the sandy compound, Rory gasped, one hand going to her mouth. "Sultan is going to kill Ghazi!"

The older male, Sultan, rapidly overcame the younger and pinned him to the ground. He was on the verge of tearing Ghazi's throat out when two keepers raced out of the lion house with whips and a wooden chair. The men managed to separate the lions and herd the young one, bleeding from bites and scratches, back into the building.

Gabriel released the breath he'd been holding, shaken by seeing nature at its most primal. "How many lions will you be sending, and which ones?"

"The young one, Ghazi," Malek said thoughtfully. "If he stays here, he'll keep challenging Sultan until he's killed. Most young males never make it to adulthood, and that would be a shame. Ghazi is an impressive young beast and will grow into a true king if he has the time."

One lion would be easier to transport than several. "I'll try to arrange the cages so the lion scent doesn't drive the other animals mad. Predators and prey do not make good neighbors."

"Discuss that with my animal keepers."

Malek pushed away from the fence. "They will know best how to arrange the beasts."

"Are there any other animal passengers to join us?"

"Yes, and they will be the most difficult." Malek led the three of them to the right until they reached the end of the walkway. A wide enclosure held a mud-edged pond, where the dark bulk of massive bodies could be seen dimly below the surface. Only the tops of their broad heads and small ears were visible.

"Hippopotami?" Gabriel tried to judge their size from the parts that were visible. "Are they young ones? They seem small."

"They're pygmy hippopotami from West Africa, very rare," Malek said with pride. "They're about a quarter the size of the common hippo. There may be no others of their breed in the Ottoman empire."

"But they're still far from small, and you're right that they'll be difficult to transport," Gabriel said. "Surely they'll need tanks of water to survive? That will be very heavy and potentially dangerous if the sea is rough."

Malek shrugged. "They came here by ship. Surely you can do as well?"

Ignoring the gibe, Gabriel said, "Barring the unforeseen, they can be safely transported to Constantinople."

"Very good. Can you leave in three days?"

Wondering why Malek was in such a hurry, Gabriel said, "Yes, but only if you can immediately supply men and materials for refitting the ship to accommodate you, your men, and your animal cargo."

"You will have all you need," Malek said tersely. "Three days, then."

As the men turned away from the hippo pool, Rory said to Malek, "Sir, before we leave, I'd like to speak to the crew of the *Devon Lady* to tell them what is happening."

Malek frowned, but Gabriel said quietly to him, "It would be a kindness and would cost you nothing. When one is imprisoned, ignorance of surrounding circumstances can drive a man mad."

Malek nodded reluctant agreement. "This is their day of rest so you may visit them in the bagnio after you leave here, Lady Aurora."

"I'd like to go with her," Gabriel said. "Since I'm another sailor, they can be rude to me if they feel the need."

"Very well. After, meet me in my office so we can discuss the material, labor, and supplies that will be needed. My majordomo will direct you." He turned and stalked away with the same tension he'd been showing since Gabriel had arrived.

"Thank you for being willing to accompany me, Gabriel," Rory said with a smile that briefly disabled his wits.

As she pulled her mantle close around her and followed Malek, Gabriel couldn't help thinking how much he looked forward to having her on his ship, no matter how awkward or difficult it would be to travel with such an appealing lady in close quarters.

Chapter 6

The bagnio was cramped and stuffy with the scents of too many men in too small a space, but it wasn't as bad as Rory had feared. High, narrow windows just below the level of the ceiling provided some air circulation, and there were a sink and water pump in the corner, and sufficient sleeping mats for the entire crew of the *Devon Lady.*

Still, when the guards unbarred the massive door to admit Rory to the bagnio, she was grateful for the quiet presence of Gabriel Hawkins behind her. Because it was a day of rest, many of the sailors were drowsing on their mats, but as soon as she entered, the occupants leaped to their feet and crowded around her, their expressions eager as they bombarded her with questions.

"Lady Aurora, you're all right!"

"Is Miss Constance well?"

"Do you have news?"

"Are we ransomed?"

"Have you come to free us?"

As Gabriel rested a protective hand on her shoulder, a shaggy Captain Roberts ordered, "Let the lass talk." He'd always commanded the respect of his sailors, and at his words, they stepped back to give their visitors more space.

Breathing more easily, she exclaimed, "I'm so glad to see you all! Captain Roberts, I almost didn't recognize you with a beard."

His smile was humorless. "They aren't about to let slaves have razors."

She should have realized that. Her gaze moved over the sailors, trying to recognize the faces under the beards. "Did everyone recover from the wounds received when we were captured?"

"Aye, everyone survived, and our special thanks to Miss Constance for bandaging us up." As eager as his men, Captain Roberts shifted his gaze to Gabriel. "Have you come to Algeria to deliver a ransom?"

Rory's throat closed at the realization that she'd have to explain that the men weren't about to be freed. She shot an agonized glance to Gabriel.

Accurately interpreting her silent plea, he said succinctly, "I'm Gabriel Hawkins, captain of the *Zephyr.* You are not yet ransomed, but the situation is hopeful.

Malek Reis demanded an exorbitant amount of money, more than Lady Aurora's family could pay. I have the amount that was raised, and I came here to negotiate the freedom of Lady Aurora. At her request, the negotiation includes the crew of the *Devon Lady.*"

A sigh of disappointment went through the room, but Rory also saw cautious optimism on the faces around her. Gabriel had the ability to inspire trust. He continued, "Malek Reis and I have reached an agreement that requires my ship to transport him, a group of his guards, and a number of rare animals to Constantinople. On our return to Algiers, he has pledged to free all of you so the *Zephyr* can take you home to England."

After absorbing that, Roberts sighed. " 'Tis not an ideal solution, but as you say, hopeful. How long will your journey take?"

"A minimum of six weeks, likely somewhat longer because I don't know how long Malek will want to stay in Constantinople," Gabriel replied.

"So likely another couple of months, assuming your ship doesn't run into foul weather, sea monsters, pirates, or the *Flying Dutchman,*" Roberts said, giving Gabriel an ironic captain-to-captain smile.

"The *Zephyr* has weathered her share of storms and attackers, and I hope to avoid the *Flying Dutchman,*" Gabriel said with matching irony. "I'm sorry I don't have a better estimate, but Lady Aurora and I thought we should inform you all of how things stand before we leave Algiers."

The sailors nodded. "Aye, it's better to have some idea than none," Roberts said, looking tired.

"What sort of work have you been doing?" Rory asked. "I've wondered."

The first mate replied, "Making bricks, my lady. Not so bad as working in the mines or being a galley slave, I reckon."

They'd been doing heavy labor in the Barbary heat while Rory and Constance had been sitting in the shade by a fountain in a courtyard. On the other hand, they hadn't been forced to parade naked before drooling lechers. Rory asked, "Is there anything I might be able to do for you before we leave? There isn't much within my power, but I'd like to try."

Gabriel said, "Perhaps letters to your families? If you give us the addresses, the ladies can write notes saying that you're well and I'll give them to the British consul to post back to England."

The suggestion was well received. Rory

should have thought of it herself.

Gabriel pulled a small notebook and pencil from inside his coat. "Lady Aurora, can you take down the directions and any special notes?"

A crewman named Jones said fervently, "I want to tell my wife that I'm looking forward to seeing the new babe, and that if I get home, I'll find a job on a coastal vessel!"

"She'll be happy to hear that, Mr. Jones," Rory said as she opened the notebook and carefully wrote the message. "Now where shall I send this?"

Jones told her where while the other men lined up to give her messages and addresses for their families. When Rory had all the addresses and notes, Gabriel rapped on the door to notify the guards that he and Rory were ready to leave. It was a relief to escape into the cooler, fresher air outside the bagnio. Besides the regular guards, a harem guard waited for her, and Malek's majordomo for Gabriel.

Carefully, she removed the pages with the sailors' information and returned the notebook to Gabriel. "Constance and I will have all the notes written by tomorrow. Thank you for accompanying me."

He nodded and tucked the notebook and pencil back inside his coat. "A bagnio is an unnerving sight, but they're being treated well as these things go."

She pulled her mantle tight around her. "They seem to be holding up."

"And they'll be happier for knowing their families will be informed of where they are and how they're doing." He inclined his head. "Until later, Lady Aurora."

Thoughts churning, she let the harem guard guide her through the labyrinth of the palace. It was a relief to be back in the privacy of their quarters.

When Rory entered the courtyard where Constance was working under a tree, her friend leaped to her feet. "Thank heaven you're back! You were gone so long that . . ." She took a deep breath, forcing herself to calmness. "I was afraid Malek Reis had sold you to one of the horrid men he'd invited to come and leer at you."

Remembering what Gabriel had said about the terrors of not knowing what was happening, Rory pulled her cousin into a hug. "I'm so sorry you were worried, Constance! Much has happened since I was taken out, some of it good."

"I could use some good news." Constance stepped back, wiping her eyes with a fold of her loose robe. "I'm sorry, too. The longer we're here, the more easily I'm overset. Now change into proper clothing and tell me the good news."

Rory gladly divested herself of the mantle and indecently transparent silk layers. Then she pulled on her flowing, mercifully opaque day robe. Algerian clothing was far simpler and quicker to don than European garments.

She joined Constance in the courtyard under the shady trees. Seeing the papers, she said, "You were working on your language lessons?"

Her friend nodded. "Master Selim says that my accent is improving and will soon be as good as yours, but he despairs of my ability to write Arabic or Turkish." She poured a cup of cool fruited water for Rory. "Good news, you say?"

Rory sank onto the cushioned bench and took a deep swallow of the water. "While I was being ogled by today's group of lechers, an English sea captain named Gabriel Hawkins arrived to discuss our release with Malek."

Constance's face lit up. "Your father sent the ransom?"

"No, my mother sent half a ransom, which was all the money she could beg, borrow, or pawn her jewels for," Rory said wryly. "Apparently Malek needs more money than that for some mysterious purpose, but he and Captain Hawkins were able to negotiate a bargain where Hawkins will transport Malek, a group of his guards, and a number of animals from his menagerie to Constantinople."

"Why?" Constance asked, baffled. "The Barbary states are nominally a part of the Ottoman empire, but in practice they're independent. Men like Malek don't even obey their local dey unless they feel like it."

"He isn't bothering with explanations, but it's obviously important to him. The really interesting part is that we're going along, too. Malek says the animals like me, and Hawkins said it wouldn't be right for me to be the only woman on the ship, so — you!"

Constance's brows rose. "I'll certainly be glad to get out of this cage, but my first thought is that Malek might want to take us along to sell if he needs more money. He might get better prices in Constantinople."

Rory grimaced. "I hadn't thought of that. You may be right. But sailing to Turkey represents opportunities that we don't have while we're caged up like chickens."

"What is this Captain Hawkins like?" A dove landed nearby, and Constance tossed it some crumbs she'd saved from breakfast. "Is he an honorable man?"

Rory didn't think she should blurt out that she thought she'd met one of her romantic heroes in real life. Better she should stick to the facts. "He seems to be. We had a chance to talk for a bit while Malek was busy with something else. From what Gabriel said, he's had a wide range of seafaring experience, including blockade running."

"I hope he's a good negotiator as well," Constance said.

"He and Malek know each other from the past somehow, though there wasn't time for him to tell me about it," Rory replied. "He was such a good listener that I told him about our writing, and he thought the stories sounded very marketable."

"Really?" Constance said eagerly. Then she laughed. "We are so desperate to find readers! Do you think he meant it, or was he just humoring you?"

"I think he meant it. He was intrigued by the idea of our bold heroines, so maybe we really might find an audience, if we ever manage to return to England." She pursed her lips thoughtfully. "Talking to him, I realized how difficult it would be to rewrite the early books to make the heroines more ladylike."

"I've been thinking about that, too,"

Constance said. "Perhaps we should write two kinds of books under different names. The books we've done so far could be by the Countess Alexander, an Adventurous Lady. and books with better behaved heroines can be by . . ." She thought, then grinned. "Miss Smith, a Well-Bred Victimized Lady."

Rory laughed. "That might be true of the heroines in that sort of story, but I'm not sure it's a good writing name. Miss Smith, an Innocent Miss?"

"That's would appeal to more readers," Constance said with a smile. "We'll need to think about this."

"I came up with a plot that will suit An Adventurous Lady. My imagination doesn't seem to run toward Innocent Misses."

"No, it usually doesn't," Constance agreed. "Tell me about your story idea."

"Sisters," Rory said. "One is a bold and dangerous blockade runner. The other, elegant and beautiful and ladylike, is captured by corsairs."

"I assume you are the bold and dangerous sister and I'm the ladylike and useless one?" Constance said with a smile.

"Nonsense, the characters have nothing to do with us." Rory leaped grandly onto the bench, her arm swept upward as if she was holding a cutlass aloft. "When Lady Lovely is sold into a harem in Barbary, Lady Bold uses her blockade-running skills to race to Algiers!"

"I expect Lady Bold will be wearing breeches when she swings into the rigging," her cousin said. "If she's in a dress or robes like you have on, she'd probably trip and fall on her perfectly shaped little nose."

Rory chuckled and stepped to the ground again, sheathing her imaginary sword at her side. "Indeed, costume is very important in Adventurous Lady books."

"She enters the harbor as if her ship is a trading vessel," Constance said encouragingly. "Making sure the pilot doesn't lead her to a berth under the guns of the fortress, because then she won't be able to escape after she rescues her sister."

"Exactly. No stranger to danger is Lady Bold." Rory pulled a fold of her robe over the lower part of her face and bent to a crouch as she slunk around the courtyard, her eyes darting around shiftily. "Dressed as a servant, I make my way into the harem to free you and any other of the females who would like to escape. Lots of derring-do."

"I can see you've abandoned the pretense that the characters aren't us," Constance said with amusement. "Who is the love interest?"

"Lady Bold's hero is a Royal Navy captain who falls in love with her and is so entranced that she persuades him to help in the rescue." And why had Rory immediately thought of a Royal Navy captain? Probably because she'd just met a man from a Royal Navy family . . .

Constance rose and clasped her hand above her heart with demure excitement. "My beloved sister, here to rescue me!" She fluttered her lashes madly. "Who is that handsome man by your side? May I have him?"

"No, you may not! He's mine!" Rory folded gracefully onto the bench again. "We may need to write a sequel. That can be An Innocent Miss book that will actually have a chance of being published."

Constance laughed. "Lady Lovely sounds so boring. Can you have her be an expert fencer who learned to use a blade by skirmishing with her big brothers?"

"That would be much more amusing!" Rory chuckled ruefully. "I fear we're doomed to never write a respectable book."

"Perhaps we should try amateur theatricals when we return to England since we enjoy the playacting." Constance gathered her study papers together. "When will we leave for Constantinople?"

"Three days, apparently. Malek Reis is in a hurry and Captain Hawkins said that would be possible if Malek helped with the refitting necessary to carry caged lions, hippos, and so forth."

Constance blinked. "So soon? Though I suppose it doesn't matter. It isn't as if we have much to pack."

"True, but we have another task. I asked Malek for permission to visit the *Devon Lady* crew to tell them the end to their captivity might be in sight. Captain Hawkins went with me and explained the situation," Rory said. "Even though there are no guarantees of release, they were glad to hear that there's hope."

"How are the men who were wounded in the corsair attack? Several of the injuries were serious," Constance said.

"They've all recovered and thank you treating them. All the sailors have grown beards and look rather alarming, but they're still the nice men we became friends with. Here are addresses and messages from them to their loved ones."

Rory handed over the pages from Gabriel's notebook, thinking she should write her parents, but that might not be wise if her father didn't know that her mother had gone behind his back to attempt to ransom her. "I promised we'd write up the messages, and Gabriel will give them to the British consul to send home. Can we do them all by tomorrow?"

"I should think so." Constance accepted the notebook pages, but her attention was on Rory. "You get a certain note in your voice when you mention this Captain Hawkins. What is he like besides apparently honorable?"

To her vast annoyance, Rory found herself blushing. "He's . . . very nice. I like him."

Constance grinned. "It's about time our lives got a romantic hero." She rose from the bench. "Now to work!"

CHAPTER 7

Packing a lion wasn't easy. Because the *Zephyr* was within an hour or so of her planned departure time, Gabriel was prowling over his ship, making sure all was in order, but he paused to watch the lion being loaded. The other animals had been boarded the previous day so they would have time to settle in before the lion came to upset them. The pens were so new that the scent of freshly sawed lumber still floated through the ship.

The cage containing Ghazi was slowly winched up from the dock, but despite the hoist operator's care, it swung and twisted in the hot afternoon air. Ghazi was *not* happy, and his furious roar sent primitive tingles of fear down the spines of everyone within hearing distance, Gabriel included.

Malek's two lion keepers had already boarded carrying long poles. When the cage swung over the open hold, they used their poles to steady and guide the cage as it was lowered into the depths of the ship. Then they headed below to get Ghazi settled while the animals already on board reacted with nervous bleats and brays and honks.

The animals were safely aboard with their keepers, and supplies for men and beasts were loaded. All they needed now was Malek, his guards, and the two captive ladies. Hoping they'd appear soon, Gabriel returned to his cabin to go over his long checklist of requirements for the journey. He'd learned early that double and triple checking was never a bad thing.

He'd privately thought it would take a miracle to modify the ship and load everything necessary in three days, but they'd managed. Malek had been true to his word about supplying the necessary men and materials; he must have terrorized everyone involved to get such excellent cooperation in a part of the world where everything took longer than it should.

As expected, the hippos were the most difficult. They and their heavy water tank were securely installed a little aft of amidships since that was likely to be the most stable position, and least likely to disturb the ship's handling.

The pens for the miniature animals were

behind the hippos with an aisle running between them, and their feed and bedding and keepers packed in between the enclosures. The scent was ripe. Gabriel could only image what it would be like by the time they reached Constantinople, but the keepers seemed capable and were clearly dedicated to their charges.

Hammocks and sleeping mats had been tucked into corners wherever there was space for Malek's guards. Gabriel assumed that many of them would end up sleeping on the deck when the weather was fair.

Gabriel was in his cabin finishing his list check when Landers rapped on the doors, then entered. Gabriel glanced up. "Is everyone and everything on board?"

"Some of Malek's guards have arrived, but Malek and half a dozen more guards and the two ladies haven't boarded yet," the first mate replied. "Maybe they were waiting for the lion to be loaded first. I'm looking forward to meeting the beast."

"Just don't put a hand in the cage to tease him. Ghazi looked angry and hungry when he arrived." The ship's cat was sleeping on the desk, and he now raised his head and shoved it against Gabriel's hand in a blatant demand for petting. He scratched between the soft gray ears. "This fellow here is a much more reliable companion. Even if he tries to bite your hand off, he won't succeed. Though he might draw blood."

"I wonder if he'll be upset by the lion."

"More likely, we'll find him in the hold making friends with the ostriches or dozing on the back of one of the little donkeys. When he isn't working, he has a talent for sleep." Gabriel glanced at the clock mounted on the wall. "Malek and his retinue had better arrive soon. It would be ironic if, after all his pushing for greater speed, he delays our departure time."

"I look forward to meeting him, too, though maybe not as much as the lion," Landers said. "Malek sounds . . . contradictory."

"He is. The lion is more predictable." Gabriel frowned. "I wish I knew why he's so compelled to go to Constantinople with his men, animals, and very marketable slaves."

"Surely once the ladies are aboard a British ship we can save them from slavery!" Landers said.

"Malek's guards are double the number of our crew and they're more experienced fighters. Plus the young ladies are hostages for the fate of the crew of the *Devon Lady.* If we run off with them, those sailors will be sent to the mines or slaughtered outright.

Lady Aurora would never accept that, and I suspect that's also true for her cousin. Very honorable young ladies."

"Now I want to meet them even more!" Landers said with a gleam in his eyes.

The noise out on the dock increased and Gabriel rose to look outside. Finally, Malek and his entourage were arriving. The amount of baggage didn't look bad. As a seaman himself, Malek must remember that space was limited on a ship. "Time to go out and greet our passengers."

By the time he reached the main deck, Malek was stepping aboard from the gangway. Behind him were stern-faced guards with the two women in the middle of the group so there was no chance of escape. They were thoroughly veiled and wrapped in pale, fluttering robes with only a slit over their eyes. It was impossible to tell them apart.

No. The second woman was Lady Aurora. He was sure of it even though they appeared virtually identical.

He stepped forward and inclined his head. "Welcome aboard the *Zephyr,* Malek Reis. Now that you're here, we'll be casting off immediately."

"I'll join you on the quarterdeck for the departure," Malek said.

Gabriel beckoned to his bosun, who was standing by. "Mr. Harris, show Malek Reis's guards where they will be hanging their hammocks and where they can stow their belongings." He turned to Landers. "Lady Aurora, Lady Constance, this is my first mate, Mr. Landers. He'll escort you to your cabin."

Looking pleased, Landers ushered the ladies away. With everyone aboard, Gabriel gave orders to cast off, and the *Zephyr* sailed away into unknown seas.

Rory eyed Mr. Landers, an attractive young man with dark red hair. If they needed a second romantic lead, he'd do, though she might darken his hair to chestnut.

Unaware that he was being cast in an improper novel, he smiled and said, "This way, ladies. You're sharing a cabin. I'm sorry there isn't space to give you each a cabin of your own."

"No matter, Mr. Landers," Constance said. "We're very used to sharing."

Two guards followed Rory and Constance below decks. Rory wondered how long guards would be assigned. They wouldn't need a lot of guarding in the middle of the Mediterranean; where would they go?

The cabin was on the starboard side with

bunk beds. Storage drawers were built under the lower bunk, and there were a tiny washstand and padded storage bench under the porthole. Very compact — Mr. Landers's head almost touched the ceiling — but it would suffice. "I imagine a couple of junior officers were evicted so we could use this cabin?" Rory asked.

"Yes, but they were happy to let you have it," the first mate assured them.

One of Malek's guards showed up with the chest that held their joint possessions. After glancing around to find space, he set it on the lower bunk, then withdrew.

Landers evaluated the chest. "You should be able to get most of your belongings into the storage spaces here. Let me know after you've unpacked so the chest can be stored in the hold."

"Thank you," Rory said as she impatiently pulled the door shut, closing just the three of them inside. The cabin was large enough, barely. As soon as they were private, she yanked down her veil and head covering.

Constance did the same, shaking out her soft, dark blond hair with a sigh of relief. "If Malek thinks that we're going to travel all the way to Constantinople trussed up like steamed puddings, he has another thing coming!"

Landers's admiring gaze moved from Rory to Constance. "The captain said there was a beautiful lady and her cousin, but he didn't tell me there were two beautiful ladies. Which of you is which?"

Constance smiled. "You're a flatterer, Mr. Landers. I'm Constance Hollings, but no one notices me when Lady Aurora is in the room."

"That's because I'm the talkative one," Rory explained. "I'm usually called Rory rather than Aurora because I'm not good at being formal, and I sometimes roar. Constance is the true lady."

"I can see that she is," Landers said, his gaze still fixed on Constance.

Rory watched with satisfaction. This story needed another hero, and it was to Landers's credit that he was drawn to Constance's quiet loveliness rather than to Rory's more flamboyant looks.

"Rory is right, Mr. Landers. You're a flatterer," Constance said with sweet mischievousness. "I like that in a man."

Landers laughed. "It's a real pleasure to have you aboard for this voyage, ladies. One of the drawbacks of a sailor's life is the lack of female company. At home in America, I was raised with sisters and cousins and neighborhood girls all around me. I've missed that."

"You're an American?" Constance asked with interest.

"Yes, and I'm glad that the war between our countries is pretty much over. I'm from St. Michaels, a little fishing and sailing town on the Chesapeake Bay. My father is a shipbuilder now, but he and Captain Hawkins sailed together. They . . ." He stopped. "That's a long story. I need to get topside since we're setting off."

"Can we join the captain on the quarterdeck as we sail away?" Rory asked, "We *really* want to be sure we're leaving!"

"I'm sure he won't mind," Landers said. "As long as you don't get in the way."

Rory and Constance exchanged a glance. "We'll find our way up there after we get settled," Rory said. "Thank you, Mr. Landers."

He inclined his head, then withdrew from the tiny cabin. As Constance sat on the lower bunk, Rory opened the small porthole to let fresh air in. "Good-bye, Algiers!"

"If all goes well," Constance said, "we'll be back here in several weeks collecting the crew of the *Devon Lady* and then heading for home."

Rory gazed out the porthole as the *Zephyr* glided away from the dock. Boats of all sizes and shapes crisscrossed the wide harbor, and a babel of sounds and languages gradually faded as they moved away from the shore. "I hope so, Constance. I can't begin to imagine what lies ahead, and I'm generally thought to have quite a good imagination."

"Indeed you do." Constance cocked her head to one side. "What do you think about casting Mr. Landers as the romantic lead for Lady Lovely?"

"I had the same thought," Rory said. "Mentally I darkened his hair to chestnut."

"I think he looks fine just as he is!"

Rory suppressed a smile. So the first mate had indeed caught Constance's eye. Well, a shipboard flirtation with a very nice man would be pleasant after weeks in harem captivity. "Time to unpack. I'll take the top bunk."

"A good thing you were a tomboy and like climbing," Constance said as she turned and unlatched the precious chest of belongings that had traveled from England to India and now to Barbary. The clothing was out of date, but it was *English.* "Now to return to our proper selves!"

The Algerian pilot expertly guided them to the open sea, then transferred to the small following pilot boat and departed. Though he hadn't been at the helm, Gabriel had spent his time on the quarterdeck watching for potential problems. That was the captain's job, after all.

Malek was also nearby, gazing at the sea in stone-faced silence. Gabriel wondered how long it would be until the other man revealed the purpose of this voyage.

A good wind was blowing so the sails were adjusted and the helmsman headed the vessel eastward. Relaxing, Gabriel turned and saw that the two ladies had been quietly standing behind him in their pale robes.

Seeing his glance, Rory smiled saucily and peeled off her Arabic robes and headdress, then tossed them behind her. The wind caught the fabric and the garments fluttered over the deck before hitting the taffrail. Dressed in an apricot-colored gown and with her hair pinned up, she looked like herself again. Like a European lady.

Her companion did the same, revealing a soft green gown. Constance Hollings was a remarkably pretty girl with a sweet face and a distinct resemblance to her cousin Rory.

Gabriel smiled at them. "You two look like the sun and the moon. Welcome to the *Zephyr.* I hope your quarters are satisfactory?"

"Entirely," Rory assured him.

Malek turned with a frown. "You are my captives and should be properly robed!"

Gabriel said mildly, "But they are on an English ship and surely they have a right to dress as Englishwomen. They will behave equally well no matter how they're garbed."

"Or equally badly," Rory said cheerfully.

Malek growled. He was not a man who appreciated defiance. Gabriel said, "Let me show you to your quarters, Malek Reis."

"I trust you gave me the captain's cabin?"

"Not exactly." Gabriel beckoned and Malek followed him from the quarterdeck, then into the captain's cabin, which ran the width of the ship's stern.

When Gabriel opened the door to his quarters, he said, "No one displaces me from my own bed, but in deference to your rank, I had the ship's carpenters erect bulkheads to divide the space. My bed is on the starboard side, a room has been created for you on the port side, and we can share the area and the cannons in the middle."

Malek opened the door to the portside cabin, which was compact but nicely furnished. "This will do," he said grudgingly.

"It will have to. This is the best my ship has to offer." Gabriel hesitated, but now that they were on the open sea, it was time to ask the question. "Malek, it's time to tell me why you're undertaking this voyage. What demons are driving you?"

Chapter 8

At Gabriel's question, Malek swung around, his dark eyes blazing with rage and menace. "Damn you, Hawkins!"

"I've already been pretty thoroughly damned," Gabriel said dryly. He'd given up being intimidated by other men after his grandfather had disowned him. "You're very different from the man I once knew. All humor and humanity has been burned away by anger. Why did you return to the corsair trade when you swore you were giving it up forever? Why are you making this journey the length of the Mediterranean with men and beasts aboard? Whatever the problem is, I can be more useful if I know your purpose."

Malek's anger ebbed away and his expression became despairing. "Damned noticing, prying Englishman," he said, but the heat was gone from his voice.

"My ship and my crew are at risk on this

voyage and I don't even know what the dangers are," Gabriel said quietly. "Don't I deserve to know, for the sake of everyone on board? Even your damned lion that wants to kill everyone who comes near."

"Ghazi is a reflection of me because I want to kill everyone, too." For a moment, Malek showed a trace of the humor he'd once had. Then he stalked over to the small windows that were set across the stern of the ship, his tense gaze on the sea.

"My wife and children," he said abruptly. "A thrice-cursed son of a dog in Constantinople has them."

Gabriel sucked in his breath, understanding how this horror lay under all of Malek's actions and the changes in his behavior. "I didn't know you had a family."

"I didn't take a wife until after you had left Barbary. My Damla is . . . lovely as a gazelle. Wellborn, well educated, a pearl beyond price. She told her father that she would not wed unless she could meet her proposed husband face-to-face, with the right to refuse if he did not appeal to her. But when we met . . ." His voice softened. "We both knew within a heartbeat."

Gabriel thought of the lightning-struck moment when he had first seen Rory, though unfortunately she was not being presented to him as a possible bride. "You were blessed," he said with matching softness. "And blessed also with children?"

"My son, Kadir, a little man with the soul of a warrior. And a small girl child, Meryem, who is the joy of our lives." Pain was palpable in his voice

"How were they lost to you?"

"Damla's father, Qasim, came to Algiers as an official from Constantinople. He made a life here, took an Algerian wife. They had only the one child, Damla. His wife had died and he'd not seen his family in Constantinople for many years, so when he received word that his mother's health was failing, he wished to take his daughter and grandchildren to meet her before it was too late. I planned to go with them, but at the last minute some important business came up and I was unable to leave. I intended to follow a week or two later. There seemed no harm in their going without me."

"They were abducted somewhere along the way?"

Malek nodded. "Do you remember my cousin Gürkan?"

"Yes, and I have the scars to prove it," Gabriel said. "Did he decide that taking your family was the best path to revenge?"

"Exactly. After his disaster in Algiers, he

acquired new corsair galleys."

"Bought in blood?"

"What else would that foul swine do? He established a home in Constantinople, but he sailed his galleys out of Tripoli and kept spies in Algiers. When he learned of my family's journey, he stalked them with his swiftest corsair ship and captured them at sea." Malek's voice roughened. "If only I had been there to defend them!"

"If you were there, you'd surely be dead and perhaps your family with you," Gabriel pointed out. "Since you were his target and you were not there, he must have realized your wife and children had value as hostages. From what I remember of Gürkan, he would never waste anything of value."

"I pray that is so." Malek's voice was tight. "Shortly after Gürkan captured them, I received a letter from Damla describing what had happened. It was written in her own hand so I know she and the children survived the attack. Her father fought to protect them, but he was killed. He was a gentle man, a scholar. Brave, but he was no warrior."

"While you are, but one man could not defeat a ship full of murderous corsairs."

"I would have *tried.*" Malek's voice was barely a whisper.

And died in the attempt. Being English and pragmatic, Gabriel preferred to survive and find some way to defeat the enemy at a later time. "So you needed that outrageous ransom in order to free your family?"

"Gürkan chose an amount that he knew was beyond my power to pay. So I returned to the corsair trade to raise more. I hoped Lady Aurora's ransom would give me enough, but it didn't, and I took no other prisoners with such value."

Gabriel's brow furrowed. "Will the rare animals make up the difference?"

"I hope so. Gürkan likes novelty." Malek swallowed. "I created the zoo for the children. Visiting the animals in the cool evening was one of our great family pleasures."

Gabriel thought of a small boy and a smaller girl happily playing with the donkeys and tiny goats. A child's delight. "I'll do what I can to help you get your family safely back."

"I believe you will try. But make no mistake, Hawkins." Malek returned to staring out the window. "If necessary to save my family, I will sell the English ladies into harems and see you and your crew dead on a blood-soaked deck."

Melodramatic but sincere. "Let us hope it doesn't come to that."

Malek made an odd sound that was almost a chuckle. "Such appalling English calm. Does nothing perturb you?"

"Very little." Because Gabriel had been numbed by losing so much when he was young, he'd lost the habit of railing at fate. "Calm is less tiring than anger, and it has the benefit of annoying others."

Malek gave a bark of laughter. "Indeed it does."

"To return to business, your goal is clear — to rescue your family and take them home whatever the price. Mine is to help you succeed, and for me and my ship and crew to get home safely." Privately he included Rory, Constance, and the crew of the *Devon Lady* in that number, but he didn't say that aloud. There was enough tension in the atmosphere already.

Malek said brusquely, "The ship must be turned toward Mecca five times a day when we pray."

Gabriel suspected that Malek was making the demand as a way to feel he was in control of something when, in more important ways, he was helpless. "That can be done, but it will cost the *Zephyr* sailing time at every prayer. We'll reach Constantinople a day or two sooner if we sail on and use a compass to point to Mecca."

Malek frowned, then said grudgingly. "I suppose it is best to use the compass."

"It shall be done. When is the next hour of prayer?"

"My muezzin will give the call in about half an hour."

"I'll talk to the deck crew so they can prepare. Now I'll leave you to settle into your cabin." Gabriel inclined his head, then headed out.

Just what his ship needed: two angry lions aboard.

Restless on her first night in a new place, especially since she and Constance were packed in like sheets in a linen press, Rory quietly descended from her top bunk, where she'd been dozing in her shift. She pulled on her simplest gown in the darkness, wrapped a shawl around her shoulders, and slipped out of the cabin. Luckily Constance was a sound sleeper.

She saw no one below decks. Moving carefully because it was so dark, she made her way up to the main deck. The low bray of a sleepy donkey sounded deep in the bowels of the ship. The mere thought of the creatures below made her smile. She'd visit the animals the next day after the ship had settled into a routine.

The air on deck felt cool and clean, with a sea breeze teasing her hair loose from its night braid. A sliver of moon combined with starlight illuminated the ship reasonably well. The crew members on watch saw her and nodded acknowledgement when she raised her hand in quiet greeting, but no one attempted to speak with her or stop her from roaming. Night on a calm sea was a time of peace and silence.

She headed aft, automatically adjusting her steps to the ship's gentle rolling. As she climbed the steps to the quarterdeck, she was surprised to see a broad-shouldered figure leaning on the taffrail with his arms crossed as he gazed into the night.

Even in the minimal starlight, she recognized the captain. Hoping he wouldn't mind company, she joined him at the taffrail and took up position to his right, also crossing her arms on the railing and saying nothing. If he didn't want to talk, she'd be quiet, but she liked being near him and enjoying the motion of the sea, which, on a quiet night like this, was like a mother's cradling arms.

He turned his head and gave her a smile of welcome. "Restless in the night?"

She nodded. "I like to explore a ship when I first embark so I know what is where. It feels so good to be out of the harem!" She smiled ruefully. "The quiet gives me time to fret about what this voyage will bring."

"As do we all," Gabriel murmured.

Curious, she asked, "Do you know why Malek is making this great, complicated voyage? You might not know yourself, or if you know you might not tell me, but my epitaph will say, 'It never hurts to ask.' "

"That's not always true, but curiosity is a hungry beast." Gabriel glanced behind them, scanning the length of the ship. The helmsman was at the wheel not far from them, but his back was turned and the splashing sounds of the ship cutting through the sea would mask quiet speech. "Malek told me after we embarked. It's not precisely a secret, but I doubt he wants it bandied about. You can tell your cousin and I'll tell Landers, but it's up to Malek to give a general announcement if he wishes."

Rory assured him, "Constance and I are both discreet."

"Given your adventurous life, I'd be surprised if you hadn't learned discretion along the way." Gabriel's serious gaze caught hers. "Malek's wife and children were kidnapped by an enemy, one of his cousins. He hopes that a combination of money and exotic beasts will be enough to persuade the cousin to release his family.

He said in as many words that he would do anything to get his wife and two children back."

"Good heavens!" Rory said, barely remembering to keep her voice low. "No wonder the man looks ready to explode all the time. This is his favorite wife?"

"I don't think he has other wives. From the way he spoke, he is devoted to his Damla. Though Europeans are fascinated by the idea of harems, many Muslim men have only one wife." Gabriel's eyes lit with amusement. "Several have told me that one wife is more than enough trouble and expense."

"The same could be said of husbands," Rory said tartly.

Gabriel chuckled. "And yet marriage remains popular."

"There are compensations, especially on cold nights." Her comment was light, but as she felt the warmth radiating from his broad, powerful form, she felt a shiver at the thought of sharing a bed with him, and not only for comfort on cold nights. Though she had long since decided that marriage was not for her, the thought of taking a lover was suddenly appealing.

Needing to change the subject, she said, "Does Malek have reason to believe he can appeal to his cousin's better nature and free his family? Along with a massive bribe, of course."

"I had some dealings with his cousin Gürkan once, and I'm not sure he has a better nature." Gabriel hesitated, then said slowly, "He's greedy and a large ransom might suffice, but I suspect it's going to be much more complicated than that and you must prepare yourself for any possibility. Malek said in as many words that he'll do anything — *anything* — to bring his family home. As he charmingly explained, he'll see me and my crew dead on a blood-soaked deck if need be. And if he needs more money, he will sell you and your cousin to the highest bidders."

CHAPTER 9

He will sell you and your cousin to the highest bidders. The words were like a splash of icy seawater. Rory drew a shuddering breath, trying to conceal her fear. "Thank you. I needed that reminder of how precarious our situation still is. Out here on the sea on a British ship, it's easy to feel that I'm free. But I'm not."

"I hope that the worst won't happen. But as you say, the situation is precarious for all of us."

"Malek's men outnumber your crew and are probably better trained in combat, and of course the crew of the *Devon Lady* is still within his power. In Constantinople, we'll be outsiders in an ancient and alien capital city." She sighed. "My overactive imagination offers far too many ways this might turn out, and most are not happy outcomes from my point of view."

Gabriel asked, "Is it a nuisance to have a

vivid imagination?"

"No one has ever asked me that, though sometimes I've been scolded for it!" She thought. "Imagination makes it far too easy to picture disaster, like a long-dormant sea monster awaking from the bed of the sea to drag this ship to the drowning depths."

Gabriel smiled. "An interesting possibility, though I'd consider it unlikely."

"So do I, but we might be struck by a monster storm that would be as destructive as any leviathan. I always have such ideas dancing through my head. I can entertain myself indefinitely by considering *'what ifs?'* and creating stories."

"Very useful if you're a passenger on a long sea voyage," he commented.

"That's why Constance and I have written so many stories! Another good result of imagination is that very few things surprise me because I've already considered so many possibilities." She made a face. "I casually imagined what it might be like to be captured by a corsair, though I never expected that to happen. Yet here I am, shocked and very annoyed, but not really surprised."

"The situation is volatile, but not hopeless." He smiled wryly. "In my first week in Portugal, I was sentenced to death twice, yet here I am."

She blinked, distracted from her own concerns. "How did you manage two death sentences, and more importantly, how did you survive?"

"I'd been asked to undertake a commission for a friend. It should have been simple, but I had the bad luck to arrive in Porto just as the French were invading. Some of the local troops caught me. They were in a bad mood, and since I didn't look or talk like a Portuguese, they decided to hang me as a French spy."

"How did they reach that conclusion?" she asked, appalled.

"As I said, they were in a bad mood," he explained. "So I was strung up from the nearest tree, but my hands had been tied very badly and I managed to free them as I was strangling. I caught hold of the rope above my head and contrived to keep breathing while I performed some wild acrobatics to free myself. I'm not too clear on the details, but several of the men shot at me, and one of the balls severed the rope."

Rory touched her throat, almost feeling the strangulation. "I guess you weren't meant to die that day!"

"That's what my would-be executioners decided, particularly since a storm was roaring in and an earth-shaking crack of thunder blasted right over our heads," he said, amusement in his voice. "Someone shouted that it was God's will I should survive and they ought to turn their attention to the oncoming French army. So they left me gasping in the mud and went charging off in search of the enemy. I'm not sure if it was God or good luck, nor did I care."

Gazing at him in fascinated horror, she said, "I'd use that in a book except that no one would believe me. Were you badly injured by the near hanging?"

"I could barely talk for a couple of days." His voice dropped roughly. "And my voice was gruff as a bear's for a fortnight, like this, but I felt I'd got off lightly."

"I should say so! How did you get condemned to execution the second time?"

"The city was in turmoil as the Portuguese fought the invaders. The local troops destroyed the main bridge over the Douro River to stop the French advance, but the civilians on the north side were desperate to escape when another French troop came in on the southern bank."

"I don't blame them. At the time, the French seemed like an unstoppable force that would conquer the farthest corners of Europe."

"They almost did. Eventually Portugal became the first step on a road that led to Napoleon's defeat, but at the time, Porto was screaming chaos," he said grimly. "Did you ever hear of the bridge of boats?"

Her brow furrowed. "This was about five years ago, wasn't it? Yes, I did read a report written after the battle. Small riverboats were lashed together to create a temporary bridge to the southern shore, but it broke apart as people were fleeing from the French. A vast number of people were drowned — no one knew how many."

He nodded, his expression as grim as his voice. "By chance, I was on the south bank within sight of the bridge when it broke up. Women and children fell shrieking into the river, drowning in front of our eyes. I joined the rescuers who went into the water to try to pull them out."

She shivered as his description brought the chaos and panic to vivid life. "Were you able to save at least some?" she asked in a hushed voice.

"A fair number of people were rescued. I saw a group of nuns and their students go into the river and went after them. I'm a good swimmer and pulled several out, and other men were doing the same." His gaze was distant, as if he was remembering the victims who hadn't been saved.

"I was so busy diving into the water and pulling people to the riverbank that I didn't see a company of French soldiers charging into the crowd on the south side. Some of the rescuers escaped, but many of us were rounded up at gunpoint. The French let the women and children and the elderly go, but they arrested adult men of military age."

"Which is how you were condemned to death again?"

"Yes, a really vile French colonel discovered that five among the rescuers were British, so he locked us all in a windowless cellar and ordered that we be shot as spies the next morning. Easier to shoot us than to take prisoners." His mouth twisted with wry amusement. "The guards were a decent pair. They gave us two bottles of rather bad brandy to help us make it through the night."

"Yet again you survived," she said faintly. "How did you manage that time?"

"One of the men in the cellar was an engineer, and he discovered an old escape tunnel," Gabriel said. "We managed to crawl out and get away on stolen French horses. Before we went our separate ways, we declared ourselves the Rogues Redeemed and promised to keep in touch through

Hatchards bookstore in London. There was a vague plan that any of us who survived the war would meet up and tell each other lies of our adventures over bottles of really good brandy."

Rory laughed. "How very, very male! I create adventures in my mind, but you've lived them. Did you succeed in the mission that took you into Portugal?"

"Yes, a British wine shipper and his Portuguese wife who feared the French invasion asked me to bring her parents to London. Once I escaped my second execution, I located them and we were able to reach my ship safely. Since they were Portuguese, no one accused them of being spies. They said I was their simple grandson who couldn't talk." He smiled. "Leaving Porto was much easier than entering it."

"Have you met any of your Irredeemable Rogues again?"

"Yes, the man who chartered my ship to go to the United States was a fellow rogue, redeemed rather than irredeemable. He said that two of the others are alive, so that's at least four. Now that the fighting is over, maybe we'll manage to get together and share that brandy."

If he'd been able to rescue an elderly couple from Portugal in the middle of an invasion, perhaps he could rescue her and Constance. It was a cheering thought. Wanting to learn even more about him, she asked, "How did you come to be disowned? I have trouble imagining you as such a disreputable youth that your family would wash their hands of you."

His face shuttered. "I've talked enough about myself. Tell me about India. I've never been there."

Ignoring his request, she said quietly, "I'm sorry. I shouldn't have asked you that."

His expression eased. "It's much easier to talk of death than dishonor."

And that long-ago estrangement from his family still hurt deeply. Without thinking, she laid her hand on his where it rested on the railing. She meant it as a gesture of comfort, but when they touched, she was shocked by a surge of energy between them. Of feeling. She remembered the thought she'd had when she'd first seen him. *This man. Now.*

Unnerved, she would have pretended the moment hadn't happened, but before she could withdraw her hand, he interlaced their fingers. That clasp felt deeply intimate and she wondered if he could feel the pounding of her heart through their touch.

He gazed at her with an intensity that

made the rest of the world fade away. "I knew returning to the Barbary coast wasn't wise," he said in a husky whisper. "But as soon as I saw your picture in your mother's locket, I agreed to go. I had to."

Glad that he wasn't denying the unexpected connection between them, she said, a little unsteadily, "This is really inconvenient, isn't it?"

His intensity eased into a smile. "So it is. This far astern in the dark, I doubt that anyone will notice us holding hands, but if we were seen by Malek or one of his men, it could cause trouble. Anything more than hand holding could prove disastrous."

She swallowed, imagining what it would be like to move into his arms for a kiss. That warm, powerful male body, enfolding and protecting hers. The wildfire energy would throb through her whole body, her heart beating in time with his. . . .

She forced herself to withdraw her hand. "I write outrageously romantic characters who are entranced by each other after a single glance, but I've never experienced anything remotely like that myself. Until now."

He exhaled roughly and made no attempt to retrieve her hand or touch her in any other way. "Whatever is between us may be fleeting and sparked by our circumstance, but it is real. And impossible for us to act on it."

She swallowed hard, knowing he might be right about circumstances triggering this firestorm of emotion. But she didn't think so. She would always have been drawn to Gabriel Hawkins. The circumstances just quickened the process. "I shall dream up a new story with bold rescues and characters who escape to live happily ever after."

His smile was warm and teasing, almost as intimate as a touch. "Please do. I've heard that sometimes dreams come true. What do your dreams look like?"

She thought about it. "I dreamed of traveling to far distant lands. I've done that and I don't need to keep doing it. Now that Napoleon has abdicated, I'd like to visit places on the Continent that have been closed to the British for so many years. But even more, I want to go home to England and live close enough to my family to enjoy them, but not so close that we annoy each other."

He laughed. "You've thought of this, I see."

"There is nothing like being trapped in a harem to make one dream. I want to continue to spin tales, and perhaps get them published. I want to have a comfortable home with cats and dogs and horses and pigmy goats and a garden. Simple pleasures."

She also realized that she was beginning to find the idea of a husband appealing. And perhaps children, though she could not say that. "What about you? You must love the sea. Is it your dream to continue sailing the world like a free wind blowing?"

"I love the sea, but I also love the land. I like horses and riding and long walks in the woods and along the ancient ridge ways. Perhaps I'll retire from the sea and start a new life on the land. Maybe I'd even visit those members of my family who would still receive me."

His voice thinned on that last sentence, and she realized that was approaching too close to the subject of his being disowned. It was a relief to feel something rub against her ankles. She looked down to see a large, odd-looking cat, mostly white below and splotches of gray on top. "Who is this come to visit?"

"The ship's cat," Gabriel said, accepting a topic less personal. "Peculiar looking, isn't he? His eyes are crossed and he has long legs like a deer and there's something unusual about the angle of his ears, but he's very good at his job. We hired him as soon as he applied for the position."

"What are his duties?" She bent and made small feline noises in an attempt to coax him closer, but he skittered back, watching her warily.

"He's the official ship's mouser. Cats have gone to sea on sailing ships for as long as men have sailed, I think."

She smiled. "So useful for keeping the ship's supplies from being ruined by vermin. How did he apply for his position?"

"He presented himself to me with a still-struggling rat in his mouth. Then he looked me in the eye and snapped its neck. I hired him on the spot."

She laughed. "A fierce fellow! What is his name?"

"He doesn't have one. He's the only ship's cat."

"Surely he deserves a name of his own!" She bent and again tried to lure him closer. Once more, he skipped away. "How about The Spook since he's spooky?"

"The name does suit him," Gabriel said thoughtfully. "He can be quite friendly when he becomes accustomed to you. He likes to sleep on my desk when I'm working there, but he'll bolt if a stranger comes in."

"So very easily spooked. Do you like your

new name, Spook?"

This time, the cat drew nearer and allowed Rory to scratch his head. His fur was bunny soft.

"He likes you," Gabriel observed. "Malek said that his menagerie animals like you, too."

"Because I like them." She smiled as The Spook wound around her ankles, a pale, ghostly shape in the darkness. She might not be able to touch the ship's captain, but she could caress the ship's cat. That was something.

She straightened and covered a yawn. "I should return to my bunk. It's been a long day. Is there any chance that The Spook will join me?"

"Probably not." Gabriel smiled. "But it never hurts to ask."

CHAPTER 10

Gabriel watched the sea for a long time after Rory left. Strange to feel such attraction to a young woman he'd only just met and barely knew. Yet there was an undeniable understanding between them. He'd never met a woman who attracted him so, and not only because of her beauty. She had intelligence, imagination, and warmth.

But she was as far out of his reach as the crescent moon in the sky above. He hoped to God he could free her from captivity, but even so, the gulf between them was unimaginably wide. If he hadn't been disowned and had stayed in the Royal Navy and survived all the battles, he might be a captain by now, and not wholly ineligible for an earl's daughter. But that hadn't happened.

Realizing he was sliding toward self-pity, he pushed away from the taffrail and did a last circuit of the ship. The *Zephyr* was on course, the sailors on watch were alert,

Malek's guardsmen were not causing trouble, and the Mediterranean was cooperating with excellent weather. If these winds held and nothing went wrong, they might be in Constantinople a day or two before his estimate of three weeks.

Then what? Like Rory, he could think of many possible outcomes, most of them alarming.

Since all was shipshape, he headed down to his cabin, weary but unsure how well he'd be able to sleep.

As soon as he descended into the captain's quarters, he smelled the smoke. An instant of a sailor's fear of fire at sea was followed by his recognition of the scent of tobacco. In the darkness of the cabin, he saw the small flare of light that came from inhaling a pipe.

Malek, of course. Now he could see the outline of the other man sitting on a bench seat under the windows in the common area between their private cabins.

The aft windows were directly below where he and Rory had been talking. Keeping his voice casual, he remarked, "You couldn't sleep either?"

"No." Another small flare of burning tobacco before Malek said menacingly, "If you despoil my prize captive, I'll take the loss of her value out of your swinish English hide."

"There was no despoiling going on," Gabriel said dryly. "If you heard me talking with Lady Aurora, surely you know that."

"I couldn't make out the words, but the tone was intimate. Like lovers whispering in the night."

"We talked of our pasts and her fears of what the future held. Lady Aurora met the ship's cat and decided he should be called Spook. It was not the conversation of lovers." Which was less than the truth. Though the words were not lover-like, under the surface had been something more.

"She might find that she likes life in a harem. My English mother did."

"Yes, but Lady Aurora loves her freedom. Any man who buys her and brings her to his bed had best take care not to leave any knives around her."

"I should give her to Gürkan as a special gift and make sure that she has a knife on her when she's delivered," Malek mused.

Uneasily, Gabriel realized that Malek might actually do something like that. "It wouldn't work. Unless one is a trained soldier, stabbing a man to death in cold blood is almost impossible. Particularly for a woman, I think."

Malek sighed. "Sadly true. I cannot imagine my Damla committing murder except perhaps to save our children."

"Let us hope that Gürkan will be satisfied to bankrupt you and start his own menagerie with the beasts you're bringing."

"That would be the best solution," Malek agreed. But he didn't sound as if he thought it was likely.

Constance smiled as she awoke to the gentle rocking of a ship. She'd been having a horrid dream about being captured by Barbary pirates and locked in a harem.

Then she came to full wakefulness and realized it wasn't a dream. Every muscle in her body tensed at the knowledge that she and Rory were sailing to Constantinople, where they might live out the rest of their lives in captivity. She forced herself to relax, muscle by muscle, one of the useful tricks for calming that she'd learned in India.

When her nerves were under control again, she sat up carefully, since there was barely headroom for her below the upper bunk. When she stood, she saw that Rory looked half awake. "Did you have a nice walk about the ship last night? It's not like having open countryside, but it's certainly more space than we had in Malek's harem."

"Sorry, I hoped not to disturb you." Rory awoke fully, looking tousled and tired in the morning light. "I was having trouble sleeping so I went exploring."

"I didn't hear you leave, but the door squeaked a bit when you came in." Constance frowned as she started to dress. Given the cabin size, only one of them could change clothes at a time. "Was it wise to go wandering about at night on a ship full of strangers, more than half of whom look at women very differently from the way the British do?"

Covering a yawn, Rory swung her legs over the edge of the bunk, though she didn't descend since Constance was dressing. "It was very quiet. The crew on deck just waved, and the only person I talked to was Captain Hawkins, who was watching the sea from the stern of the ship. We talked for a bit, then I returned to our cabin."

Her tone was carefully neutral, but Constance saw deep sadness in her cousin's eyes. Softly, she said, "You like him a great deal, don't you?"

Rory bit her lip. "Too much, under the circumstances. When I'm with him, I feel . . . understood. Accepted. Not just admired for the good looks I inherited from my mother, and which I can't take any credit for."

Acceptance and understanding were gifts beyond price, especially for a woman who was considered eccentric and far too independent. Constance was less eccentric and independent, but enough so that she understood the appeal. "He's very good looking as well, which never hurts."

Rory perked up. "Isn't he? So strong and solid and reliable."

"And handsome."

"I suppose he is, but that matters less than the rest."

It was a sure sign of liking when a woman noticed a man's character more than his good looks. Constance turned her gaze away, thinking the grief in her cousin's eyes was too private for anyone else to see, and perched on the edge of her bunk to pull on stockings and shoes. "I'm going below for a quick look at the menagerie before breakfast. I was never allowed out to visit the animals, and I was always envious that you got to see them."

"Remember that having to display myself indecently in front of lecherous strangers went along with seeing the menagerie," Rory said dryly.

Constance shivered. "I know that you loathed having to do that, but you managed it far better than I would have. I'd have collapsed in shrieking humiliation."

Rory sighed. "One can endure a great deal when there is no choice. I found it useful to pretend that I was one of my fictional characters, not myself. When I'm dressed, I'm heading straight to the officers' mess for breakfast. I'll see you there. Later today, we can go down into the hold and spend more time with the animals."

Topside, Constance heard Malek's muezzin calling the faithful to prayer, so she waited for the rumbling footsteps of men climbing to the main deck to end. She guessed that they'd pray, then eat their breakfast, so this would be a good quiet time to visit the menagerie. "I'll see you soon then. Now I leave the dressing room to you."

"A good thing neither of us is very large!" Rory said as she slid down from the upper bunk to land in the crowded space beside her cousin.

Constance heard shuffling and footsteps overhead. Captain Hawkins had attached a large covered cabinet on the main deck to store the prayer rugs used for the five-times-daily ritual. When she heard the soft slapping sounds of rugs being laid down on the planking, she left the cabin.

With so many men above, the passage

amidships was deserted. The large hatch on the main deck was open, admitting light to illuminate the companionways, the steep stairways connecting the decks all the way down to the hold. Outside, the weather was sunny and pleasant, and from what she could see of the sails, there was a brisk breeze. The *Zephyr* must be making good time.

Turning her back to the sunshine, she descended the ladders to the menagerie, making use of the railings since the water was choppy and the ship was rolling more than the day before. The steps ended just a few feet from a sizable structure in the center of the ship. It was the hippo home, with a small pool and a lounging ledge at the aft end.

Splashing could be heard, and the light of the carefully shielded lanterns polished the dark, glistening hides of the two pigmy hippos. One hippo was mostly submerged in water only eyes and ears visible, while the other dozed on the ledge like a dark, smooth rock.

As Constance rounded the hippo enclosure, the one on the ledge suddenly plunged into the pool, splashing water in all directions. Laughing, she dodged backwards and avoided most of the flying water. She had seen the hippos lowered aboard in vast, heavy-duty slings the morning before. They hadn't been happy about it, but they seemed to have recovered nicely.

The familiar aromas of horses and donkeys mingled with the scents of other, more exotic creatures. An aisle ran down the center of the ship with pens for the different species, and each pen was enclosed with grids of solid wooden bars that went all the way to the ceiling so that no agile inhabitant could leap out.

Four silvery-gray miniature horses trotted up eagerly when she stopped by their pen. "Oh, my beautiful darlings!" she crooned as she reached between the bars to stroke the velvety muzzles. "Next time I'll bring sugar for you."

The pigmy goats were adorable, as were the little donkeys. The ostriches eyed her with disdain, and the male's head almost touched the ceiling. It was strange to see them gracefully maintaining their balance as the ship rolled. She'd love to see them running wild across the African plains.

The lion was all the way back in the stern of the hold. In order to put space between the predator and the other animals, food and hay and other supplies were stacked in storage areas on both sides of the ship.

Some of the keepers had made up beds among the hay bundles, she noticed.

She caught her breath when she reached the cage of the lion. He was beautiful and wild as he paced restlessly back and forth, muscles rippling beneath his tawny hide. His mane was magnificently full, and he eyed her with an intensity that suggested he was sizing her up as a possible meal.

His cage was secure so she didn't feel threatened, but it was easy to see why the lion was called the king of the beasts. Rory had told her that the females of a family group did the actual hunting while the males lounged about and looked decorative, but no matter. This one still looked like a king.

Lost in admiration, she was unaware that a man had emerged from the storage area or that he was approaching, his footsteps obscured by the sound of splashing hippos and bleating goats.

She didn't notice until arms encircled her and calloused hands clamped onto her breasts.

Chapter 11

For a moment, Constance was paralyzed by the unexpected assault. Then she jerked away and whirled around to see a wiry little man with a gap-toothed smile. From his dress, she guessed he was one of the animal keepers. She tried to dart away, but he had her cornered against the lion's cage.

She flattened her back against the bars and tried to remember the Arabic words for "Go away!"

When he grinned and continued pawing her, she pushed violently at him. He jerked back from her. She hadn't thought she'd pushed him hard enough to knock him so far, but then she recognized the rangy figure of the first mate, Mr. Landers, behind her attacker. Half a head taller than the keeper and furious, he snarled some words that sounded like curses and made a throat-cutting gesture.

Looking confused and babbling defensively, the keeper scuttled away along the aisle until he disappeared from sight around the hippo enclosure. Ignoring him, Landers turned to Constance, who was pressing her hands to her mouth and trying to avoid strong hysterics.

"Miss Hollings, are you all right?" he asked, concern on his face.

"I . . . I think so," she stammered as she lowered her hands, struggling for calm. "Just . . . shocked."

Since she was shaking, he steadied her with a light, firm grip on her upper arm. He was so wonderfully tall and kind and English. Except he wasn't English, but American. Close enough. She wanted to lean into him and cling while she wept out her misery and fears for the future, but of course she couldn't.

"Why did he assault me?" she choked out. "I did nothing to invite that!"

"Forgive me for saying this, but when he saw you with a bare head and face, he must have thought you were a . . . a comfort woman brought on the voyage for the convenience of Malek's men," Landers said, his voice soothing. "A misunderstanding, and a very upsetting one."

She blushed violently and squeezed her eyes shut. "I should have realized. Just this morning, I warned Rory about wandering the ship alone at night, particularly since so many of the men are from a different culture. Then I did exactly the same thing here. But I never thought I'd be attacked in broad daylight!" She pulled herself together and stepped away from Mr. Landers.

"Men can be unruly brutes, and as you said, many of the ones on this ship are from a different culture and have different expectations." His expression was serious. "Do you want to report him to the captain?"

She hesitated. "Since he's one of Malek's men, that would cause complications, wouldn't it?"

"I believe Malek Reis would want to see him punished, perhaps violently, for offering such insult to one of his prized prisoners."

The mate's voice was neutral, but she heard the unspoken implications. "So that man might be flogged or worse. That seems too great a punishment for what was a misunderstanding. You did a good job of terrorizing him, so best not to report the incident, I think."

"That's a good decision, Miss Hollings." He offered Constance his arm. "Allow me to escort you up to the officers' mess. I'll speak to the captain unofficially and he can ask Malek to warn his men how to behave around European women."

She took his arm gratefully since her legs were still unsteady and the rolling of the ship didn't help. The aisle was barely wide enough for the two of them, but she didn't want to let go. "You seemed to know Arabic curses."

He chuckled. "They're the first words a sailor learns when he arrives in a new port. Very useful they are, too."

She smiled and gave Landers a sideways glance as they walked to the companionway that led up to the next deck. He really was a very fine-looking man, as well as a calming one. She liked the rich, warm shade of his auburn hair. That, along with his brown eyes, meant that he tanned rather than burned in the sun like lighter redheads. His lean, fit body was also worthy of further study.

Which she shouldn't be doing. On this ship of different nationalities and goals, she was beginning to realize that having two youngish females aboard only stirred the volatile mix. "Would the ship's stores have fabric suitable for making a pair of long scarves that Rory and I can use to conceal most of our faces when we go about the ship? Those would be more comfortable than the wrappings we wore when we boarded, while making it easier to avoid confusing any more animal keepers."

Landers gave an approving nod as they climbed the companionway side by side. "That's an excellent idea. In Algiers, I bought a number of long scarves as gifts for my mother and sisters and female cousins, so I can give you a pair. They're long enough for local standards of modesty and light enough to be comfortable in a hot climate."

"That will be perfect. Thank you."

They reached the top of the first set of steps and crossed the short distance to the next set. Landers said as they ascended, "It would be wise always to have a companion when you go down into the hold to the menagerie. Just in case."

Constance frowned. "I hate being so constrained because men can be such brutes, but that's good advice."

"I apologize for my gender," Landers said regretfully.

"I should have said present company was excepted!" she exclaimed.

He chuckled. "Don't worry — I've been called a brute by my sisters any number of times."

"How many sisters do you have?"

"Two, plus a younger brother. I'm the oldest." He shook his head. "I've been away from home too long. I wanted to see the world, and now I have. After this voyage, I'm returning home for good."

"Where is home? Is it like England?"

"St. Michaels is in Maryland on the eastern shore of the Chesapeake Bay. It's a fishing and seafaring town. There are several shipbuilders, including my father, and the bay has some of the best fishing in the world." His voice turned mischievous. "We've also built fine privateers for capturing British merchant ships in the war. I've not lived in England so I'm not sure how alike the countries are, but I expect it's similar since so many of us in the town are of British stock."

She could hear the yearning for home in his voice. She had no real home, except for Rory, who had taken her in and made her a friend when she had nothing else. "What about the war between our countries? From what I've read in the newspapers, there have been dreadful battles."

"Yes, but they say the peace negotiations in Ghent are close to finished with no great changes to the borders or anything else, so the war should be over soon. Stopping the Royal Navy at Baltimore in September evened the balance, I think." He smiled ruefully. "I've never understood what this war is about so I'm glad to see the end of it."

"As am I!" she said fervently. "I don't like the war with France, but I can understand since we've done it for centuries. But why fight Americans, who are our brothers and cousins? I'm hoping that with Napoleon gone, we can have a long and prosperous peace."

"We can but hope." He didn't sound terribly optimistic.

They'd reached the main deck so she reluctantly released his arm. "Time for breakfast. Later, Rory and I will go down to watch the animals again. Together."

He touched the brim of this hat. "Till later, Miss Hollings."

"Constance," she said shyly. "Since we're shipmates and you're my rescuer."

"Constance," he said with a slow, warm smile. "My name is Jason." He inclined his head and left her.

As she crossed the deck toward the officers' mess, she realized she was doing the same thing as Rory: finding one of the men on this voyage far too attractive. She'd have to bury those feelings.

But she would enjoy them, and the memory of his smile, for a little longer.

■ ■ ■ ■

Rory thought Constance looked distracted when she arrived at the officers' mess, but she didn't find out why until they returned to their cabin. Hanging on the outside knob was a canvas bag tagged with their names.

When they entered the cabin, Rory opened the bag and found a pair of neatly folded scarves. Her brow furrowed. "These are very pretty, but who gave them to us?" Constance took the shimmering green scarf and let it fall open to reveal bands of gold embroidery at both ends. It was about a foot wide and easily six feet long. "They're from Mr. Landers. When I was looking at the lion, I was assaulted by one of the animal keepers who apparently thought I was a . . . a woman of ill repute." She tried to sound casual, but her voice was less that steady.

"What!" Rory stared at her cousin, shocked. "Can you identify the man who attacked you? He must be reported to Captain Hawkins and punished!"

Constance sank onto her bunk and pulled the green scarf through her fingers nervously. "Mr. Landers rescued me before any damage was done and explained that having a bare head and face made me look like I wasn't a respectable woman. When I suggested wearing head scarves when we're out and about, he said he'd send over a couple that are suitable. After he terrorized the fellow, he asked if I wanted to report the incident, but when I thought about it, I said no."

"Why? Even if you *were* a prostitute, he shouldn't have assaulted you!"

"Since the assault seemed to be a misunderstanding, I thought it best not to make an official report, which might increase tensions on the ship. Mr. Landers said he'd discuss it unofficially with the captain to ensure nothing similar happened again." She wrapped the light, silky fabric experimentally around her neck, lower face, and head. "If I must wear a scarf, this one is very pretty."

"It brings out the green in your eyes." Rory perched on the bench seat below the window and examined the other scarf, which was similar in style but blue instead of green. "Thank heaven that Mr. Landers was available to rescue you."

"There are brutes about, but we're lucky that many men are kind and honest and protective."

Hearing an unexpected note in her cousin's voice, Rory asked, "And Mr. Landers is such a man?"

Constance blushed. "Like you, I'm finding myself too attracted to one of the men on this ship."

"I wonder if we're susceptible because we know this voyage might end in our being forever separated from our own kind?" Rory said thoughtfully.

"I suppose that's possible," Constance said. "Yet I think I would find Mr. Landers attractive under any conditions."

Rory wondered if she'd be so drawn to Gabriel Hawkins if she wasn't in danger of lifelong slavery. No, she'd find him appealing anywhere because he wasn't like any other man she'd known. He lived in a broader world than the one in which she was raised, the world she'd spent years trying to escape.

Scratching sounded at their door. Constance said warily, "Do you think that's some other idiot male who thinks our cabin is a brothel?"

"I think such a man would knock or rattle the doorknob or croon sweet nothings in Arabic." Rory moved to the door and cautiously opened it, then reflexively jerked backward. Sitting outside on his haunches was The Spook, and in his mouth was a still-struggling gray rat. A *large* rat.

"Good heavens!" Constance said, pulling her feet up onto her bunk bed. "What is that creature? A refugee from Malek's menagerie?"

"He's the ship's cat. I met him last night. Since he didn't have a name, I christened him The Spook. Captain Hawkins said this is exactly how he applied for the job of ship's cat. He showed up on the *Zephyr* with a struggling rat in his teeth and broke its neck to prove his credentials."

"He must like you," Constance said, relaxing a little. "He's brought you a gift."

Rory winced as The Spook crunched down on the rat. There was an audible snap, and the rodent stopped struggling.

In her travels, Rory had seen many sights that would be considered unfit for a lady's eyes, but she had to steel herself to say, "What a very efficient mouser you are, Mr. Spook. Are you waiting for an invitation to come in?"

She stepped aside and the cat entered and dropped the dead rat at her feet. "I suppose an honest rat is a better gift than bad poetry from some idiot boy who thinks I'm a perfect lady. Spook, you don't seem inclined to eat your prey. May I throw it out?"

He sat down on his haunches again and began washing his face. Rory asked, "Constance, you're one with medical experience. Do you wish to do the honors?"

Her cousin shuddered elaborately. "No, thank you! You're the one he fancies."

After Rory unlatched the small porthole, she used the canvas bag the scarves had come in to gingerly pick up the limp body. Then she hurled it out as hard as she could.

After closing the cabin door, she sat on the bench seat and extended a hand to the cat. "He really is an odd-looking creature, isn't he? Strange proportions, with a head too small for that rather large body, absurdly long legs, and the splotches of gray on his head and back are two distinctly different shades."

"And cross-eyed. He looks like he was made of spare parts left over from other cats," Constance observed. "Are you sure he isn't some exotic African breed?"

"As far as I know, he's a standard alley cat. But he's rather endearing, isn't he?"

"If you say so. I'll concede that he's an interesting-looking fellow. Mr. Spook, will you come here so I can scratch your head?" Constance stretched out a hand invitingly.

Ignoring her, the cat crossed to Rory and sat in front of her, his cross-eyed gaze fixed on her face. Moving slowly so as not to startle him, she scratched between his ears.

He leaned into her and began purring.

She smiled and continued scratching his head and neck. "Last night when I asked if he might spend the night with us, he must have realized it was an invitation."

"He could have showed up without the hostess present!"

"True." Rory laughed. "But he has guaranteed we'll never forget meeting him."

Chapter 12

Diplomacy was required when traveling with potentially hostile passengers who outnumbered one's own crew. Gabriel would have preferred flogging the man who had assaulted Miss Hollings, but he and Malek were in agreement that handling the matter unofficially was wisest. Gabriel commended Landers on his good sense, and Malek gave a lecture to his men about the proper ways of regarding European women, since many of them had never seen such exotic, apparently brazen creatures before.

Later in the day, Gabriel observed his female passengers moving about the ship with discreetly wound head scarves that covered all of their faces except for their eyes. Oddly enough, he had no trouble telling the cousins apart even though they were of similar size and shape. He had a feeling he could find Lady Aurora in a coal cellar at midnight, and wasn't that a foolish thought for a hard-bitten sea captain?

One crisis averted on the voyage, but Constantinople was still at least two and a half weeks away. He wondered what the next crisis would be, but shrugged. Dealing with crises was a captain's job.

At dinner in the officers' mess, the ladies removed their scarves so they could eat, and Lady Aurora entertained the table with her tale of how the ship's cat had invited himself into their cabin and given proof of his hunting skill in the process. She seemed to have reacted to the struggling rat more calmly than he'd done when The Spook had first joined his crew.

After dinner, the ladies donned their scarves again and withdrew to their cabin together. He watched them go wistfully. Foolish of him to wish that Rory would roam the ship every night, but he couldn't help but hope.

It had always been his custom to make his rounds of the ship before retiring, ending at the taffrail where he would unwind and sense the weather for the coming hours. Tonight, the waves were rougher than usual and it felt as if there would be rain by morning, but nothing serious.

As he eyed scudding clouds across the waxing moon, his thoughts obsessively returned to the subject of how to successfully free Malek's family and the two captive English ladies. He didn't know Gürkan well, but in his previous dealings, he'd judged the man to be a bully who enjoyed causing pain. Malek was hoping that ransom money and gifts would free his family because he had no other hope, but Gabriel suspected that Gürkan would accept the money and gifts, then slam the door in Malek's face.

Though Gabriel didn't know much about the Ottoman legal system, it was a fact of life everywhere that men of great wealth and power were usually able to commit crimes that would get lesser men executed. If Malek accused his cousin of kidnapping his wife and children, Gürkan could claim they were slaves given as gifts. And if Malek protested too much, his family might die of some mysterious fever in Gürkan's harem. Malek knew that as well as Gabriel did. The situation was damnable.

He hadn't realized how tense he'd become until a faint fragrance of rosemary pulled him from his thoughts. Rory. He turned and smiled as she approached, moving gracefully from one handhold to another because of the rough seas.

"Captain," she said, voice demure but giving him a smile that blazed like a candle in the night.

He suspected that the smile he returned made him look like a babbling idiot. "Lady Aurora. Are you and Miss Hollings settling in well?" Had he asked her that last night? Probably.

"Yes, your crew has been all that is kind."

"Since it's windy, shall we move here?" He motioned to the leeward side of the quarterdeck, which was a little calmer, and also out of sight of any crewmen.

Rory wasn't wearing the head scarf, and there was just enough light to reveal the classical purity of her features. Searching for a neutral topic, he asked, "Has the cat moved in with you and Miss Hollings? He needs to remember that his first duty is patrolling the ship and providing summary justice to vermin."

She laughed. "He spent some time lounging on Constance's bunk, but left when I came out and went off to report for duty. I expect he is even now searching out mice and rats. Cats are really valuable at sea, aren't they?"

"Very. The cook dotes on him because vermin can destroy a ship's supplies very quickly. There is no better antidote to that than cats."

"I shall be sure to include a cat onboard with my blockade-runner heroine. Constance was doing sketches of me looking brave and dashing." She frowned. "I need to learn more about cutlasses. Do you have yours on you?"

"As a matter of fact, I do," he admitted. "For all that the sea seems quiet tonight, these are potentially dangerous waters. If a galley full of pirates approached and tried to board, one wouldn't want to be without weapons."

"I must remember to put that in my story. May I see the cutlass?"

He pulled the blade from its sheath, which was mostly concealed under his long coat, and showed it to her. The curving blade glinted briefly as the moon emerged from behind passing clouds. "Have you had any experience with swords?"

She studied the weapon with interest. "I sometimes fenced with my older brothers, but we used lightweight fencing foils."

"A cutlass is shorter and much heavier. Heavy enough to cut through ropes and canvas and even wood if necessary." He showed her the proper grip and demonstrated several cutting motions. "It's good for close-quarters work and doesn't require as much training as a long sword. That's why they're so useful on ships."

"May I hold it?"

He didn't usually allow others to handle his sword, so it seemed very personal to give it to Rory. Handing it over hilt first, he said, "The blade is very sharp, so use care."

The weapon briefly sagged in her hand when she took hold of it. "This really is heavy!"

She ran her fingertips over the subtle engraving on the curved blade, then took a firm grip on the basket handle. As she raised the cutlass and moved it carefully through the air to get a sense of how it felt in her hand, she observed, "Brandishing a cutlass is harder than it looks. My heroine is going to have to have strong wrists!"

There was a heavy bench by the mizzenmast so she hopped gracefully onto it, catching a line with one hand for balance as she swayed with the ship's motion. "Behold the brave and beautiful captain of the swiftest blockade runner on the high seas!"

He beheld a goddess of wind and sea. And he knew the image of vital, laughing Lady Aurora with a cutlass in hand and her golden hair and full skirts billowing in the wind would remain with him until the day he died. Throat tight, he said only, "No need to brandish it unless you're being boarded.

Hold the cutlass by your side as you look nobly into the sea, eyes narrowed while you scan for enemy sails."

She chuckled. "It's hard to see myself as a danger to anyone."

She was certainly a danger to male hearts and wits. He lifted his hand to retrieve the weapon. "Tomorrow you can examine it more closely in daylight."

She passed the cutlass back, hilt first. He liked that she was a quick learner and respected the potential danger of weapons. After sheathing the cutlass, he raised his hand again to help her down from her perch.

As he did, the *Zephyr* lurched into an unusually deep wave. In the act of descending, Rory lost her balance and a bundle of warm, soft female tumbled into his arms. He barely managed to keep them both from crashing to the deck, but years of sailing experience came to his aid and he stayed upright, holding her hard against him with one arm.

He froze, flooded with sensations. How long had it been since he'd held a woman like this? Far, far too long, and that woman had not been Rory Lawrence.

She could have pulled away, but instead she gave a small sigh of pleasure and melted against him, her arms sliding around his chest and her cheek rubbing sensuously against his throat. "I shouldn't want this so much," she said huskily.

"Nor should I." Yet he literally could not force himself to let her go. He'd seen her lovely, graceful body barely concealed by silken veils, and he remembered every detail of her tapering waist and slim limbs and perfect breasts. Immobilized by an intoxicating blend of desire and emotion, he ran his hands over her sweet curves and wished they were skin to skin, intimate as Adam and Eve.

Seeking, his mouth met hers in a kiss of wonder and delight. Her lips were warm and soft, not wholly inexperienced but far from practiced. His reaction flared into shattering need. He wanted to claim her, protect her, bind her to him forever.

The ship's bell rang through the darkness. Eight bells. Midnight, the changing of the watch, and far past time to put distance between them. Dear God, what was he doing kissing her on his quarterdeck with his helmsman on the other side of the mizzenmast?

He forced himself to release her and step back, one hand still steadying her against the ship's endless rolling. "That shouldn't have happened," he said roughly.

"Yet I find it impossible to say that I'm sorry," she responded, her voice uneven and her eyes wide with shocked delight. She was warm and willing, impossible to resist.

Yet he must. *He must.*

He drew a deep breath and removed his steadying hand, clenching his fingers into a fist. "This way madness lies."

"I prefer madness to reality." She shivered and moved away till her back was braced against the mast. Her face was a pale oval as she gazed at him. "If only I was a free woman, I could explore this madness! But I'm not, and I can't."

Gabriel had fought hand to hand on decks slippery with blood, and his imagination supplied paralyzing images of such a battle on the *Zephyr.* His men being cut down by Malek's. The cook, the cabin boy, Landers. And God only knew what would happen to the women.

He could not allow reckless desire to risk everyone on the ship. Though he could not regret that embrace, as fragments of control returned, he swore he would not let it happen again. "Are there any safe topics we can discuss while our brains return to better function?"

Her smile was rueful. "I don't think there

are. Talking about the present is dangerous. The future is depressing. Perhaps the past is safe?"

"The past has its dangers as well," he said wryly.

She cocked her head to one side. "Your past has the Royal Navy and being disowned. Are they too dark to discuss?"

He hesitated since they were topics he preferred to avoid. Yet he cared for Rory a great deal. Though they had no future or much of a present, he wanted to reveal something of himself in an act of trust and intimacy. "Dark, but not too dark to discuss."

"You said that you hadn't done anything you felt was wrong, even if it was against the rules. What did you do that was so terrible you were disowned at a tender age? Gambled away too much money? Drank too much? Fell in love with a wholly unsuitable female?"

"Nothing so benign. I left the quarterdeck of a vessel I commanded in the middle of a battle."

She stared at him. "Not from cowardice, I'm certain."

His tension eased a little. "It was more in the nature of an accident. I was a newly fledged lieutenant on a frigate. We had the bad luck to encounter a much larger French warship and it was pounding us to pieces. One of the midshipmen was wounded so I carried him below to the ship's surgeon."

"Surely that's allowed?"

"Not if one is the captain. All three officers who outranked me were killed at virtually the same time, leaving me in command. I was charged with abandoning my post and would have been court-martialed, but because of my youth and honored family name, I was allowed to resign in disgrace."

"That's not fair!"

He shrugged. "The articles of war aren't about fairness. They're about duty. I failed in my duty. My grandfather said in as many words that he wished I'd died honorably in action."

She gasped and instinctively touched his hand, then drew her own back quickly. But the feel of her fingers, and her compassion, lingered.

Gabriel turned his attention to the sea. "My father died honorably in a sea battle when I was five. I barely knew him because he was so often at sea, but I have a few fond memories of him. My mother was already gone, so I was raised by my grandparents. My grandfather had very high standards. I didn't live up to them."

"How old were you when he disowned you?"

"Eighteen."

She frowned. "That's a very young age to be cast off! Young people often make mistakes. It's part of growing up."

"The Royal Navy has a low tolerance for error. My grandfather's was even lower," he said flatly.

"Would you have been happier if that hadn't happened and you'd stayed in the Royal Navy?" she asked unexpectedly.

He hesitated. "I haven't thought much about what might have been. My life has been more complicated and more interesting than if I'd followed the expected course. I suppose my greatest regret is the estrangement from my family. I've occasionally exchanged letters with an aunt who passes them on to my grandmother, but I've seen no members of my family since the day I was disowned."

Her mouth twisted. "You're making me grateful for my own family. Have you thought of going back to see if enough time has passed to heal the breach?"

"No," he said flatly. "My grandfather is not the forgiving kind, and he would not approve of the choices I've made."

"That's his loss then." She touched her

fingers to her lips and blew him a kiss. A wise decision since if they touched each other, it would be very hard to let go. "Sleep well, my captain," she said softly. Then she turned and moved away, catching handholds for balance.

He watched her leave and wondered if there had been any way they might have met and been able to act on their attraction in an honorable, sensible way. But they wouldn't have met if she hadn't been captured.

He supposed there was a chance that Malek would be able to persuade Gürkan to release his wife and children without having to sell his English prisoners. But that was damnably unlikely.

Instead of howling at the moon about the unfairness of meeting the right man at the catastrophically wrong time, Rory tried to analyze the mysteries of attraction. In her stories, all she had to do was tell her dashing hero to fall madly in love with the beautiful, adventurous heroine — they were her characters and jolly well had to obey her.

Real life was so much more complicated. She'd observed improbable people becoming besotted with each other, but why? Was it a physical reaction, the way cats reacted to catnip?

Gabriel would laugh if she told him he was her catnip. Her innards knotted with the thought. She wanted to spend time with him, to unravel the mysteries of attraction. To *act* on the mystery of attraction.

Better to spend time considering ways to escape a harem.

When she descended to her cabin, a pale shape appeared from the shadows and stropped her ankles. She bent to scratch his head. Such a sweet Spook to sense when she needed comfort. She whispered, "Has anyone ever mentioned that your face is rather long and horse-like? You're the oddest-looking cat I've ever seen, but such a darling. Will you come sleep on my bunk?"

He continued at her side so perhaps she'd be lucky and have someone to sleep with tonight after all. If she couldn't have Gabriel, she'd like to have Gabriel's cat.

CHAPTER 13

Constance enjoyed sea voyages and would have found more pleasure in this one if she hadn't been so aware of how it would end. They'd had eight days of sunny, pleasant weather and were probably within a fortnight of Constantinople. She tried not to think of that; she'd learned early to live in the moment rather than waste herself on worry.

After breakfast, she and Rory returned to their cabin and Rory worked on her current story, which was not going well. Casually, Constance said, "I think I'll go down to the menagerie with my drawing pad. Would you like to join me?"

Rory shook her head. "I expect you'll be escorted by your handsome first mate?"

Constance blushed. "We don't plan it, but he seems to be available around this time every morning and he does think we shouldn't go about alone."

"A very honorable fellow," Rory said with a smile. "I'll see you later."

Constance lifted her head scarf and wrapped it around her head and lower face. She'd become quite adept at it. Then she collected her bag of drawing materials and climbed up to the main deck.

Since the incident with the animal keeper, she'd kept a wary eye on Malek's men. There were fifty or so, about double the number of the *Zephyr*'s crew, and their hammocks and sleeping mats were all over the ship. They carried themselves like soldiers, and she didn't doubt that they would acquit themselves well in a fight.

But they were well behaved. They prayed, talked together, dozed in the sunshine on the forward part of the deck, and engaged in what looked like gambling games. Though they regarded Constance and Rory with interest, the head scarves prevented them from showing too much interest.

She glanced toward the sea and caught her breath when she saw a school of porpoises leaping behind the ship. Unable to resist, she pulled out her drawing tablet and a pencil and started a swift sketch, working to catch the graceful arc of their shining bodies as they propelled themselves into the air, then slid sleekly back into the water.

"They do seem to have a great deal of fun," Jason Landers said from behind her.

She jumped, and her pencil squiggled in the wrong direction. "A good thing my protector has arrived," she said with a wry glance at the first mate. "When I'm drawing, I often lose track of what's going on around me."

"Which is why I'm here to escort you to the menagerie, if that's your destination."

"It is, so I thank you, sir." The words were formal, but their eyes danced when they looked at each other. She felt safer and happier with him near.

As they headed down the companionway, she said, "I'm going to sketch goats today. Usually Rory is the writer, but I've been thinking about writing a story myself."

"Gothic adventure tales about goats?" he asked doubtfully.

She laughed. "No, just a simple tale for children. I leave the adventure stories to Rory." Harems always had children, so wherever she ended up, perhaps her stories would find an audience. "Can I persuade you to pose with them?"

"I'm to star in a story about a man and his goats?" he said with a grin.

"Oh, no, the goats are the stars. The lead character is Blackie, the small, mischievous fellow. You're just furniture," she said with wide-eyed innocence.

He laughed. "You'll need to make a second sketch that I can take home to show my family so they can admire my worldly success."

She laughed with him, sorry she wouldn't see when he showed his mother the picture. She loved his stories of growing up in America. The Chesapeake Bay was a constant presence in the life of his community, which seemed simple and sane. More relaxed and down to earth than the life she'd known in England.

When they reached the menagerie, he unlatched the goat enclosure and went inside. "Will you be coming in with me?"

"No, the goats would eat my drawing pad and pencils." Constance pulled the head scarf down around her shoulders and settled cross-legged outside the enclosure. She had a gift for making swift thumbnail sketches that she could expand on later.

He chuckled as he latched the door so the nimble little creatures couldn't escape. "So it's all right for them to eat my buttons but you won't risk your tablet?"

"Exactly," she said unfeelingly. "You're bigger than they are and I'm sure you can successfully defend those buttons."

He grinned. She loved the lighthearted banter between them. With a dozen swift strokes, she drew Jason with goats skipping around and over him. Impossible to capture the sparkle in his eyes, but she enjoyed trying.

She'd learned early that drawing a person or object made her really see them, and after that, she didn't forget. She liked the way his ears stood out just a little, and this time she noticed a very faint scar on his chin, probably the result of some childhood mishap.

As he knelt and began to play with the goats, he said conversationally, "I've been thinking about the house I'll build when I return to St. Michaels. I have some ideas. Would you be able to sketch a floor plan for me if I tell you what I want? I'm thinking something similar to my parents' house, but a little larger. More sunshine and more breezes in the summer when it's blazing hot."

"I'd be happy to sketch it out." Her tone was light, but her throat tightened at the knowledge that she'd never see that house. She didn't doubt that once Jason returned home, it wouldn't take long for him to find a girl to share his home. She hoped that unknown bride would be good enough for him. "Will you build in the town?"

"No, a bit outside. I already have the land. It's a nice-sized piece of property near my parents. It has a good view of one of the creeks and there's room for gardens and an orchard and pasture for animals."

"Will you like being so close to your family? Many people prefer a bit more distance."

"They're some of my favorite people," he said cheerfully. "Why would I want to settle anywhere else?"

She sketched a goat in mid-leap. "You're fortunate."

Hearing a tight note in her voice, he glanced over, surprised. "You don't get along so well with your family? You and Lady Aurora seem very close."

"We are, but she's the only one of the Lawrences I know. I'm from the black-sheep side of the family."

He cocked his head. "You seem respectable enough to me."

She debated with herself, then decided to explain so he wouldn't ever regret that they wouldn't have the chance to build a deeper relationship. "My father was the youngest son, and so disgraceful my grandfather disowned him. He favored all the usual excesses. Drinking, gambling." She concentrated on catching the tilt of a goat's ear exactly right. "Getting bastards on housemaids."

His expression sobered. "That was how you came into the world?"

She nodded and flipped to a new page. "My mother was a dairy maid and died when I was born. My father was killed in a hunting accident when I was an infant. Not that he would have been interested in any accidental offspring, particularly a female."

Voice soft, Jason asked, "Who raised you?"

"His mother was notified of my existence and thought the family should take responsibility for me."

"I should damned well think so!" Jason said, then apologized. "Sorry for the language. But you are a Lawrence and should have been raised as one."

Constance shrugged. "The Dowager Lady Lawrence placed me as a foster child with a physician and his wife. They were older and had no children of their own, so they were glad to have me and the stipend to cover my expenses. They found me useful. Cooking, cleaning, helping in the clinic. I was glad to learn some medical skills."

"They don't sound very warm," Jason said cautiously.

"They weren't, but they treated me well enough. I was fed and clothed and educated and almost never beaten. But the stipend ended when I was eighteen, so they married me off to an old farmer down the road."

"I hope he treated you better than your foster parents did!"

"He wanted a nurse more than a wife, but he was kind in his way. When he died, the farm went to a married nephew who said I could stay on as his mistress." She did a very quick sketch of the nephew and showed it to Jason. "You can see why I wasn't willing to accept."

He frowned. "The nephew looks like an overfed hog."

"I'm very good at caricature," Constance said dryly. "But then my fortunes changed. I'd met Rory a year or two earlier and she'd guessed that I must be a Lawrence even though her grandmother never told the rest of the family about me. Rory thought that was outrageous."

"It was! Your grandfather was an earl. You deserved more."

"That's what Rory thought. After my husband died, I wrote her and asked if the Lawrence household might need a maid because I had to find some kind of position. That's when she asked me to become her traveling companion. Of course I said yes."

Jason carefully removed a goat that had

jumped on his shoulder. "It seems to be a relationship that has benefited both of you."

Constance smiled. "Indeed it has. Her sisters are all older than Rory, nice but much more traditional. She said she needed a sister who enjoyed being as eccentric as she was. It's worked very well for us both. At least until now."

He rose and brushed straw from his knees, then regarded her gravely through the cross bars of the enclosure. "I'm beginning to understand why I've liked you so much from the beginning. Because you're strong as well as pretty. Resilient and wise beyond your years."

She looked up at him, startled. "I suppose I'm resilient, but I'm nothing special."

"Yes, you are." He gazed at her, his heart in his eyes. "I would like so much to take you home to St. Michaels so you could meet my family and help me build my house and stay with me in it until death do we part."

She bit her lip, near tears. She'd received her share of dishonorable offers, but never anything resembling a real proposal. "I'd like that, too, but it's not to be."

His gaze didn't waver. "Maybe, maybe not. We Americans aren't as willing to accept inevitability as you English are. We'll see."

Another goat tried to leap on his shoulder and failed, scrabbling its tiny hooves as it slid down him. He grinned and scooped the lively creature up into his arms. "What other poses do you need me to take with these little fellows?"

Glad to change the topic, she asked, "Is the straw clean enough to lie down in?"

"The straw is fine — it's my dignity that's in tatters." But he smiled as he lay down and the goats clustered around him.

She began to sketch. She might never join him in that house in a far land, but she'd always have these vivid memories of him, and her, and playful little goats.

Chapter 14

Rory avoided conversations with Gabriel and he'd been doing the same, though it was impossible to avoid each other entirely when they shared meals in the officers' mess. Sometimes their gazes met and she felt a small jolt of electricity, as if she'd scuffed a carpet in winter. She did her best to control her expression as well as he did, for letting her feelings show would benefit no one.

Nonetheless, when she and Constance went up for breakfast in the officers' mess after ten days at sea, she saw Gabriel at the railing and couldn't resist the temptation to join him. Surely exchanging a few words when they were in plain sight was safe enough.

Since the first mate was ambling across the deck to wish Constance good morning, Rory moved to the railing, keeping a careful yard of space between them. "Does the morning mist suggest ill weather?" she asked. "Or are you watching the sea for other ships?"

There was a smile in his eyes as he greeted her, though his face was carefully neutral. "I suspect there will be fog tonight, but my survey is more general. These are not the safest seas." He gestured at the lookout nest high above. "Which is why the sharpest-eyed men in my crew keep watch."

She shaded her eyes with one hand and looked toward the horizon. "I see small sails in several places. Fishermen, perhaps?"

His gaze followed hers. "Yes, those are fishing vessels."

Her gaze moved further out, and she squinted to get a clearer view of a distant object. Then she gasped with icy shock. "There are corsair galleys heading toward us!"

She felt him come to full alert, though he gave no outward sign of concern. After a long moment, he said, "What you're seeing is a rare kind of mirage called a fata morgana. When weather conditions are just right, images can be reflected over vast distances so we're seeing something far beyond the horizon. They say the myth of the *Flying Dutchman* was inspired by a fata morgana."

She stared at the image and her grip on the railing relaxed. "It's shimmering. Changing shape. Now it looks like a pair of upside-down ships." She gave him a sidelong glance. "But you're still somewhat concerned."

His steady gaze on the horizon, he said, "Always. We're north of Tripoli, one of the great pirate nests. Corsair attacks have been increasing over the last couple of years all along the Barbary Coast, as you know. If we were to be attacked, this is the most likely place."

Putting some pieces together, she said, "Several days ago I saw your chief officers and also Malek's heading down to your day room. Did you call a meeting to put everyone on alert?"

He hesitated, then nodded. "Yes, and also to plan for whatever might happen. My crewmen are sailors, not soldiers, but they fight well when necessary and they're very good with the ship's cannons. Malek's men are true soldiers, rather like the marine troops carried on Royal Navy ships. Anyone attacking us will regret it."

Suspecting there was still more reason to worry, she asked, "Corsairs in general are more active now, but does Gürkan have any connection with the Tripoli corsairs?"

Gabriel gave her a slanting glance. "You're very astute. Yes, he does. He's a very rich and powerful man with a high position at the Ottoman court. At one time, he had corsair ships based in all the major Barbary Coast pirate cities. He was driven out of Algiers ten years ago, and Malek was instrumental in that. Which is why going to him in Constantinople is so dangerous. But Malek is desperate and has no other choice if he wants to get his family back."

She pursed her lips thoughtfully. "So he's willing to risk his life for his wife and children. One has to admire a man so devoted to his family."

"I do, but I'm less enthusiastic about his risking all our lives," Gabriel said dryly. "The closer we get to Constantinople, the more concerned I become." His expression turned rueful. "For heaven's sake, don't mention that to anyone else! The captain of the ship is always supposed to be calm and confident."

"You play the role of confident captain very well," she assured him. "But you're entitled to your private worries."

So was she. And like Gabriel, the closer they got to their destination, the more anxious she became. On impulse, she asked, "Were you part of the situation that led to

Gürkan being driven out of Algiers?"

"Yes. A story for another day." He turned and gave her the full force of a captain's gaze. "If we're attacked, promise me that you and Miss Hollings will stay in your cabin until the battle is over. There isn't anything you can do, and your presence in the middle of the fighting would distract my men."

She hesitated, knowing he was right. "I'm not good at hiding safely."

"Sometimes we must do things we're not good at." His gaze was relentless. "And this is one of them."

She took a deep breath. "Very well. I know you're right."

"I am." His voice softened. "I don't want to be worrying about you."

She wished she didn't have to worry about him, but if fighting came, she knew he'd be in the thick of it.

Gabriel had long since learned that survival in a menacing world required a sixth sense for danger. Though the corsair galleys Rory had seen were a mirage and not nearby, he had a bad feeling that those distant galleys were seeking the *Zephyr,* and the fishing boats might be scouting for them.

Worse, the weather favored attackers; for

the first time on this voyage, the ship was becalmed in a night world of heavy fog. Perfect ambush weather.

Unable to sleep, Gabriel armed himself with cutlass, pistol, and a dagger and went above to prowl the deck and wait for the danger he sensed approaching. He was unsurprised to meet Malek in the stern of the ship, watching and listening and as well armed as Gabriel.

"You feel it, too, don't you?" Gabriel asked quietly.

Malek nodded, the gesture almost invisible in the foggy night. "Aye, there are monsters in the mist."

"Do you think Gürkan has sent Tripoli corsairs to attack?"

"Yes," Malek said flatly. "He surely has agents in Algiers who saw when we left. A very fast ship could have carried a message to Tripoli to warn them of our approach."

"The sea is vast," Gabriel said, knowing that wouldn't make them safe.

"But the best and quickest routes to the east are well known. They're out there, Hawkins. I can *feel* them."

Malek would not have survived so long if he didn't have a sense for danger equal to Gabriel's. "Your men are on alert?"

"They sleep with their swords."

"I hope the enemy comes tonight and gets it over with," Gabriel said. "Why not take some rest? Not good if we're both exhausted."

"Are you capable of resting tonight?" Malek said brusquely.

"Probably not." Gabriel turned to resume his prowling about the deck, then paused. "Have you forgiven me for escaping from Algiers with the *Zephyr* and a crew of enslaved Christian sailors?"

"No," Malek said with a hint of amusement in his voice. "But you were helpful enough at that time that I decided not to hunt you down and kill you."

"As if you could," Gabriel said with equal amusement.

Malek raised a hand in dismissal and Gabriel went on his way. He and Malek had a complicated, hard-to-define relationship. But tonight, as they faced a common danger, they were close to being friends.

Taking his own advice, Gabriel lay down on his bed without removing his boots or most of his weapons. He was going to feel like a fool if there was no corsair attack. But better to be a fool than dead or enslaved again.

He closed his eyes and tried for more cheerful thoughts. His bed was no mere bunk but wide enough to share, and the thought of sharing it with Rory was definitely pleasing. She had such life and intelligence, not to mention beauty. And amazingly, she seemed as drawn to him as he was to her.

Once he started thinking of Rory, it was impossible not to remember her clad only in veils, or the feel of her warm body in his arms and her passionate response. If only . . .

He was jarred out of his reverie by the splash of dozens of oars slicing into the sea, the tempo going faster and faster as the oars accelerated a galley to ramming speed. The unmistakable sounds of a corsair attack.

As the ship's bell began clanging furiously in warning, Gabriel leaped from his bed and slammed his cutlass into its sheath. He was halfway up the steps to the main deck when the pirate galley smashed into the *Zephyr,* its battering ram grinding across the deck from the starboard side and shuddering to a halt amidships.

His ship convulsed as if caught in an earthquake, and he had to grab the stair railing to keep from being pitched down the steps. He regained his balance and sprinted upward three steps at a time.

By the time he reached the deck, chaos

was in full cry. Screams and gunshots and stinging clouds of smoke filled the air, and gunpowder flashes illuminated the fog, revealing corsairs swarming onto the deck from their galley. They were met by fierce resistance from Malek's men, whose distinctive scarlet tunics separated friend from foe.

Bloody hell! Gabriel was knocked from his feet by another collision. There were two damned attacking galleys, the second one savaging the *Zephyr* from the port side. Swearing, he hit the ground rolling and was on his feet again in an instant.

He and Malek hadn't expected to be attacked by two galleys. Not that knowing would have made a difference. They'd already made the best preparations they could.

Gabriel had fought his first hand-to-hand combat as a fourteen-year-old midshipman, and nearly been spitted by a French sailor. A grizzled Royal Marine had saved him, and after the battle undertaken to teach Gabriel how to fight well enough to live to fight again. He'd learned how to parry with the dagger in his left hand while wielding his cutlass with the right.

Most of all, he'd learned how to use the all-consuming rage of battle. That rage burned through him as he saw corsairs swarming aboard his ship. The bastards would never take the *Zephyr*!

Time seemed to slow, allowing him to perform feats that should have been impossible, such as countering attacks almost before they began. Stabbing a blade while an enemy was still sizing him up. He knew how to kill, and how to survive.

Three pirates were charging his helmsman, who was struggling to keep the *Zephyr* stable despite the attacks and lashed galleys. Gabriel reached the attackers and took one down in a single sweep of his cutlass. Two others swung around furiously to confront him. A wild-eyed corsair attacked, scimitar glittering in the erratic light. A standard-issue blade, not superior Damascus steel.

Gabriel chose his moment, then swung his heavier cutlass, shattering the scimitar blade just below the hilt. As the corsair staggered, Gabriel continued the arc of his weapon and buried the blade in the pirate's chest. In the moments it took for him to destroy the first two attackers, his helmsman pulled his own cutlass and took down the third.

Two *Zephyr* sailors came to Gabriel's side, and together they fought off a clump of pirates. While Gabriel sliced and dodged and attacked, he automatically scanned the main deck to get an overview of the combat.

Malek was leading a squad of his men along the starboard side, mowing down the pirates who attempted to board from that side. On the port side, Gabriel's second mate had organized a similar maneuver to cut down the attackers before they could board, and his group included both *Zephyr* sailors and Malek's guards.

The ferocity of the corsairs was vicious proof that they wanted to slaughter the ship's crew and passengers, not take prisoners and sell them as slaves. These attackers were here to destroy Malek and everyone around him.

The small carronades, particularly lethal at short distances, roared below decks. Pirates screamed as huge fragments of their galley exploded into the air, accompanied by wails of agony and unidentifiable body parts. Jason Landers was in charge of the cannon, and he and his gun crews must have slept by the weapons to respond so quickly.

The port-side cannons blasted with equal effectiveness. *Well done, Jason!*

Not expecting such fierce resistance, the corsairs were falling back, leaving their dead and wounded behind. A *Zephyr* sailor hurled a torch into the galley on the starboard side.

The sails caught fire and blazed up, fully illuminating the deck of the schooner.

Retreat cut off, some of the corsairs turned and launched themselves toward Malek. Malek was a fierce, clever fighter, but his squad was outnumbered. As they fell back across the deck, Gabriel and his companions charged in, cutlasses swinging. The illusion that time had slowed allowed him to deflect blades, cut down corsairs, aid threatened fighters from his side.

A giant corsair loomed behind Malek. Too far away to use his cutlass, Gabriel shouted, *"Malek!"* and yanked his pistol from its holster.

Praying his aim would be true despite the ship's pitching, he pulled the trigger. The giant corsair crashed to the deck.

Malek spun around and bellowed a warning of his own. "Hawkins! Behind you!"

Gabriel spun about to face a corsair intent on beheading him. As he dodged out of the way, he hurled his dagger into the man's throat. As that corsair collapsed, he sensed another enemy closing in. Then shattering noise and the world went black.

Chapter 15

Rory and Constance huddled together on Constance's bunk, The Spook burrowed nervously between them as screams, gunshots, and cannon fire rocked the ship. Flames from the burning galley lashed astern of them cast lurid light and shadows across the cabin. "At what point do I break my promise to the captain to stay safely down here?" Rory asked in a shaking voice.

"If the cabin is in danger of catching fire, we leave," Constance said firmly. "Until then, we stay put. We're unarmed and would be helpless in the middle of the madness taking place above us."

Rory knew her cousin was right, but the cacophony of battle seemed endless. After what seemed like hours but was surely much less, the shouts and gunfire began to diminish. She unfolded her stiff limbs and moved to the porthole to look outside.

The burning galley was below and behind

their cabin. Though the flames were dying out, there was still enough light to see that corsairs were tumbling down into the galley and slashing through their lines to free themselves from the schooner. "The pirates are retreating as fast as they can, thank heaven!"

Constance joined her at the porthole. "The cannon have stopped firing."

Rory bit her lip, desperate to know what had happened in the brief, vicious battle. She was heading toward the cabin door when someone pounded on it, calling, "Constance, Lady Aurora, are you all right?"

"Jason!" Constance unlocked the door and threw herself into the first mate's embrace. "I was so worried!"

"I'm fine," he assured her. "I was below decks commanding the artillery so I wasn't in the thick of the fighting."

Throat tight, Rory asked, "How many casualties have we suffered?"

"Not as many as I feared from the sound of the fighting," Landers said, his arm still around Constance. "Three confirmed dead, all from Malek's troop. Those fellows fought like tigers! A fair number of our men have suffered injuries, mostly saber slashes that are bloody but not too serious."

"What about Captain Hawkins?" Rory

asked, her mouth dry.

"Wounded," Landers said tersely. "A pistol ball grazed his head and he's unconscious. That's one reason I came down here. Your medical skills are needed for cleaning and bandaging wounds, Constance. Lady Aurora, do you have any medical experience?"

"Some. Not as much as Constance, but I'm not afraid of the sight of blood." She and her cousin had already packed bags of bandages, salves, and other supplies for treating injuries in the aftermath of battle. Slinging one over her shoulder, she asked, "Where is the captain?"

"In his cabin." Landers stood aside and gestured for them to go out ahead of him. Constance took the other bag of medical supplies and the three of them exited.

Rory asked, "How is Malek Reis?"

"Some minor injuries, but nothing serious. We were lucky."

They reached the main deck, which was a fair approximation of a lower circle of hell. Splashes of lantern light revealed bodies and blood strewn across the deck. Under the supervision of Malek's captain of the guard, the corsairs who remained were being disarmed and forced down into the portside galley, which was still lashed to the

Zephyr. The bodies of dead or wounded pirates were tossed in as well. The sails and many of the oars had been blasted away by cannon, but the galley looked seaworthy.

Landers explained, "Rather than take prisoners or slaughter everyone, we're sending them off without sails or weapons. Eventually they should be able to reach land, but they won't be coming after us again any time soon."

"That's sensible," Constance said briskly. "Now where are the wounded?"

"The forecastle," Landers replied. "Lady Aurora, you know where the captain's cabin is. Our surgeon's mate is with him, doing what he can."

They split up, Rory almost running down the steep steps into Gabriel's quarters. The companionway ended in the wide area that was the captain's dining and day room. Gabriel had said his sleeping cabin was starboard so she turned that way. A similar cabin was on the port side. Malek was seated inside, impatiently waiting for one of his men to bandage his arm. Ignoring him, Rory entered Gabriel's cabin.

A lantern illuminated his limp form, and for a horrible moment, she thought he was dead. Then, thank God, she saw the faint rise and fall of his chest. His head was bandaged and blood had dried through his brown hair, and along his neck, and in alarming great splotches on his white shirt. He must have suffered a scimitar wound, because the surgeon's mate was tying off a bandage on his left arm.

Rory asked tensely, "How is he?"

The mate looked up, frowning. "Can't say for sure. I've cleaned and dressed all his injuries. The saber cuts aren't bad, but head wounds are the devil to predict." The mate got to his feet. "I've done as much as I can here and I need to tend the other wounded, but I don't want to leave him alone. Will you stay and keep an eye on him?"

She resisted the temptation to say there was nowhere she'd rather be. "I will. Is there anything I should know? Or do?"

"If he wakes and talks sensibly and remembers, that will be good. Very good. If he's in pain, you can give him a couple of drops of laudanum with water. Apart from that . . ." He gestured to the basin of water on the table tucked between bed and wall. "He'll look less deathly if you clean off some blood."

"Understood. Now go to your other patients."

As soon as the mate left, Malek entered the cabin, one arm in a sling. He stared broodingly at Gabriel. "How badly injured is he?"

"The surgeon's mate isn't sure how serious the head wound is. We'll have to wait and see," Rory replied. "You seem to have come through reasonably well."

"To your regret?" he asked, his dark brows tilting.

"I don't actually want you dead," she said cordially, "but if you were, we could turn this ship around and sail away from Constantinople."

He gave a ghostly smile. "I'm sure that would be a relief. But the ship will sail on. If Hawkins doesn't make it, I'm a good enough sea captain to get us the rest of the way."

Rory perched on the edge of the bed, then dipped a clean rag in the basin and began gently sponging dried blood from Gabriel's hair. "Captain Hawkins implied that the two of you had a history," she said encouragingly.

"An understatement. Ask him about it if he survives." Malek leaned wearily against the door frame, exhaustion in every line of his body. "Today he saved my life. Again."

"He makes a habit of that? Yet still you persist in blackmailing him for his cooperation."

Malek shrugged. "I honor what he has done for me, but a man does what he must do. I will spare no one in my quest to recover my family. Not even you or your better-behaved cousin."

Her mouth tightened. "I have to admire your honesty, though not much else."

He smiled a little. "You and my wife would like each other, I think. Now if you will excuse me, Lady Aurora, I must see to my men."

Rory resumed cleaning away blood, then realized that The Spook must have streaked out when they'd left their cabin. The cat was now stretched out between Gabriel's leg and the wall, his long, furry face looking worried. Maybe she just imagined the worry, but she was glad he'd come to keep his master company.

She kept her touch light as she washed blood from Gabriel's head and tanned neck. When she was finished, he looked less like a man at death's door. She leaned forward and brushed her lips over his. "You'd better not die on me, Gabriel Hawkins," she said under her breath. "I need you to rescue me from harem slavery!"

His eyelids flickered and opened, his sea-blue eyes gazing at her in confusion. She caught her breath. "I do hope your wits aren't scrambled. Do you remember what happened?"

He frowned; then, in a raw whisper, he said, "We fought a battle with two corsair galleys. That can't have been a dream because my throat is so sore I must have been shouting, which I generally do when in a battle. How did it turn out?"

"We won. Mr. Landers says our casualties were surprisingly light. The surviving pirates were disarmed and their ships dismasted, and they've been left to find their own way home," she said succinctly. "How do you feel?"

"As if I've been kicked in the head by a horse." He raised his hand feebly toward the bandage.

She caught his hand and gently tugged it down to the bed. "Best to leave the wound alone. Your surgeon's mate said you were grazed by a pistol ball and he wasn't sure how badly you were hurt, but that it would be a good sign if you woke and talked coherently. Which you're doing, so the head injury hasn't scrambled your wits. But you're liberally splashed with blood from other wounds."

"Most of it isn't mine. I think. Fighting with blades is messy." He started to lift his bandaged arm, then winced and lowered it.

"The mate said I could give you some laudanum if you're in pain. Shall I mix up a draft?"

"Only water, please." He gave her an uneven smile. "Holding your hand is better medicine than opium."

She realized he was still clasping her fingers, so she gave a gentle squeeze before pouring some water and helping him drink. As she settled him back on his pillows, she said, "I'm happy to oblige. And if you want to hold a tail, The Spook is lying on your other side."

His eyes lit with amusement and he turned his head gingerly. "So he is. And mercifully unencumbered by rats." He moved his left hand a few inches so he could scratch the cat's head. The Spook bumped Gabriel's hand enthusiastically.

"He spent the battle with us, then must have left to find you when Mr. Landers came to collect us. Constance is above decks treating injuries."

"Did Malek make it through the fighting?" Gabriel frowned. "I remember seeing a huge corsair coming at him from behind and using my one pistol shot on the fellow, but I'm not clear what happened next."

"Malek was here earlier. One arm is in a sling, but he's otherwise intact. He said you saved his life, so I presume your shot was accurate."

"That's right, the giant corsair went down," Gabriel muttered. "I must have been shot just after that."

"Malek said you'd saved his life *again,* but referred me to you about your shared history." She smiled wryly. "I may never learn what that history is, other than that it's a long story for another day."

He gave a breathy little laugh. "Which is still the case." His expression sobered. "It's not a story I like telling and I don't have the energy to explain it all now, but I swear I will later."

"I shouldn't be keeping you talking when you're exhausted and wounded," she said with compunction. "What matters is that there will be a later. I was rather worried about that." She raised his hand and kissed his fingers. "I should leave you to rest and see if I can help with the other wounded."

He tightened his grip on her hand. "Stay," he whispered.

She hesitated. "There is nothing I'd like more, but I don't want to cause more trouble, given how possessive Malek is about his merchandise."

Gabriel's expression darkened. "You are no one's merchandise! As for causing trouble, well, the usual rules of decorum are suspended after a battle, and Lord knows I'm in no condition to compromise you."

Giving in to temptation, she said, "Very well. If The Spook doesn't mind."

Gabriel smiled. "He likes you, and the bed is large enough for the three of us."

He tugged on her hand and she yielded, swinging her legs onto the bed. "Let me know if I hurt you."

"You couldn't," he assured her. "Not enough to matter."

She stretched out carefully on her side next to him, every part of her tense, tired body gradually relaxing as she settled into place with his right arm around her, her head on his shoulder, and her hand spread out on his chest. He released his breath in a sigh of contentment. "You feel so good," he whispered. "Soft and lovely and right."

"And you feel warm and solid and safe," she murmured. "The only other time I've slept with a male was when I was very small and crying frantically during a horrid thunderstorm that I thought would tear the house down. My favorite brother, Hal, heard me crying and took me to his room; he tucked me beside him and told me I was safe." She swallowed hard, wondering if she'd ever see Hal again.

"He sounds like a good fellow."

"He is. All my brothers and sisters are good people. I'm the black sheep."

His arm tightened around her. "Which is why you're so interesting."

"I'm glad you think so," she said with a little laugh. Then she covered a yawn. "I don't know why I'm so tired. You're the one who fought a battle."

His hand stroked her waist and hip soothingly. "Fear and anxiety are tiring, and you've been living under a very dark cloud for months."

She closed her eyes, feeling tears stinging. "I've tried to stay strong and optimistic," she whispered. "I don't know how well I've succeeded."

"I think you've done very well, my lady bright."

She liked that as a nickname. "I've had trouble believing that I might spend the rest of my life locked in a harem, all traces of Lady Aurora Lawrence obliterated and my identity reduced to 'the blond slave,' probably with a name assigned to me. But the closer we get to Constantinople, the more real it seems."

"Lady Aurora will not be obliterated!" he said firmly. "Never forget that even if you are forced into a harem, it won't necessarily be forever. Much may happen, and you have friends."

She closed her eyes, and prayed that he was right.

Chapter 16

Though Rory was exhausted, she slept lightly, always aware of Gabriel's breathing and movement in case he took a turn for the worse, but he didn't. Under different conditions, desire would have moved to center stage, but tonight deep, deep peace at being in his arms predominated.

Twice, she jerked awake from a nightmare in which the bullet that had creased his skull had struck an inch to the right. His soft breathing and the steady beat of his heart reassured her, but she couldn't help feeling a clutch of fear at the fragility of life. Then she pressed even closer to his warm sleeping body and gave thanks that he was still here.

She woke again at dawn, when the small portholes in Gabriel's cabin were pearlescent gray in the morning mist. This time it was Constance's soft voice that brought her out of sleep. "It's time to get up and return to our cabin, Rory."

Rory blinked and turned her head to see Constance standing in a narrow doorway that was concealed behind a shallow bookcase. Behind her cousin stood the rangy form of Mr. Landers, who had a supportive arm around her tired cousin's waist.

Regretfully, Rory slipped from the bed. Gabriel's arm briefly tightened when she moved away, but he didn't wake. Rory rested her hand on his forehead. No fever. Then she bent and kissed his prickly jaw, feeling deep tenderness. "I'll see you later," she promised in a whisper.

She followed Constance from the cabin, closing the door before speaking. "The captain is doing well. What about the rest of the men?"

"We were very lucky," Landers replied. "The butcher's bill is three of Malek's men dead, but all three of the medics, Constance, our surgeon's mate Lester, and Malek's man believe the rest of the wounded will pull through if there aren't complications."

"Which there shouldn't be given the amount of spirits I poured on after cleaning the wounds!" Constance said wryly. "One of the sailors stood guard over the spirits to protect them from being drunk instead of used for treatment."

"Thank heavens for such good news! Captain Hawkins will be very glad to hear that." Rory examined the door Landers had closed behind them. "This paneling is fitted so well that it appears the passage ends here. The door was designed as a secret exit?"

"Yes, it can be useful for the captain to have a less obvious way to come and go from this cabin," Landers explained. He touched an unobtrusive bit of paneling on the left side and the door silently swung out toward them before he closed it again. "This passage is very quiet so exits and entrances are unlikely to be seen."

"A good door for smuggling women in and out of the captain's cabin?" Rory asked with a touch of dryness.

"Yes, though I'm sure you're the first. The captain isn't in the habit of compromising ladies," Landers said with a tired smile. "A hidden door could also be convenient in case of mutiny. The captain has never had one of those, either, but he likes to be prepared."

"Given our current circumstances, discretion seemed wise." Constance smothered a yawn. "Let's return to our cabin, Rory. I'm ready to sleep the clock around."

"You've earned it!" Rory turned away from the secret door, thinking how much she would like to be compromised by Gabriel.

Landers and Constance exchanged a private smile; then he returned to Gabriel's cabin. Constance led the way back. This small passage opened to the larger one that their cabin was located on. It really would be easy to go to the captain's cabin without being seen.

The thought gave Rory ideas. . . .

Gabriel had always healed quickly, which was a convenient trait. By midday after the battle, he was on his feet, though his head ached and he moved cautiously. He wished he'd been more aware when Rory had spent the night with him, but his brain had been rather fuzzy. Having her there had been wonderful even though he could only hold her. Now he wanted more.

Landers reported that the *Zephyr* was on course and sailing at a good clip. He also said that the ship's crew and Malek's soldiers were more at ease with each other than they had been. Fighting side by side had that effect.

By dinnertime, Gabriel was well enough to join his officers and passengers in the officers' mess. Rory gave him one swift, warm smile, but didn't speak to him. She was being discreet, which was both wise and regrettable.

He hoped to see her when he made his last rounds of the ship, pausing at the taffrail to watch the sea, but no such luck. Tiredly, he returned to his cabin. He could use a good night's sleep. He'd try to dream of Rory instead of slashing swords. . . .

"Gabriel, it's me." A low female voice yanked him awake. *Rory.* Gabriel shoved himself up in his bed and was rewarded by a sharp pain from his head wound, but he didn't care. "Rory, what are you doing here?"

"Can't you guess?" She had come through the private door, and she closed it behind her. A faint light through the window revealed that she wore a long, dark robe, her golden hair was loose, and her expression was that of a mischievous and somewhat nervous angel. "The corsair attack made it blindingly clear just how uncertain life is here. I want to be with you as much as I can, for as long as I can."

He felt as if he'd been struck in the head again. Unable to resist her, he rose and rested his hands on her shoulders. He couldn't think of what to say, so he drew her toward him and bent into a kiss.

Her mouth was sweet and welcoming, and a little anxious. "Thank you for staying with me last night," he said softly. "I'm sure that's why I'm recovering so quickly."

She laughed and relaxed. "Mr. Landers said you always heal quickly, which is a very useful trait at sea."

"Or anywhere else." He kissed her again, pulling her close so that her richly female body was pressed full length against him. His hands skimmed down her back, feeling the lovely curves under her robe. "You aren't wearing very much, are you?"

She ducked her head, embarrassed. "I thought fewer clothes would make seduction easier."

"All you have to do is breathe to be seductive!" His body tightened, and he made himself step back, his hands remaining on her shoulders. "But full-scale seduction would be a very bad idea," he said, forcing himself to speak bluntly. "If all goes well in Constantinople, the state of your virginity will be no one's business but your own. But if the worst happens, it will matter a great deal."

She stiffened. "In other words, since I was certified as a virgin in Algiers, all hell will break loose if I'm not one in Constantinople. My value will certainly go down. Would

I be whipped?"

"Perhaps. The range of possibilities is wide." His voice turned grim. "You might be killed as tainted goods by an angry buyer, or Malek might be killed for claiming you're a virgin when you're not, or Malek might come after me with a pistol because he'd have a very good idea of who had despoiled you, as he so charmingly puts it."

She drew a shaken breath. "I hadn't realized the amount of havoc that might be wreaked. It's damnable that what should be a private matter should cause such trouble!"

"Damnable and wrong," he agreed. "But it's the reality we must deal with."

She leaned into him, hiding her face against his throat. "So I am to be denied the closeness with you I want so much."

"Not necessarily." He ran his fingers through the silky fall of her shimmering hair, finding the texture irresistible. "There is much intimacy possible that doesn't involve ending your virginity, and there can be great pleasure in exploring that."

"Oh?" Her voice brightened and she looked up at him. "I am willing to be enlightened. More than willing!"

Smiling, he drew her down to sit on the edge of the bed by him and drew her into another, deeper kiss. "Then let us explore the possibilities together, my lady bright."

CHAPTER 17

Rory felt nervous as Gabriel pulled her down to sit beside him on the edge of the bed. "This seems so . . . deliberate."

"It is," he said with a reassuring smile. "But we'll do only what you want. Just being private together is a gift. No helmsman nearby, the main door locked, just us. And you can leave whenever you wish."

"I don't want to leave," she whispered. The dim light of the lamp illuminated the strong planes of his face and the sea-blue eyes that met hers with unnerving honesty. He wore only drawers and a loose, open-necked linen shirt worn to softness.

Studying the neat bandages around his head and his arm, she asked, "How do you feel? You looked rather dire last night."

"A bit of a headache, a sore arm. Nothing to signify." He lifted her hands and pressed a kiss on the back of each. "Nothing to interfere with cherishing you."

Most of her nervousness dissipated. "You are such a lovely man. You *listen.* A lot of men don't listen much to women."

"Their loss. Women are interesting." He grinned. "And it's my gain if the fact that I listen makes you think I'm lovely."

"That's not the only reason," she said, laughing. He was also wise and kind and reliable, and the more she looked at him, the more attractive he became. Strong and masculine, with a well-muscled body and broad, powerful shoulders. "But if I say too much, you might become vain."

"I've been accused of many failings, but vanity has never been one of them."

"Then you've spent too much time at sea with only men around." She skimmed her palms across those beautiful shoulders, then down his chest. The open neck of his white shirt revealed soft brown hair beneath. She brushed her fingertips over it, thinking that the differences between male and female were so very, very interesting. She leaned forward and kissed his bare throat while resting her hands on his taut waist.

He exhaled with pleasure and stroked his large hands down her back from shoulders to waist to hips. "I love that women have curves in places where men don't even have places."

Desire began coiling through her. When they'd kissed at the taffrail, touch and taste and reaction had occurred so swiftly that there had been no thought. Now she had time to think and savor how much she liked touching and being touched by him. "I'm beginning to understand the meaning of sensuality. Of so many senses coming to life."

She exhaled a soft breath against his chest, then nibbled her lips along his throat to his jaw, his cheek, his mouth. His wonderful, warm mouth, which opened under hers.

Hesitantly she touched her tongue to him, startled by how erotic that felt. Sensuality indeed! He responded with no hesitation at all. The kiss deepened and her eyes closed as she submerged herself in her tingling senses.

His hands had come to rest on her hips, holding her firmly in place, and the strength of his clasp created a flowing, liquid response deep inside her. As the kiss continued on and on, he pulled her up onto his lap so that she was straddling him. Her lower body responded to the increased closeness with enthusiasm and began pulsing against him.

He made a rough sound deep in his throat and untied her sash so that the robe fell open over her breasts. He cupped them with his large, excitingly male hands and said tightly, "When I saw you barely clad in veils, I was ashamed that you should be humiliated so. Yet more than anything on earth, I wanted to touch you, my lady bright."

"You forced yourself to look only at my face," she said with a breath of laughter. "I appreciated that because being seen naked by an Englishman was somehow more embarrassing than being ogled by strangers. But even more, I appreciated your giving me my cloak to cover myself." She leaned forward to nip his ear. "That was then. This is now, and I love your touch and your admiration."

"Admiration is too mild a word." With his thumbs, he strummed her nipples. She gasped as electric sensations blazed through her and pooled in her most secret places. "I admired your strength and dignity, and fought a desperate battle to suppress my desire. But it has been there, waiting and hoping for such a time as this."

Wanting to see more of him, she felt for the hem of his long shirt, then slid her hands underneath. His chest was a miracle of power and firm muscles. She kneaded upward until her palms skimmed over his nipples. Curious, she tweaked them. "Do you feel this as I do?"

He sucked his breath in. "I'm not sure if the feeling is identical, but I am feeling. A *lot*!"

She laughed, a little giddy that she could affect him so strongly. "If I were a bold adventuress in one of my books, I might rip your shirt off, but linen isn't easy to tear!"

"Very true. Not to mention that replacing clothing on shipboard can be difficult." He caught hold of the shirt's hem with both hands and yanked it up over his head.

Straddling his lap gave her a splendid view of the hard ripple of his muscles and those truly magnificent shoulders. "Thank you! You look very well in your tailored sea captain's uniform, but you look even better like this."

"I'm glad you think so." He sounded embarrassed by the compliment. "Clothing is interesting, isn't it? The primary purpose is to protect us from the weather and the hazards of everyday life, but a strong secondary purpose is to identify ourselves to the world, and to the opposite sex."

She laughed. "If you've ever been to a society ball, you must know that the *primary* purpose of clothing can be preening for the opposite sex! By both men and women. Not so very different from peacocks and other creatures. Fine feathers are a vital part of the mating game."

"True. But you, my lady bright, need no plumage. You are breathtakingly beautiful just as nature made you." He peeled her robe from her shoulders. It dropped around her waist, leaving her entire upper body bare. She was glad there was so little light because she suspected she was blushing.

"You look so soft and . . . edible," he murmured, both gaze and hands caressing every visible inch of her. "I'm tempted to lick you all over, but that would take quite some time and probably wear out my tongue."

She giggled. She *never* giggled! "Is intimacy supposed to include laughter?"

"Sometimes humor is a delightful ingredient of desire. Other times, crazed passion rules and there is no time for laughter." He caught her around the waist and transferred her to the mattress, then twisted down so they were lying face-to-face on their sides. "Both are good because shared laughter can be as intimate as touch. Sometimes even more so."

"Your thoughts sound very worthy of analysis, but I'll consider them later," she murmured. "My logical capabilities aren't working just now."

"Mine are largely paralyzed as well," he admitted. "You are so shockingly beautiful, so desirable, that I can think of little else."

His gaze warmed her to her marrow. Though technically she still wore her robe, it was falling behind her so that she was bare enough for him to run his hand caressingly from breast to waist and along her outer thigh. When his hand reached her knee, he leaned into another kiss.

She rolled closer so that her bare breasts pressed softly against his equally bare chest. "I love this touching," she breathed. "I'm beginning to understand the appeal of marriage since it grants license to do this all the time."

"Marriage grants license, but true intimacy comes from trust and caring." He rubbed his chin affectionately on her temple, but his hand began to move again. Up her thigh, closer and closer to the mysteries above. She gasped when he first touched the moist, hidden cleft beneath the triangle of golden hair.

She almost cried out at the sheer raging sensations triggered by that contact. She felt as if flames burned from his fingers into the deepest, most secret places of her body. Then he began stroking gently and not only logic but all thought disintegrated into intoxicating pleasure.

Again, he kissed her deeply, distracting her from the increasing intimacy of his touch as his fingertips explored the delicate, insanely sensitive hidden folds. Deeper, sliding, probing, building unbearable heat until she was frantic with need.

With shattering suddenness, the coiling fire within exploded into coruscating flame, annihilating everything but the passion that ignited every fiber of her being. She convulsed, clinging to him desperately so that she wouldn't tumble into the abyss.

Consuming fire faded, leaving her limp and profoundly satisfied. She had never felt so close to another person in her life. "If I'm sinning," she said weakly, "I'm all in favor of it!"

He laughed and gathered her close, his hand stroking her back tenderly. As he did, she realized there was a part of him that was still tense and unsatisfied.

She said hesitantly, "I think that was the end of chapter one, but there is another chapter yet unfinished." She slipped her hand under his drawers and found that rather alarming proof of maleness. When she clasped him, she felt the shock wave through his whole body.

"You don't have to do this!" he gasped.

"Not if you don't want to."

"How can I know if I want to if I don't try?" she asked reasonably. She squeezed him gently and he almost stopped breathing altogether. "But you'll have to tell me what to do."

"What you're doing," he said in a choked voice. "Perhaps . . . pull a little."

She did as he suggested with spectacular results. He jerked in her hand and his hips thrust against her. He culminated with a spasm of release as he crushed her close. The inherent violence was alarming, but also satisfying. She loved that she could give her strong, confident sea captain such pleasure.

As his body eased, he said, "You're a swift learner, my lady bright." A small hand towel hung on a bar on his bedside table and he reached for it so he could clean them both up. He tossed the towel aside when he was done and cuddled her close again.

"I'm so glad you came tonight," he whispered. "Having you with me is extraordinary."

"It certainly was for me," she agreed. Her hand still rested on his genitals, which were now soft and intimate rather than threatening. "But surely not as extraordinary for you?"

Recognizing her barely veiled question, he said, "A man who spends most of his time at sea doesn't have a lot of opportunity for rakish behavior."

"You've never been married?"

"No, the closest I've come to that is a long-term affair with a widow in Bristol. Whenever the *Zephyr* landed there for refitting and repairs, I'd visit my lady friend. She was warm and welcoming and a fine cook. We always enjoyed each other's company."

"She's gone now?" Rory asked quietly.

"Yes, she died of lung fever one winter." He sighed. "I didn't find out until months later, when we visited Bristol again."

Sensing his sadness, she asked brightly, "Since you're talking about the past, I think it's jolly well time you told me the history of you and Malek. I can't wait to hear all about it!"

Chapter 18

"I can't avoid it any longer, can I? But, first, we reposition ourselves." Gabriel rolled Rory onto her back and tied the sash of her robe. "This is necessary or I'll be too distracted to speak coherently. Would you like a glass of claret?"

"Sharing wine with you in bed sounds deliciously decadent." She scooted up against the headboard, tucking a pillow behind her. Her unbound golden hair cascaded lushly over her shoulders and breasts.

Gabriel donned his own robe, then unlocked his liquor cabinet and removed a bottle and two sturdy glass tumblers. He poured the wine and handed it to her with a courtly bow. "To my lady bright, the most dazzling star on the Middle Sea."

She raised her glass in return and gave him a smile that made him feel ten feet tall. "And to my captain, who has taken me somewhere I've never been before."

They clinked their tumblers and drank, then Gabriel gave in to impulse and kissed her again. She kissed him back, murmuring, "I feel cherished and decadent in the best possible way!"

Unable to remember when he'd felt so content, he settled on the bed beside her. She said, "When you were unconscious, Malek told me you'd saved his life again. What was the first time? Part of your mysterious past, I assume."

He turned the tumbler absently, gazing into the ruby depths. "It was over ten years ago. I've told you about being disowned and returning to the sea on a merchant ship. The *Sea Song.* I'd worked my way up to being second mate and was hoping to have more influence with the captain, who was a little lax in his ship's security." He sipped at the claret. "Which was probably why we were taken by an Algerian corsair."

She caught her breath, shocked by the revelation. "You were enslaved? Was it by Malek?"

"No, a different reis. But Malek bought me and some other sailors to work on a ship of his." He glanced sideways at Rory. "One of the other men was Jason Landers's father, which is how I came to know the family. We've been friends ever since, to our mutual benefit."

"I see," she said thoughtfully. "So when Jason Landers was going off to sea, his father asked you to take him on and make sure he was well trained and cared for."

He nodded. "It was no hardship; Jason is a born seaman. In return, I have friends and a really good shipyard on that side of the Atlantic if I need repairs."

"So going back to the Barbary Coast and your being enslaved," she said encouragingly.

"Experienced European sailors are prized and valuable because we generally have superior ship and artillery skills. I brought a good price," he said dryly. "Malek rather liked me and regularly suggested that I turn renegade and embrace the Muslim faith. I would have my freedom and I could captain one of his ships."

She sipped her wine, her gaze not leaving him. "Clearly you turned him down."

"I'm not a very good Christian, but I realized that the faith I was raised in was too much a part of me to renounce."

Her brows furrowed thoughtfully. "When one is forcibly removed from one's own world, preserving as much of one's identity as possible must feel very necessary."

He hadn't thought of it in those terms. "That's it exactly. Despite the advantages of turning renegade, few captured Christians do so. At any rate, I worked on one of Malek's local boats that sailed mostly around the harbor of Algiers. I learned a lot about the language, customs, and waterways and considered ways to escape."

"Is that how you escaped?"

"Oh, no, the story is much more complicated! I was getting ready to make my attempt to escape when Gürkan came. He's Malek's second cousin, a rich and powerful merchant based in Constantinople. He's well known at the imperial court and has several government posts in places like the customs depart. He and his younger brother came to Algiers to build their own corsair fleet, and he called on his cousin Malek for help."

"And then betrayed him," Rory said flatly. "How did it happen?"

"Malek was flattered by the attention of his older and wealthier cousin. He thought they were allies. Instead . . ." Gabriel shook his head. "There's an old Arabic saying. *'I, against my brothers. I and my brothers against my cousins. I and my brothers and my cousins against the world.'* Gürkan didn't want an ally; he wanted Malek and his sailors. He captured all of us, including Malek, and chained us to the rowing benches of a corsair galley."

Rory sucked her breath in. "How did you escape?"

"Working together, Malek and I managed to free ourselves of our chains and take over the galley, and then the *Zephyr,* which was Gürkan's newest prize and his headquarters. Gürkan wasn't on the *Zephyr* when we took it, but his younger brother was. I killed him in the fight, thereby sparing Malek the crime of killing his own kin." Gabriel poured himself more wine, preferring to drown the memory.

"I'm sure it was more complicated than you're letting on."

"Yes, but it was a lot of years ago, and what we did was necessary. When the dust settled, Gürkan had pulled out of Algiers and Malek was in possession of all Gürkan's ships, warehouses, and trading goods in the area. He'd become a much wealthier man, so he suggested that Gürkan should stick to the eastern end of the Mediterranean."

"After all you did for Malek, did he keep you enslaved?" she asked, frowning.

"We negotiated." Gabriel smiled a little. "Or more accurately, Malek wanted to keep me so he tried to find conditions under which I'd willingly work for him in Algiers as a free man. And while he was talking, I seized the *Zephyr* and escaped with as many of my fellow Christian slaves as I could manage. Malek was not happy, but I think he felt he owed me too much to pursue us. Not that I think he could have caught the *Zephyr.* She's the fastest ship I've ever sailed in, which has proved useful in my shady career."

"Good heavens!" Her eyes were wide with admiration. "I would love to weave your story into one of my novels!"

He smiled crookedly. "It was painful, bloody, and difficult and I will not give you more details, my charming little ghoul. I claimed the ship as my prize and returned my fellow freed slaves to safety. Some are still part of my crew."

"You're a hero, my captain," she said seriously. "You freed yourself and a number of other captives and have become a man of means as a ship owner and captain. Surely your horrid grandfather would be proud of you."

Gabriel snorted. "He would condemn me for being taken captive in the first place. To him, the only kind of honor that matters comes from the Royal Navy. I find it easier to respect Malek, actually. He is a man of his time and place, as we all are, but he's also a man of honor. Which is why we haven't been at each other's throats despite that very adversarial history."

"Complex relationships are fascinating," she murmured, her eyes out of focus.

"You may take the essence of my relationship for one of your stories, but only if you change the facts out of all recognition."

She nodded. "That's fair."

He gazed at her, his gut knotted at the thought that her stories might be locked forever with her in some damnable harem. That wouldn't happen if he could help it, but he had no idea what he might be able to do to save her from such a fate. Better to think about the present. "Tomorrow morning, or I suppose it's later this morning by now, the three Muslim soldiers who died in the attack will be given burials at sea."

"Should Constance and I come, or are no women allowed?"

He hesitated. "I'll check with Malek and his imam. I think they'll let you attend the service, though in your most conservative, unobtrusive clothing."

"Long dark gown and maximum head scarf," she said with a nod. "Unless it's forbidden, I'd like to attend. Those men died for all of us."

"Exactly. I think that Malek and his men would be pleased by a show of respect from two foreign ladies."

"What is a Muslim funeral like? I'd like to know what to expect."

"The details vary greatly," he explained. "Ideally, a Muslim is buried in the earth within a day or so. If a ship is too far from land for that to be practical, burial at sea is permitted. The bodies will be sewn into shrouds with weights so they'll sink quickly, and sent into the sea facing Mecca. Prayers will be said, but the service is otherwise simple."

"We can manage that." She smothered a yawn. "I'd love to stay the night, but I think it's time to return to my cabin."

Reluctantly he said, "You're right. I'll escort you back."

"I'll probably not be seen by anyone."

"Nonetheless." He swung out of the bed and offered his hand to help her to the floor.

She slid her feet into the light slippers that she'd worn coming in and kicked off when things got interesting. After pulling her hair back in a loose knot, she tightened her sash, making sure she was completely covered.

They stood in front of the hidden door, their gazes locked. She was so beautiful, so warm and open. It seemed impossible that she could care for a man like him, but he couldn't doubt that the emotion between them was mutual. "I wish so much you could stay," he said painfully.

"There will be some other nights between now and Constantinople," she said. "If you want me, I'll take advantage of every one of them, and of you."

"I'll take you up on that, my lady bright." He drew her into a hug, engulfing her in his arms as if his body could protect her from all danger.

She clung to him for long moments, then stepped back, her face resolute. "Good night, my captain."

Silently he opened the door and gestured for her to go ahead. Then he followed her down the narrow passage and into the wider one where her cabin was. They didn't touch, because they might be unable to release each other again.

When she reached her cabin door, she looked back for one last intimate smile. Then she turned the key, opened the door, and disappeared.

He returned to his cabin, feeling gut-punched. There had to be a way to free her and her cousin and the crew of the *Devon Lady.* But he didn't know what it might be. Any chance of success must be wrenched from events as they unfolded.

When Rory quietly closed the cabin door, she was unsurprised to hear the squeak of her cousin's springs, and a sleepy voice saying, "So you're safely home again. How did your clandestine visit go?"

Rory sank wearily onto the foot of her cousin's bunk. "I think I love him, Constance. And I think he loves me. We stopped short of endangering my virginity, but I learned that there is much that can be done without going too far." She smiled reminiscently, still tingling in unnamed parts of her body.

"I'm glad," Constance said softly. "It was dangerous to meet him, but with so little time before our journey ends, I think you were wise to take the risk."

Rory turned, barely able to make out the pale oval of her cousin's face. "What about you, Constance? You also have a man you care for deeply, and you're a widow. Why not take advantage of your circumstances?"

"I hadn't really thought about that!" Constance said, surprised. "You're always the adventurous one, not me. But perhaps this time I should be reckless. Do you think Jason would be interested?"

"Of course he would! I've seen the way he

looks at you. Seize the day, cousin, and seize the man!" Rory's mouth tightened. "For the next week or so, we can call our bodies are own if we're careful enough not to be caught."

Constance drew a deep breath. "Perhaps . . . perhaps I'll have the courage to proposition him tomorrow when we're visiting the menagerie."

Remembering the funeral service, Rory said, "You may have to make your visit later than usual. Gabriel said that tomorrow morning the soldiers who died will be buried at sea. I asked if we might come, and he thought it would be allowed."

Constance made a small sound of distress. "I hadn't really thought about the fate of the men who died, but of course it's necessary. I hope we can go to pay our respects."

"Not to mention that it will be interesting. Fodder for our adventure tales!" Rory gave a twisted smile in the darkness. "We're incorrigible, aren't we?"

"I prefer to think of it as creative," Constance said with dignity. "We've collected a great deal of material on this journey, haven't we? It's a silver lining."

"So it is." Rory stood, yawning again before climbing up to her bunk. A silver lining to a very dark cloud. But better than no light at all.

Chapter 19

Rory woke from a sleep filled with too vivid dreams to find Constance already dressed and reading a note. "This was just delivered," her cousin said. "Your captain says that we may attend the funeral service and our presence will be appreciated."

Rory yawned and swung down from the upper bunk. "How soon?"

"Very, I think. The service will be announced by the tolling of the ship's bell."

"I'd better get dressed, then."

As Constance curled up on her bunk to give space, Rory pulled on a dark blue gown and added a sober shawl. She wrapped the head scarf with particular care so that nothing but her eyes and a bit of brow were visible. Constance had done the same.

As Constance drew on gloves, she said, "I regret the deaths of three brave men, but I do think this will be interesting."

"We both have too much curiosity, which

is why we're here," Rory said with a chuckle, remembering how Gabriel had teasingly called her a little ghoul in a voice that made it an intimate endearment. "Time to ascend to the top deck."

The seas were rough, and they needed to use the railing as they left their cabin and walked to the companionway. "It feels like a storm is moving in."

"I suppose we're overdue for one," Constance said without enthusiasm. "I hope it's just an average storm, not like the one that hit when we were crossing the Indian Ocean. I was saying my final prayers that time."

"That was a pretty dreadful storm," Rory agreed. "But we survived." The *Zephyr* lurched heavily to port and she grabbed the railing again.

Constance asked, "Do you think the service might be postponed?"

"The captain said the custom is to bury the deceased as soon as possible. I gather the ceremony isn't too long, so it might be over before the storm hits."

As they started up to the main deck, the ship's bell began tolling with the slow solemnity of an ancient church. At the top of the stairs, they were greeted with overcast skies and a sharp wind that carried a spattering of raindrops.

Gabriel was on the quarterdeck studying the sky. Frowning, he gave orders to his second officer. The second officer relayed more orders, and sailors began climbing the rigging and reefing sails.

Rory had spent enough time at sea to know that taking in sails was the best way to deal with foul weather. Doing it now not only would prepare the *Zephyr* for the coming storm, but would steady the ship for the solemn ceremony that was about to begin.

Jason Landers saw them and came over with a special smile for Constance. "Ladies, allow me to escort you to the overhang of the quarterdeck. You'll have a good view of the ceremony and be more protected from the weather that's coming in."

They'd also be fairly unobtrusive in case some of Malek's men were disturbed by the scandalous sight of females. They followed Jason to the area he'd suggested. As he'd said, they were protected from the wind. He stayed near them, probably under orders from Gabriel to make sure nothing untoward happened.

A section of the starboard railing had been removed, and judging by the low voices Rory heard from the helm, the ship was altering its course so that the burial zone faced Mecca. Members of the *Zephyr* crew who weren't on active duty were gathering on the deck in formal lines, faces sober.

Gabriel joined them in his navy-blue full-dress uniform. None of Malek's men were present until a slow, mournful drumbeat began. Led by Malek, a double line of soldiers marched up the companionway to the deck, the three shrouded bodies carried on their shoulders. Rory held her breath, hoping the motion of the ship didn't cause trouble, but the soldiers managed to keep their balance.

The bodies were set gently on the deck. Malek's troops surrounded them and sang a funeral prayer. Then the first body was lifted and transferred to the edge of deck that was open to the sea. The imam, Hajji Asad, a dignified older man, nodded to Malek.

First Malek, then Gabriel spoke brief tributes to the courage and honor of the fallen warriors. The imam intoned a short prayer and the first body was consigned to the sea, falling swiftly because of the weights that had been wrapped in the shroud. The ship's crew saluted, and several Catholics among them crossed themselves.

The second body was accorded the same somber ritual. The wind was getting stronger and so were the gusts of rain.

Almost everyone was watching the service, but concerned by the weather, Rory scanned the sea. On the port side of the vessel, a strange black circle of water was spiraling. Wondering if it was a whirlpool forming, she said in a low voice, "Mr. Landers, is that water formation to port normal?"

Jason looked in the direction she indicated and sucked in his breath. Then he moved forward and spoke to Gabriel in a low, tense voice. Gabriel frowned and looked to port.

The third body had been brought forth to the edge of the deck and the imam was saying his prayers when disaster struck. A blast of wind and water caused the *Zephyr* to roll so violently to starboard that men and objects were flung across the deck.

Rory and Constance were both knocked off their feet, and Rory was sliding toward the open section of the railing.

"Rory!" Constance managed to clamp a secure handhold with one hand while hurling herself across the deck to catch Rory's wrist with the other. The jerk almost dislocated Rory's shoulder, but she barely noticed as delayed panic at what might have happened flooded her body.

As she crawled back toward her cousin, the third shrouded corpse shot precipitously over the edge of the deck and into the sea. And the imam tumbled after him.

Gabriel lunged toward the gap in the railing shouting, "Hajji Asad!"

Rory's heart almost stopped when she saw him going after the imam. Barely in time, he caught a corner of the holy man's flowing robe and pulled him back toward safety, but their position was still precarious. A half-dozen strides behind Gabriel, Malek added his muscle and a secure grip on the railing to help drag Gabriel and the imam back to safe territory.

The rescue had taken only seconds, but screams and cries said there was other damage. Two crewmen raced to the section of railing that had been displaced and slammed it back where it belonged just in time to save one of Malek's soldiers from sliding overboard.

The ship was rolling back to port and no one else seemed to be in danger of being lost. As Rory stumbled to her feet, her gaze returned to the disturbance in the water. Aghast, she saw that the viciously swirling waterspout had spun up to connect with the bottom of a low, dark storm cloud. Another spout was forming beyond it. Rory had seen waterspouts before, but they'd been small and harmless compared to these monsters.

Gabriel's hat had vanished overboard and his hair was blowing in the fierce wind, but there was no question who was the captain when he bellowed, "Men aloft, down to the deck quick as bedamned! Malek, get your men to safety below! Landers, take the ladies to their cabin, then down to the hold and pump out the water from the hippo pool!"

Having given his orders, Gabriel pivoted and raced to the helm. The ship was pitching so violently that the helmsman was unable to control the wheel and the *Zephyr* was dangerously close to foundering. When Gabriel reached the helm, he added his strength and between them the two men were able to force the wheel to port. The *Zephyr* sluggishly came around to a more stable course.

Obeying his captain's orders, Jason Landers latched on to Constance and Rory. "Below decks *now*!"

He hauled them to the nearest companionway through the chaos that reigned all around them. Everything had happened so *quickly*!

As the three of them half fell down the steps, Rory was struck by several flying objects. Fish! Small fish that must have been sucked up in the waterspout and hurled onto the ship. A little wildly, she wondered whether they would be served for dinner if the ship was still afloat then.

Dodging a silvery minnow, she asked, "Mr. Landers, is the weight of the hippo pond unbalancing the ship?"

"Yes." His expression was grim. "Giant waterspouts are rare, but they can sink a ship without a trace. The captain and I were concerned that the weight of all that water in the pool could be trouble in a bad storm so we have a pump rigged next to it. With the sails reefed, we should be able to ride this out."

"Do waterspouts last long?" Constance asked in an unsteady voice.

"Luckily, no. All we have to do is stay afloat until they fall apart. Now I have to go down to the hold and get that water pumped out before the ship founders," he said briskly. "You two go to your cabin and hang on until the sea is back to normal."

Not waiting for acknowledgment, he spun about and plunged down the next flight of steps, skimming his hand along the railing to keep from breaking his neck.

The ship was still pitching so Rory and Constance hung on to the railing at the side of the landing while soldiers and sailors stamped about overhead and passed them on the steps as they sought refuge below decks. They could hear the banging of objects being tossed around, but the noise diminished as loose items were secured.

Rory took a deep breath, telling herself that the worst was over. Probably. "Thank you for catching me! Even a harem is preferable to feeding the fishes."

Constance smiled crookedly. "If I hadn't caught you, your captain would. He's impressive in action, isn't he?"

"Indeed. How are you doing? I've acquired numerous bruises in unmentionable places, but nothing serious."

"The same here. I'm more padded than you, so I probably bounce better."

Now that she was taking time to breathe, Rory heard the bleats and cries of frantic animals coming from the hold. "I'm going down to the menagerie. Maybe I can help quiet the animals. They must be terrified."

"I'll go with you," Constance said firmly. "I'm almost as good with them as you are. Not to mention that I have no desire to sit alone in our cabin and terrify myself about what might happen."

"Doing something useful should help keep fear at bay," Rory agreed. "Down we go, and hang on to the railings! We don't need broken bones."

Constance flashed a swift, dimpled smile. "Maybe that would diminish our market value."

Rory smiled as she started down the steps, her right hand firmly gripping the railing. The possibility of breaking bones was no joke. Several of Malek's soldiers were nursing injured arms and legs and heads as they made their way below.

She had a moment of panic as she imagined the ship sinking with the two of them trapped below decks, drowning. She drew a deep breath and reminded herself that even if they were on the top deck, they'd still drown. The exact place and time would be merely a detail.

More steps, and the closer they got to the menagerie, the louder the complaints from the animals. They reached the hold only a couple of minutes behind Jason Landers, but already he and some of the animal keepers were setting up the pump to drain the water from the violently sloshing pool. The hippos were making frantic noises, and while they might be pygmies, they were still very large and heavy as they pitched about in their pool. She hoped they wouldn't be injured.

Keeping out of the way of Jason and the

animal handlers, Rory and Constance darted by the hippo tank and into the aisle that ran between the other animal enclosures. "I'll visit the goats," Constance said. "They've always been favorites of mine."

She unlatched the door and slipped inside, latching it behind her again. Then she sank into the hay and opened her arms. The little goats pressed into her, bleating pitifully as she put her arms around them. "Come to mama," she crooned. "You're safe here."

Her cousin made a lovely Madonna of the Goats. Smiling, Rory moved along. Unable to stand in the pitching vessel, the ostriches were huddled together in a corner of their pen. They were mighty mounds of black feathers and they looked seriously annoyed, but there were no apparent injuries.

The lion was pacing back and forth and periodically roared with shivering menace. Rory flinched back. Ghazi was one beast that should be left to the experts!

The little donkeys were not happy, but they weren't as upset as the miniature horses, who churned around their enclosure, sweating and frantic. One was limping.

She was particularly fond of the miniature horses, so she entered their pen and settled down with her back to the wooden grid that made up the front wall. "Come to me, my beauties," she said coaxingly. "This will be over soon, so you mustn't hurt yourselves."

She continued talking softly. First to come was the limping horse. She guessed his fetlock was strained, but nothing seemed broken. He was trembling, but as she stroked his muzzle and mane, he relaxed and folded down against her.

Another horse came over enviously and gave her a solid head butt. "Of course you're worried, little friend," she murmured as she scratched between his pointed ears. "It's been a very difficult morning."

He soon settled down, and it wasn't long until all four of the miniature horses surrounded her. They were safer lying in the straw than standing. The *Zephyr* was still pitching, but perhaps not as badly as it had been.

The men talking by the hippo enclosure sounded less upset now. They must have pumped the water out so that it was no longer destabilizing the ship. She leaned back against the wall and relaxed as she continued to pet the horses. If she had a chance to write more stories, she'd have plenty of new material to draw from!

Chapter 20

The sea was as violent and dangerous as Gabriel had ever seen it, so he stayed at the wheel until the swift, ferocious storm had passed, the waterspouts had collapsed, and the *Zephyr* was steady on her course again. By then, it was mid-afternoon, but he needed to inspect his ship before he ate or rested.

Since it was still raining and he was already saturated to the skin, he didn't bother to change, though he briefly visited his quarters to get another hat. He found The Spook burrowed into his bed, unhappy but safe. He was glad to see that; he was fond of the beast.

When he started his inspection, he found that one of the smaller sails had been ripped beyond repair, but reefing early had spared the other sails and no masts were seriously damaged. A cage of chickens lashed to the deck has been swept away along with an assortment of small objects, but it was a tribute to his crew's knot-tying abilities that more objects hadn't been lost overboard. The fish that had rained down had been collected, and the top deck was on its way to being shipshape again.

Methodically, he worked his way down the lower decks, with a side trip to the cabin shared by the ladies. He frowned when there was no response to his knock. They must be all right, though; he'd seen Jason escort them below decks. Since these particular ladies were curious as cats, he guessed they'd gone exploring after the worst of the storm had passed.

He stopped by the galley and appropriated a chunk of cheese, then continued his inspection. He talked to Malek and his officers and checked out damage, but still no ladies. He reminded himself that a ship had many stray corners, and descended to the hold. There, he found Jason Landers and most of the animal keepers working to repair the hippo pen, which had suffered serious damage.

"Good work, Mr. Landers," he said formally. "I could feel the ship stabilizing as you pumped the water out. We might not have survived if that hadn't been done so quickly."

Jason was as saturated as Gabriel. Dripping quietly, he said, "I'm glad we'd prepared for the worst so the pump was ready to go." He gestured to the pen. "As you can see, the hippo enclosure needs repairs. The poor beasts kept getting thrown against the walls like battering rams. Hard on them, harder on the walls."

"Did they come through safely?"

"Their keepers say so, but they seem upset As you can see, they're huddling in their pen."

The head animal keeper came up to Gabriel, gesturing and talking so quickly that Gabriel had to ask him to slow down. After listening and asking a couple of questions, he said to Landers, "The hippos need water to survive. They can accept a certain amount of seawater, but it should be mixed with fresh water to keep them healthy."

Landers sighed. "A good thing our water supplies are in reasonable shape. Tell him we can do that, and as soon as the pen walls are repaired we can start bringing buckets of water down to splash over the beasts until the pool is full again." He looked over at the large, huddled hippos. "The poor critters didn't ask for this."

"Nor did we," Gabriel said rather dourly. "Do you have any idea where the ladies are?

Not in their cabin."

Landers grinned. "They came down here to help calm the animals, and they did a good job." He waved a hand down the aisle toward the stern of the ship, then returned to supervising repairs to the pen.

Realizing he should have expected this, Gabriel went deeper into the menagerie. He found Constance Hollings first, surrounded by goats. "Miss Hollings?"

She looked up with a smile. Her head scarf had fallen around her shoulders and one of the goats was quietly munching on it. "Good day, Captain! Thank you for keeping the ship afloat."

"I had a personal interest in our survival," he commented. "You may want to separate your head scarf from that little black goat."

She laughed and tugged the scarf away from the creature. "Thank you, I need this to stay respectable."

He asked, "Is your companion in mischief down here also?"

"Try the horse enclosure. Or possibly the little donkeys."

Gabriel did just that and found his lady bright, covered in straw and surrounded by small silver-gray horses. Like Constance, she'd lowered her head scarf. She was leaning back against the wall and seemed to be dozing, so he quietly let himself into the pen. "Lady Aurora?" he said softly.

She opened her eyes and gave him a melting smile. "My captain. I'm happy to see that you've survived the storm intact. Though you squish a bit." She patted the straw next to her. "Join me and rest a moment. I imagine you've been working nonstop all day."

He took her suggestion and sank down in the straw after gently pushing one of the little horses aside. He did indeed squish when he leaned back against the wall in his saturated clothing. "That's what a captain is supposed to do."

Remembering the cheese he'd picked up, he pulled the chunk from his pocket and broke it in two. Offering her half, he said, "You must be hungry. The galley fire was shut down when the ship was pitching so violently, but now that we're steady, the cook is at work again and promises a hot meal."

"Thank you, I'm ravenous!" Keeping the cheese away from an interested little horse, Rory bit into the chunk. "Let me guess. Fish soup with very, very fresh fish?"

He laughed. "I believe you're right. I've heard of the sky raining fish, but never experienced it before. By the time I left the helm, all the fish had been removed from the deck. They should be simmering soon."

"I've never seen anything like those waterspouts," she said with a shiver. "I had no idea they could appear in clusters."

"I counted five today." He ate a bit of his cheese. "That's rare, but not unknown. Several centuries back, a famously violent group of waterspouts rose in the harbor of Valletta in Malta. Several ships sank, a lot of people died, and there was a huge amount of damage."

She shuddered. "How much damage did the *Zephyr* suffer?"

"Surprisingly little. We lost a sail and a cage of chickens, and there are some broken bones and bruised bodies, but it's something of a miracle that no lives were lost."

"We would have lost the imam if not for your quick action." She looked up at him, her gaze stark. "And could have lost you as well."

"Close calls don't count except as dinner conversation." Since they were fairly private here, he moved his hand over to clasp hers in the straw. His voice quiet, he said, "I keep thinking about what might be done to rescue you and your cousin. As soon as we reach Constantinople, I'll visit the British embassy. It's said to be a large one because a number of British visitors come through the city. Since I'm a temporary British consul to Algiers, I'll talk to the ambassador and see if he has any influence in a situation like yours."

"Perhaps, though from what I've heard about the Ottoman empire, its leaders are not particularly concerned with the opinions of Western European countries." She chewed and swallowed the last of her cheese. "The fates of Malek's family, Constance and me, and the crew of the *Devon Lady* are all linked together. I don't know if it's possible to separate out any of us without freeing everyone. Or failing to free anyone."

"You may be right," he said grimly. "But if only some of you can be freed, that's better than none."

Her hand tightened on his. "Don't get yourself killed trying, Gabriel," she said quietly. "I'd rather be in a harem and know you were alive than have my freedom at the price of your life."

He gazed down into her mesmerizing blue eyes and marveled at how quickly she'd come to know him. "I have a feeling that the situation when we reach Constantinople will be volatile. Anything might happen, and success will rest on seizing whatever opportunities arise."

"I'm sure you're good at that." She dropped her gaze. "You're going to be exhausted by the end of the day. Do you think you'd like some company tonight? Late?"

His heart speeded up. "I'd like nothing better, my lady. Just be careful."

"I will." Her smile was rueful. "It would be so much wiser to stay locked in my cabin with Constance. But wisdom has never been one of my talents."

"One of the reasons you're so irresistible." He wanted rather desperately to kiss her, but that could lead to discovery and disaster. Instead, he cupped her face with one hand, falling into her gaze. "I need to return to duty. I'll see you later."

"So you will." Her smile was a private promise.

The fish soup served for dinner that night was excellent. With very, very fresh fish.

Chapter 21

It was near sunset by the time the hippo pen was repaired. Jason didn't speak the same language as the animal keepers who helped him repair the pen, but they were hard workers. He'd be happy to sit down and have a beer with them any day, except he didn't think that Muslims were allowed to drink.

They didn't know what they were missing. Back in his cabin, Jason had a really excellent bottle of brandy that the captain had given him on his last birthday. He saved it for special occasions, and he was pretty sure that surviving the most dangerous storm at sea he'd ever seen qualified as such.

The pen was repaired, and precious fresh water from the ship's supply was being brought down and poured over the hippos. Adding seawater to get the level high enough to make the hippos happy would be easy since they were surrounded by the stuff.

Leaving the menagerie in the capable hands of the Algerian animal keepers, he walked down to the goat pen. He hadn't seen Constance pass him on her way up, though admittedly he might have missed that while working. But, happily, she was still there, surrounded by goats and looking quite content.

Smiling, he unlatched the cage and stepped inside. "Do you need help extricating yourself from your little friends?"

She looked up with the sweet smile that went straight to his heart. "That would be very helpful. I'm so stiff from sitting here and hanging on to the cross boards to keep from being tossed around that I'm not sure I can stand!"

Recognizing an invitation, he extended his hand. She clasped it firmly and came lightly to her feet. The goats decided it was time to play and started scampering about their pen.

"I'm afraid one of the goats damaged your scarf," she said apologetically as she showed him a mangled corner.

"I'm glad he didn't eat more." With reluctance, he let go of her hand. "But the scarf is yours, not mine. It was a gift."

"Thank you." She stroked the silky folds. "I'll cherish it always." The gaze she gave him said wordlessly that it would be a memory of Jason even if she spent the rest of her life as a harem slave.

He opened the door to the aisle, blocking two of the miniature goats who tried to follow her out. When the little creatures were safely locked up again, she paused to adjust the scarf so it covered her head and face.

"I'll escort you to your cabin, Miss Hollings," he said politely.

"Thank you, sir. Though I imagine everyone on board is too tired to plot mischief just now," she said with a weary smile.

"True, but I'm under orders not to risk your safety."

As they headed toward the companionway, he wished he could take her arm, but the captain had impressed on him the need not to be seen touching either of the ladies; anything perceived as immodesty might backfire on them.

Though he understood the necessity, he yearned to treat Constance like a cherished woman of his own kind. To offer his arm, to talk easily with her whenever he wanted. To kiss her discreetly and know that if they were caught, the viewer would be indulgent rather than wrathful.

Instead, he stayed a safe yard away as they climbed and then turned into the passage that led to the cabin she shared with Lady Aurora. As they walked in single file because the passage was narrow, she said, "Your cabin is along here also, isn't it?"

"Yes, though it's more the size of a travel trunk than a cabin," he said with a smile. "But at least I have it to myself. There was quite a bit of shuffling when Malek's men came aboard since his senior officers needed cabins."

"Your cabin is smaller than ours?" she said, mischief in her eyes. "I wouldn't have thought that possible. Can I have a brief look?"

He glanced along the passage but there was no one else in sight. "If you like, but you will not be impressed."

He led her to his door and unlocked it, revealing the room with a flourish. "Behold my castle!" Luckily, he'd left it looking neat because it was too small to allow any amount of clutter.

She peered in. "Goodness, you weren't joking about the size! Is the storage cabinet above your bunk something that can be removed and another bunk added if necessary?"

"Yes, exactly that. A ship needs flexibility." He closed and locked the door. "Just like the temporary cabin that was constructed for Malek Reis in the captain's day room."

She looked up at him and said very softly, "Have you ever wished for a bit of company at night?"

Startled, he said carefully, "It depends on the company. There are some visitors who would be very welcome."

She held his gaze for a long moment, enough to prove that she meant what she was saying. "Perhaps some welcome company might call tonight."

She retraced her steps to her own cabin, but turned and looked at him with solemn hazel eyes before she disappeared from sight.

He took a moment to duck back into his cabin so he could steady his breathing. Was Constance feeling reckless because her future looked so bleak? Whatever the reason, he'd give ten years of his life to have private time with her. To talk. To hold her hand, and maybe even kiss her.

Something, anything, to hold in his memories.

Maintaining the captain's log usually took only a few minutes, but the events of a day with burials at sea and waterspouts took longer. As always, Gabriel worked in his day room since his sleeping cabin didn't have enough space for a proper desk.

He was finishing his entry for the day when a weary-looking Malek came down the steps to the common area they shared. Gabriel wouldn't have been surprised if the other man had only given him a nod of acknowledgment, but instead Malek came over and sank into the chair opposite the desk.

Gabriel cleaned his pen and set it into its stand. "Is there something you or your men need? The worst of the storm damage has been cleared up, but there's bound to be more than we've taken care of so far."

Malek made a dismissive gesture. "Nothing important. Your ship and crew did a remarkable job of weathering the storm. What I want to discuss is what happens when we reach Constantinople."

Gabriel became very still. "How do you intend to negotiate with Gürkan?"

"I've been able to come up with nothing but the simplest of plans. Call on him with two or three of my soldiers. Enough for a proper escort but not so many as to seem threatening.

"Then I'll tell him what gifts I have brought for him in exchange for the release of my family. The large amount of money I've brought, though it's not so large as he would like. The rare and interesting animals for his menagerie. And then I shall grovel." Malek smiled humorlessly. "He'll enjoy the groveling because he'll know how much I loathe doing it."

"Where do the English ladies come in?" Gabriel asked with an edge to his voice. "Did you include them with the animals for his menagerie?"

Malek shook his head. "I promised you that I would try to spare them. They will be the last of the gifts I will offer."

"Damnation!" Gabriel swore. "You said if necessary you'd sell them for the highest price possible to raise more money. Much as I hate that idea, it would be preferable to becoming the possessions of a brute like Gürkan!"

"That is what I thought, but I remembered that my cousin likes fair European women, so offering them to him directly might be more persuasive than merely giving him more money. The golden Lady Aurora will appeal greatly."

When Gabriel swore again, Malek pointed out, "At least they would be able to stay together. I have seen the friendship between them, so sharing the same harem would be some compensation for their continued captivity."

Gabriel felt rage perilously close to battle fever rising in him, but he forced it down. Killing Malek wouldn't help, and being killed by Malek's men would leave his ship without a captain and wouldn't benefit the ladies at all. "Will giving Gürkan two Englishwomen be enough to achieve your goal?" he said tightly. "Surely he holds you responsible for the death of his brother even though you weren't the one who killed him. Will anything less than your death appease him?"

"Very likely not," Malek said calmly. "The last thing I can offer is my life in return for the freedom of my wife and children. That might appease him as nothing else could."

Malek's cool acceptance was chilling. "I realize that Muslims are fatalistic, but I'm sure your family would rather have you alive and with them rather than a martyred sacrifice to their freedom."

Pain flickered in Malek's dark eyes. "I would prefer that also, but it might not be possible for all of us to return safely to Algiers."

Which was true, but Gabriel preferred optimism to fatalism. "Is my death one of the items you're prepared to offer Gürkan? After all, I'm the one who actually killed his brother."

"He doesn't know that. I need you to be ready to take my wife and children home to Algiers before Gürkan can change his mind about releasing them."

Gabriel sighed. "I presume that you know your cousin is a lying, vicious snake who might take everything you have to offer, including your life, and still not release your family."

"I'm very aware of that, but what other choices do I have? Gürkan has Damla and the children in his harem, which is in a grand and heavily fortified palace in the oldest part of the city. The only way my family will be free is if Gürkan releases them voluntarily." Malek shrugged and got to his feet. "I will do what I must do, and I must trust that you will do your part."

"Even if part of the cost is the freedom of Lady Aurora and Lady Constance?"

"Even then," Malek said in a steely voice. "I captured them before you appeared on the scene. They are the currency for buying my family's freedom. Will you take Damla and the children back to Algiers even if your English ladies must spend the rest of their lives in Constantinople?"

At least Malek wasn't enjoying the suffering he was causing, as Gürkan would do. Gabriel admitted to himself that if Rory was his wife and she and their children were held captive, he would do anything to free them.

He hated situations where there was no good solution. Stiffly he said, "I'll convey them home safely if it is within my power. But in return, I will hold you to your part of the bargain we made in Algiers. If it is possible to leave Constantinople with your family, you will free the crew of the *Devon Lady.*" Rory would be glad for that even if she was enslaved herself.

"I will. I left instructions with my steward in Algiers." Malek smiled faintly. "If I'm dead, I'm perfectly willing for them to be freed."

Gabriel got to his feet. "For what it's worth, I intend to call on the British ambassador to see if anything can be done to free the British subjects you've enslaved."

"Call on the British ambassador if you wish. But it will do you no good. European ambassadors have little influence in the Sublime Porte." Malek turned and disappeared into his sleeping cabin, walking as if he carried the weight of the world on his shoulders.

It was a wrenching end to a deeply tiring day. Gabriel dowsed the lamp he used when writing in the captain's log and took another smaller lamp to light his way into his bedroom. Would Rory come? This late, it seemed almost too much to hope for.

But when he entered his room she was there, curled up against the headboard of his bed and reading a book, her gilded hair spilling over the shoulders of her dark robe. He closed and latched the door behind him, unable to take his eyes from her. Rory lit up his life as nothing and no one ever had.

"You look exhausted," she said softly as she uncoiled herself from the bed and walked into his arms.

He embraced her as if he were drowning and she was his lifeline. She was so warm, so present, so *real,* that it was hard to imagine she might be wrenched away from him. But it was equally hard to imagine how he could stop a troop of armed men from carrying her and her cousin away to a place where they might never again see anyone from their own country.

"Malek has been telling me his plans, such as they are," he said in a hoarse voice. "He's prepared to offer everything he has, including his life and your freedom, to get his family out of Gürkan's clutches. And I don't think there is any way I can prevent it."

"There might not be any way," she said in a voice that had only the slightest of tremors. "Not when Malek has the power and we are foreigners in a strange land. I know you will do your best. That is all anyone can ever do."

She raised her face in invitation, and he kissed her with all his churning emotions. His lady bright, a swift shooting star who would soon spin out of his grasp forever.

Her intensity matched his and passion swiftly unfurled between them, building higher and higher until it drowned out all thought and reason. In a few stumbling steps, they came down on the bed together, kissing and caressing as frantically as if the world would end in the next hour. This was not the wondering exploration of the previous night, but the white heat of lovers who were born to be together.

Yet even in the middle of their mutual madness, they did not take the final, irrevocable step that might destroy her.

It was the only thing he could do to protect her.

Chapter 22

Rory had already left, and Constance didn't expect her back any time soon. She'd learned the watches and the ship's bells and knew what time Jason Landers went off watch, so she waited about half an hour after to give him time to return to his cabin.

She was a tangled skein of nerves. Rory was the adventurous one, and it had taken her cousin to point out that as long as they were on this ship, they enjoyed some degree of self-determination. Since she wanted very much to spend time with Jason, she must take advantage of this limited, furtive freedom. The days were running out, and in another week or so, they'd be in Constantinople.

Wanting to act before she lost her nerve, she silently opened the cabin door and peered out. The passage was empty. There were areas of the ship that were always busy, but this wasn't one of them. She closed and locked the door with only a tiny click that couldn't be heard more than a yard away.

Then she soundlessly glided down the passage to Jason's door and scratched on it. He opened the door immediately, a wide, slightly nervous smile on his handsome face as he stepped back so she could enter. The cabin was even smaller than what she shared with Rory, and Jason took up a lot more space.

He closed the door, saying, "Visitors to my humble abode never have to wait long to be admitted because I can open the door from anywhere in my cabin."

Which wasn't quite true, but close enough. She smiled and began to relax. "May I sit on the bunk?"

"You'll have to since there are no chairs," he said wryly.

She perched on one end of the bunk and studied her surroundings. She'd had only a quick glance earlier, but the tiny room was neat, every inch of space was used, and the only personal item was a sketch of a family. His family, she saw, because he was in the middle of the smiling group. "Your family looks happy."

"Mostly we are," he agreed. "That picture was drawn by a cousin who is almost as good an artist as you. You'd like Nancy. And my family would love you."

She smiled a little sadly, knowing they would never have the chance to form an opinion of her. Changing the subject, she said, "I brought you a small present. From a bazaar in India. I don't have many things, but I wanted to give you something to remember me by. Like I have the scarf from you."

"A token from my lady!" He sat down on the other end of the bunk, a yard away. "Thank you."

She handed him the small, fabric-wrapped object. "It's just a little trinket."

"But it's from you." He unwrapped the scrap of calico cloth to reveal a small carved stone hippopotamus. It was painted red with little designs drawn on the exaggerated shape, and it had a happy expression.

She wanted to apologize because it was so silly, no more than two inches long, and . . . silly. But Jason smiled with delight. "What a charming fellow! Or maybe it's a female hippo. Should I call it Constance?"

Relieved, she smiled back. "I'd like to think I'm not shaped like a hippo! How about calling her Harriet?"

"Harriet it is." Jason looked like he wanted to kiss her, but he refrained. Tucking the carving in his pocket, he said, "I'm not able to provide much in the way of refreshments for a visiting lady, but I do have some good brandy. Would you like a glass? Suitably watered."

"That would be lovely," she said. "Definitely watered!" Having a drink would give her something to do with her hands.

He took two glasses and a bottle of brandy from the storage cabinet overhead, then poured a small measure for each of them and stirred in water, more for her than for him. He handed her the drink and raised his glass in a toast. "To friendship!"

"To friendship," she echoed. "And unexpected meetings."

Holding his gaze with hers, she sipped at her brandy. Even watered, it had a kick, but the flavor was very nice.

"Tell me your story about the goat," he suggested. "The one in which I play furniture."

She smiled, liking how he eased the awkwardness of this meeting. "It's just a short story for small children. Blackie, the little goat, is an orphan who was raised with calves. They thought he was small and useless and didn't know what to make of him, so they ignored him. Because he's so lonely, he finally runs away from the cow pasture to seek his own kind."

Looking thoughtful, Jason asked, "Does he succeed?"

"Oh, yes, but not before he meets with donkeys and ostriches and hippos and has a dangerous encounter with a lion. He thinks there is no one in the world like him. . . ." She stopped suddenly as her throat choked. Looking down at her brandy, she said, "I'm exposing myself, aren't I?"

He closed the space between them and wrapped a warm arm around her shoulders. "Everyone wants a home. A place to be with their own kind."

"I've found that with Rory." She wiped at her eyes. "I hope we're not separated in Constantinople. Without her, I will have no one."

His arm tightened. "A heart as warm as yours will create a family wherever you end up."

"I hope so," she whispered.

He brushed a kiss on her temple. She looked up into his strong, honest face, loving the auburn hair and the spattering of freckles across his cheekbones. He was both dear and desirable, an irresistible combination. "I didn't come here just to talk."

His face became serious. "What did you come for?"

Recklessly, she swallowed the rest of the

brandy, hoping for courage. "I'm a widow, and widows traditionally have a certain amount of freedom."

She swallowed hard, horrified by her brazenness but wanting him so much that she was willing to risk utter humiliation. "My husband was old and clumsy and not very interested in me as a wife. I was grateful for that lack of interest. Now I face a future as a slave. For once in my life, I . . . I'd like to lie with a man I desire."

He caught his breath, his eyes widening. "If you are choosing me, it's the greatest honor I've ever known."

"I choose *you,*" she said firmly, feeling more confident. "Only you of all the men I've ever known."

"An honor beyond any I deserve." He took the empty brandy glass from her hand, set it in the bowl of the tiny built-in washbasin, and set his own glass next to it. Then he cupped her face in both hands and studied her, as if trying to memorize her image forever. "You are so lovely," he murmured. "And so brave."

"Not brave at all. But I want you so much." He kissed her gently, then with increasing intensity. It was all she'd hoped and dreamed of. A virile young man she desired, and who desired her.

Already, her heart wept that she could have him for only a handful of days at best. But she would never regret seizing this last chance.

As his hands moved over her, caressing, she said in an almost inaudible voice, "There is just one thing." She needed to speak before she became lost in sensation. "I don't want to have a child. I couldn't bear to have one born into slavery."

He winced. "A child of mine born into slavery. No, that won't happen, I swear." He brushed her hair back. "Now let us take advantage of this night, and a bunk so small that we'll have to be ingenious to make it work!"

As he drew her into his arms, she laughed the way he'd intended. He was right about the size of the bunk and the care and ingenuity required for them to come together. But that didn't mean that lying with him wasn't as wonderful as she'd dreamed and more. In this narrow bunk, she discovered passion, and love.

No one could take these memories away from her for as long as she lived.

Chapter 23

The *Zephyr* sailed into Constantinople at dawn, and most of the ship's complement was on deck watching as they entered the city's vast harbor. Byzantium, Constantinople, Istanbul, a city of legend and many names. Veils of mist floated above the water and the first rays of sunshine gilded towers and minarets to gold.

Rory and Constance were both at the bow, modestly dressed and swathed in their head scarves. Rory was painfully aware that the relative freedom of being on a British ship was almost at an end. She and Gabriel had spent their secret nights in talk and sensuality and sometimes sleeping in each other's arms. She felt so close to him that it was hard to imagine how actual intercourse could draw them closer. Though she would love to find out.

She cast a glance to her left, where Gabriel was looking at the crowded harbor.

His controlled face was unreadable, but when he felt her gaze and returned it, she saw despair in his eyes.

But there could be no emotional displays in public. He said calmly, "We've left the Strait of Bosphorus and are entering the Golden Horn, the harbor of Constantinople. It's a drowned river valley and one of the finest harbors in the world." He gestured at the endless stretch of ships and piers and warehouses ahead. "All the treasures of the east and west flow through here."

"I thought once it would be interesting to visit the city. I never expected to do so under these conditions." She tried to keep her voice cool, as a brave, indomitable British lady should, but didn't think she was very successful. In a matter of hours, she might be dragged away from the world she knew and the man she had come to love.

Not that she had said those words to him. Her freedom might end here, but his didn't. Perhaps someday he'd meet another woman he could love, and he shouldn't be cursed with guilt because Rory had loved him and he had been unable to save her.

Constance was in a similar state. She stood to Rory's right, her tension palpable despite the swaddling head scarf. On her right was Jason Landers, his expression grim. Like Gabriel, he was very carefully not touching his lady.

Malek stood apart from the Britons, his gaze bleak. He had to know how long the odds were on retrieving his wife and children, but he would carry through on his determination even if it destroyed them all.

The number of his men who also watched their approach to the city was a reminder of the power Malek held. The city around them magnified that power. It was the *Zephyr* and her crew and passengers who were the foreigners here, with only the limited safety that Constantinople was willing to grant them.

Such bleak thoughts. Rory returned her focus to the brilliant, ancient city. It had seen civilizations come and go and been the capital of two great empires. When she'd first sailed into Bombay and Athens, she'd been almost jumping up and down with excitement. Now mostly she felt fear and regret.

Maybe she and Constance daren't touch their men, but surely they could touch each other. She laid her hand over her cousin's. Constance's fingers were ice cold. Rory's were much the same.

Her cousin squeezed Rory's hand back. Whatever was ahead of them, Constance would probably deal with it better than Rory. Constance had already survived so much with grace and resilience. Rory prayed the two of them would end up in the same harem, because she was going to need her cousin's strength.

A pilot boat brought customs and health officials, then guided the ship to a berth. As soon as the *Zephyr* was docked and cleared, Malek pushed himself away from the railing and turned to Gabriel.

"I assume that, like me, you are in a hurry to get started. My lieutenant, Mülâzım Boran, is a native of this city. He will hire a carriage and guide you to the British embassy. I will take two of my men to Gürkan's palace and beg the favor of an audience." Face like granite, Malek offered his hand. "You have been a good friend, Hawkins. For an unbeliever. May Allah favor your endeavors."

After a hard handshake, he turned and walked toward the gangway that led down to the pier. Gabriel watched him leave, and knew that Malek was not optimistic about how his meeting with his cousin would go.

Malek was likely a fool — and perhaps the bravest man Gabriel had ever met.

Gürkan's palace was as lavish and grand as

Malek remembered. A fortress built long ago to defy all enemies, it had been expanded in more recent generations and furnished lavishly to flaunt the wealth and power of its owners.

Malek's grandfather had grown up here, a lesser son who had joined the army, done well, and settled in Algiers. Now Gürkan ruled in the family palace, exercising the deadly power and caprice of a sultan with less power, but more cruelty.

Malek had thought this visit might be only paying his respects and asking for a future meeting, but instead Gürkan said he would grant an audience today. He must be keen to play the last moves in the game they'd engaged in for half their lives.

Not unexpectedly, Malek and his two soldiers were disarmed and left to cool their heels in the least grand of the reception rooms. They were not offered refreshments despite the increasing heat of the day. Malek bore the insults stoically. They were mere pinpricks, scarcely worth noticing.

Finally, Malek was called for his audience. His men were not allowed to accompany him. That was not a good sign, but again, not unexpected.

The reception hall had ceilings four times a man's height and was richly decorated with polished marble and towering columns. Gürkan greeted his visitor from a carved, gilded chair intended to mimic a throne. His layered robes of velvet and gold-threaded fabrics screamed that this was a rich, arrogant man.

Malek had heard that his cousin aspired to join the powerful council of advisors called the Divan. For the sake of the empire, he hoped the viziers would reject him.

A beautiful serving girl, probably a concubine, wielded a great plumed fan of ostrich feathers to waft cooler air over her master. Less alluring were the ten heavily armed guards watching the visitor with bloodthirsty eyes.

Though a few years older than Malek, who was not quite forty, Gürkan looked regrettably healthy. Malek bowed deeply. "I rejoice to see you again, cousin, and in such good health." He'd rehearsed the courteous lies beforehand so that he could speak with a straight face.

Gürkan inclined his head sardonically. "I cannot say the same of you, cousin. The years weigh heavily on you."

It was an opening. Malek said, "I grieve for the absence of my wife and children, cousin. I know you enjoy the company of beautiful women and children and understand why you are loath to relinquish them, but they are needed in my home. So I have brought many gifts to console you for the sadness you will feel when they are gone."

Gürkan perked up. "You have brought me the ransom I requested? I am impressed. I thought the amount far beyond your means."

"It was not easy, but my greatest desire is to please you." So many lies when Malek's real desire was to hack Gürkan into small pieces and feed him to Ghazi, the young lion.

Instead, he bowed again. "Though I was not able to raise quite the sum you requested, I have brought other rare gifts to compensate for that lack."

He sank to one knee in front of Gürkan and, with a flourish, produced his first gift from the velvet bag he carried. "First a priceless antique clock from France that plays music so the gilded figures can dance." He reached under the clock for a quick wind of the mechanism, then offered it with both hands.

Made of precious metals and gorgeous enamels, it was an exquisite piece of craftsmanship that would bring a high price in any European market. Malek had acquired the clock in the first phase of his piracy and kept it because of its beauty. He'd given it to Damla on the first anniversary of their marriage because she loved the music and dancing figures. When she came home again, she'd scold him for giving it away. He looked forward to that.

Gürkan took the clock in both hands because it was heavy. The lord and lady, dressed in the rich style of the French court, danced to the bright tune. Then Gürkan hurled the clock to the marble floor. It shattered, pieces of the enameled figures and glass clock face skittering across the floor. Eerily, the music continued to play until it reached the end of its cycle. "Heathen trash! It is forbidden to use the human figure in Muslim art. You insult me by offering such a gift."

Malek's rage almost overwhelmed him, but he called on every shred of control because losing his temper would certainly be fatal. He bowed deeply. "My apologies. I had hoped such a trinket would please your wives."

"How much money did you bring?"

Malek told him. He'd hidden the vast treasure in Hawkins' ship and would not hand over a single gold coin until he was sure Damla and the children would be freed.

He continued, "I've also brought rare and

valuable creatures for your menagerie. A pair of pigmy hippopotami, perhaps the only ones in the empire. A magnificent young lion, a matched team of silver gray miniature horses and a special chariot, perfect for your sons. And also . . ."

Gürkan cut him off with sudden fury. "That is all? An insufficient ransom and a few beasts? Hardly enough to compensate for the loss of my favorite new concubine. Your Damla lacks beauty, but after I trained her, she has proved adept at all amatory arts. She has begged me not to allow you to take her away should you come seeking her. She says she cannot bear the thought of lying with any man but me."

Though he knew that was a lie, Malek almost gave in to his annihilating rage at the words. That was what Gürkan wanted.

It was time to play his last cards. *I'm sorry, Hawkins.* "I have heard tales of your masculine prowess, Gürkan. That is why I chose my last gifts so carefully."

He lowered his voice dramatically. "I have brought you two British women of high birth. One is a stunning golden-haired maiden who is daughter to a great lord. Her beauty is beyond description, and she is a virgin." *And you damned well better not have changed that by having her in your bed, Hawkins!*

Having Gürkan's attention, Malek continued, "She is accompanied by her lovely fair-haired cousin, the great lord's niece. Though she is a very young widow, I'm told she is already a mistress of sensuality."

Gürkan's eyes were glittering. "They are here on your ship?"

"Yes, but you'll not have them until we can arrange an exchange."

Gürkan leaned back in his throne chair and smiled with vicious pleasure. "The women sound interesting, but there will be no exchange, my stupid, gullible cousin! After your woman wrote her letter to you, I had her strangled along with the two brats. I will not have such tainted blood in my harem."

It took a moment to understand the shocking words. Then agonizing grief blazed through Malek. Maddened with pain and with nothing left to lose, he lunged at Gürkan, wrestling his cousin from the chair, then slamming him with his fists and knees and howling with rage as he tried to kill the other man with his bare hands.

Gürkan screamed and clenched his groin, blood streaming from his face. Before Malek could throttle the monster, his cousin's guards rushed forward and dragged him away, then slammed him to the marble floor. Malek fought back with every dirty fighting trick he'd ever learned, hoping he'd hurt them before he died.

But he was not granted the mercy of death. "Don't kill him!" Gürkan screamed as four guards hit and kicked their prey. "I want to keep him alive. He must *suffer*!"

Face twisted with pain, Gürkan staggered to his feet and lurched to his captive's side. Malek was pleased to see that his cousin was bent over from the damage to his genitals, his nose was broken and bleeding, and he'd have black eyes and massive bruises. The damage was far less than he deserved, but better than nothing.

"Your family died quickly," Gürkan growled, "but you will go into my black hole until you rot and rats gnaw your bones!" He spat into Malek's face with bleeding lips.

"Take him away!" Gürkan said to the four guardsman who had captured Malek. To the other half-dozen guards, he said, "Go to the men who came with him and give them beatings, but not so badly that they can't stagger back to their ship. Tell their fellows that their master and his family have died like dogs, and the ship must sail by noon tomorrow, or I will have it impounded and everyone on board imprisoned."

Malek was half unconscious, but as he was dragged from the throne room, he wondered dispassionately how long it would take him to die.

Perhaps, Allah willing, Hawkins would be able to escape with the English ladies. He hoped so.

Chapter 24

Gabriel was grateful for Malek's guide. Compact and heavily bearded, Boran had a quiet air of authority. Besides knowing his way around the great sprawling city, he spoke some English and good French. As they made their way to the embassy, he occasionally pointed out sights such as the magnificent mosques.

At any other time, Gabriel would have enjoyed the journey through a fascinating new city, but today his attention was on reaching the British embassy. Someone there should be able to tell him the legal situation of Rory and Constance, and if anything could be done to free them. If the embassy could not help, there would be nothing else to do but pray that Malek would be able to negotiate an agreement that would free his wife and children without bringing his English slaves into it.

Maybe when the animals were transferred

to Gürkan's menagerie, the lion would eat him. One could hope.

The British embassy was large, and walking inside was like stepping into an English manor house with numerous people busy about their business crisscrossing the large entry hall. Granted, there were splendid Turkish carpets laid down, but the same was true of English manor houses.

Sitting at a desk near the front door was what looked like a young gentleman of good family who was learning the diplomatic trade from the bottom up. Behind him stood a couple of British soldiers in red uniforms, their eyes alert as they scanned visitors.

Using his most commanding voice, Gabriel presented his consular credentials and asked to see the ambassador. The young man frowned. "I'm sorry, Captain Hawkins, but the ambassador is away for the next fortnight. Is there anyone else you'd like to see, or is this just a courtesy call?"

Gabriel needed to find someone with intelligence and experience. How should he word the request? Direct was usually best. "I'm here to discuss the situation of two wellborn English women who were captured and enslaved by corsairs. Who is the best person to speak with?"

"The ambassador's secretary for special projects," the young man said immediately. "I believe Mr. Ramsay is in." He beckoned to a footman who was on duty. "I'll send someone to see if he's free."

Gabriel couldn't bring himself to sit still, so he paced the entry hall until the footman returned and gave his report. The young receptionist nodded and said to Gabriel, "Mr. Ramsay is free now. If you'll follow Stevens, Captain Hawkins?"

Stevens led him up the stairs and to the back of the building, announced the visitor, then left. When Gabriel entered the office, he scanned his surroundings while waiting for the man working at the desk to look up. Ramsay's office actually showed signs of being in a foreign country. The expected Turkish carpets were supplemented by Ottoman statuary and pottery and even older artifacts. Large maps of the city, the Mediterranean, and the Ottoman empire were pinned to the walls.

Glad that this man might know the city, Gabriel said, "Thank you for seeing me, Mr. Ramsay."

The dark-haired, hard-featured man at the desk looked up, and there was a moment of mutual shock. Gabriel said, "It's been five years since we met in that cellar in Porto.

I'm glad to see that you're alive and well, if not named Chantry."

Ramsay rose and came around the deck to offer his hand with a grin. "When the five of us parted company the next morning, it was acknowledged that we might be using names that don't show up in our family Bibles. But you're still Hawkins, I see."

"Yes, though I admit it's a middle name. There's an additional name in my family's Bible." Assuming his existence hadn't been scratched out by his grandfather.

Ramsay waved him to a seat. "I'll ring for refreshments. Then I want to hear what you've been doing these last years. I gather you're here on a matter of some urgency."

Gabriel sat and began tersely describing how the ladies had been captured and enslaved, and Malek's complicated situation. By the time a tray with tea and Turkish coffee and delicate Turkish pastries arrived, he'd covered the main points.

He stopped talking until the servant left, then asked, "If I were able to get the two ladies here to the embassy, would they be safe until they could return to England?"

Ramsay, who had been listening intently, frowned. "In theory, yes, but diplomatic immunity is not as strong a tradition here as it is in Europe. I know of Gürkan, and he's an extremely powerful man with a reputation for bowing courteously to the viziers and behaving ruthlessly to his inferiors. Which means almost everyone. It's not impossible that he would conjure a mob to attack the embassy, steal away the women, and then burn the place down to cover his tracks. Needless to say, the embassy would not like to be put in that position."

Gabriel sighed. "I was afraid of that. If the women are handed over to Gürkan and put in his harem, would Britain have any success in demanding their return?"

Ramsay shook his head. "Harems are the most personal and private places in any household, particularly for a rich and powerful man. At this point, it's best to see how the meeting between Malek and Gürkan goes." His thoughtful gaze moved to the map of the city. "But if negotiations fail, there might be an unofficial way to help the ladies."

"I hope to God you're right!" Gabriel rose and offered his hand. "I'll let you know how this plays out."

"Please do. We can still hope the ladies will be freed from durance vile with no loss of lives on either side."

Gabriel nodded agreement and left. But as he climbed into the carriage with Boran, he didn't believe that would happen.

The *Zephyr* was quiet after Malek and Gabriel headed off on their missions. Rory and Constance visited the menagerie in the morning, then worked on their current story. As noon approached they decided to stretch their legs and get some fresh air by strolling around the main deck.

"It's a fascinating city," Constance said as she stood by the railing and gazed out over the glittering domes and minarets. Multiple languages floated up from the sailors and dock workers. "So diverse!"

She had her drawing pad and was making quick sketches of the skyline. "I wish we could go out and explore."

"So do I." Rory suppressed a smile and adjusted her head scarf. Since it was possible they could be seen by men on the shore, they were at their most demure.

Jason Landers ambled up to join them. "Would you ladies like to look more closely? I brought my spyglass and the captain's as well."

"Oh, yes!" They each accepted a spyglass happily. The three of them chatted about what they could see, and avoided talk of the future.

Midday was a quiet time. Some of the

ship's crew and Malek's men had gone ashore to sample the delights of an exotic new port. Half a dozen soldiers were on the deck standing guard, but most of the rest were below decks eating, repairing clothing, doing their laundry.

The quiet was disturbed by the sound of marching feet as a company of local soldiers emerged from one of the streets that led to the waterfront. Rory studied them with the spyglass. In their turbans and uniforms, they looked official and dangerous.

She lowered the spyglass, cold fear enfolding her. The soldiers were marching directly to the *Zephyr's* berth.

Because crew members were coming and going, the gangway was down, guarded by two men at the top and two more at the bottom. The company marched to the foot of the gangway and the officer in charge announced himself to one of the guards on the wharf. Frowning, Jason said, "I'd better see what they want."

He crossed to the gangway and was joined by Gadil, Malek's captain of the guard, who could act as a translator. A discussion began, with voices getting louder and louder.

Rory and Constance set the spyglasses aside and moved closer so they could hear what was going on. The word "customs" was repeated several times.

Constance said, "Didn't the ship go through customs when we reached the port?"

"Yes, but the inspection was fairly casual. They may have reason to want to go over the ship more carefully." Though Rory was trying to be reasonable, the knot of anxiety in her chest was growing tighter and tighter.

Jason's voice was very clear when he refused to allow the soldiers aboard. More words were exchanged through the translator. When Jason offered to show the inspection paperwork, he was told they had received information that the *Zephyr* carried contraband.

The customs official produced papers of his own. Gadil frowned as he scanned them. "Mr. Landers, they have authorization to search the ship and say they will bring up artillery and blow the *Zephyr* out of the water if you don't allow them on board."

Jason hesitated, then said reluctantly, "I'll allow ten of them on board. That should be enough men to conduct their search."

His offer was grudgingly accepted, and the captain of the customs men and several of his soldiers marched up the gangway. When they were on deck, the leader stood still and scanned the deck with narrowed eyes. He spotted Rory and Constance and shouted something in Turkish.

With sudden horror, Rory realized this was what the so-called customs inspection was really about. "They're here for us, Constance! Split up and run!"

As she bolted to the left, Constance ran to her right toward the nearest companionway. Peace shattered into shouts and threats. The men who had boarded sprinted after Rory and Constance while the rest of the troop surged up the gangway and onto the ship.

Malek's guards sprang into action and their shouts brought more of them from below deck, but they weren't as prepared as the invaders. When Jason tried to stop the officer in charge, the man smashed his skull with the heavy barrel of his pistol.

Jason collapsed, blood splashing over the ship's deck. Constance had been caught before she could go below, and she screamed when she saw him go down. Rory was also seized before she could get below decks.

As she fought, a heavy net was thrown over her, immobilizing her limbs and making resistance futile. She thrashed and screamed, hoping that some of the people on the wharf would respond, but the gathering crowd kept a wary distance.

A broad soldier tossed her over his shoulder, making it a struggle to breathe. He carried her down the gangway and dumped her unceremoniously into some kind of closed carriage with Constance and two soldiers. Only a couple of minutes had passed from the beginning of the assault to their removal from the ship.

As the carriage whipped away from the *Zephyr* at the fastest speed possible on the busy streets, Rory realized that the abductors must have been sent by Gürkan. The worst had happened, and she and Constance were doomed to a life of slavery.

Chapter 25

Gabriel returned to the *Zephyr* to find his ship recovering from battle. The guards at the bottom and top of the gangway had grim expressions and their weapons ready to hand. He raced up the gangway to discover blood on the deck and battered men being bandaged. Shocked, he snapped, "What the devil has happened here?"

Lane, his second mate, joined him, one arm in a sling. "A troop of official-looking soldiers arrived and said they had orders to search the ship for contraband," he said succinctly. "Mr. Landers wouldn't allow them to board till they threatened to blow the ship out of the water, so he let a few on."

Once again aware of the weight of the alien empire surrounding him, Gabriel said, "It sounds like he didn't have much choice. What then?"

Lane rubbed his forehead, leaving a streak of blood. "As soon as the devils were onboard, they rushed at the ladies while the rest of their troops stormed the ship. There was a bloody great brawl until the ladies had been dragged to shore and carried off in a carriage. It was over almost before it started."

Gabriel felt as if he'd been hit in the gut by a savagely swinging spar. No, this couldn't be possible — Rory should be safe on his ship!

But she wasn't. She and her cousin had been seized by brute force and taken to God only knew what future. He wanted to howl with pain, but a captain must always seem to be in control. "Were there any deaths or serious injuries among our people?"

"No, though Mr. Landers took quite a blow on the head. He was knocked out for a time, but the surgeon's mate just told me he's starting to wake up and doesn't seem to have lost his wits."

"I'll talk to him. Has Malek returned?"

Captain Gadil, head of Malek's guard, was approaching and he heard the question. "That swine Gürkan imprisoned Malek Reis! He may be dead already!"

He gestured to where two of his bloodied soldiers lay on the deck being treated for numerous injuries. "My men who escorted him were attacked and beaten and thrown out on the street. They were told to return to the ship and that we must leave the city by midday tomorrow, or everyone on board will be imprisoned and the ship impounded."

It was another body blow. Gabriel asked tightly, "Was there any news of Malek Reis's wife and children?"

The tough officer's face crumpled. "*Dead!* All dead! Gürkan's captain said that his master had them strangled not long after they were captured."

Gabriel decided to hell with calm and swore with all the furious eloquence of a lifetime at sea. He wanted to invade Gürkan's palace and slice the monster into small, bleeding pieces and feed them to pigs.

But what could he do? He forced himself to take a deep, slow breath and started to consider the possibilities. Assault was useless; even the combined forces of the ship and Malek's guard wouldn't stand a chance. Official intervention by the British embassy would also be useless.

Grimly he realized the only faint hope was Ramsay, one of his companions on that long-ago night of terror and courage. He'd listened with intelligence and sympathy this morning. Maybe, just maybe . . .

Boran had followed Gabriel onto the ship,

so Gabriel turned to him. "Catch the carriage before it leaves, Mülazım. We're going to the embassy again. The ladies are too valuable for Gürkan to kill, and if we act quickly, Malek might still be alive. I'll join you on the wharf in a few minutes."

Boran nodded, his expression grim. "Yes, sir."

Gabriel turned back to his second mate. "Take me to Mr. Landers."

Lane led him down to Malek's cabin. Gabriel understood the bleak practicality of putting the injured man there since Malek might never return.

His first mate had bled copiously from the head wound and had a scarlet-drenched bandage around his auburn hair. The Spook was curled up on the far corner of the mattress, tail twitching and an anxious expression on his long furry face. He was good at offering comfort when times were dire.

Seeing Gabriel, Jason struggled to sit up, but the surgeon's mate shoved him flat again. "Lie still, Mr. Landers!"

Jason obeyed, but his eyes were wild. "Captain, they took Constance and Lady Aurora!" he said raggedly. "I couldn't stop them!"

"With the numbers they had, no one could have. I'm guessing the attackers were

Gürkan's men. Did you hear anything to confirm that?"

Jason took a deep breath, struggling for control. "I heard the name Gürkan mentioned. Captain Gadil was acting as translator so he can tell you more."

"I'll talk to him, then return to the embassy. The man I met with there said perhaps something could be done unofficially. Mr. Lane has the command. Don't try to get up too soon." He touched Jason's shoulder. "All hope isn't gone yet."

Jason exhaled roughly. "I'll see if I remember any prayers."

Gabriel turned and headed up the steps to talk with Gadil. The captain of the guard confirmed that the attackers had surely been sent by Gürkan. Malek's cousin held a high post in the customs service, and it wouldn't have been difficult for him to forge papers and send men to the *Zephyr*.

Having collected what information he could, Gabriel descended to the wharf and joined Boran in the carriage. As they set off again, he said, "Malek told me you're a native of Constantinople. Do you have any ideas or knowledge that might be useful?"

Boran showed his teeth in what was not a smile. "I was once part of Gürkan's guard, until he had my brother unjustly executed. I would have killed the devil swine if I could have met him face-to-face. Since I couldn't do that, I left and traveled to Algiers to beg a position of Malek Reis. I'd met him when he visited his cousin and knew him to be an honorable man. I will do anything to send Gürkan to the hell he deserves."

Gabriel felt a spark of hope. "Knowing Gürkan's household will be vital. Come into the embassy with me while I meet with Mr. Ramsay."

Now to find if Ramsay could work miracles.

Gabriel swept into Ramsay's office, with Boran a step behind. "Sorry to interrupt you again, Ramsay," he said bluntly. "But the situation has turned catastrophic."

Ramsay's eyes narrowed and he set his papers aside. "Tell me."

Swiftly, Gabriel explained what had happened to Malek and the abduction of the English ladies. He ended by asking, "What kind of unofficial help can you conjure up? Mülazım Boran here is second in command of Malek's guard, and he was once part of Gürkan's household."

Ramsay offered Boran his hand. "Excellent. Knowledge of the household is vital if anything is to be done, Mülazım."

Brow furrowed, Ramsay moved to the large map of the city on the wall. After a moment of study, he tapped a location. "This is the site of Gürkan's palace, in the heart of the old city. It was built as a fortress centuries ago, and there is no way to attack it directly to free your prisoners. Unless you know otherwise, Mülazım?"

Boran shook his head. "It would take a full assault with artillery, and even that would likely take days to succeed."

"Someone would be bound to notice an artillery bombardment," Ramsay said dryly. "But there might be another way. This is a very ancient city, and below the surface are cisterns and pipes and sewers that go all the way back to the Roman emperor Justinian. These days, most of those structures are unused and largely forgotten, and the odds are decent that there's a way to break into the cellars of Gürkan's palace from below. Mülazım Boran, do you know of any such passage?"

Boran frowned as he thought. "Not of my personal knowledge, but it was said in the guardroom that there was a secret way to leave the palace from the cellars."

Gabriel caught his breath. "If there's a secret way in, perhaps we could strike quickly and be away before the deadline for leaving the city."

Ramsay pursed his lips. "It's possible, though it will be difficult. The crucial first step is finding that cellar entrance. I know a man who is very familiar with the labyrinth of tunnels below the city. He might be able to help us."

"Is Siçan the tunnel rat still managing to escape justice?" Boran asked with interest. "He helped me leave the city for Algiers."

"The man in question had his hand cut off for theft, which made it harder to steal things himself," Ramsay explained. "So he took the name Siçan, which means rat, and became a master of thieves with connections to half the illegal activities in Stamboul. He's spent years exploring what lies beneath the city. His knowledge is available for a price, and he has no love for the great lords of the court."

The spark of hope Gabriel had felt earlier brightened. "Then let's find him!"

Ramsay opened a tall wardrobe and pulled out a pair of voluminous Turkish robes. He tossed one to Gabriel. "Put this on. A European will be too conspicuous where we're going."

Gabriel obeyed. "You routinely keep robes around for undercover missions?"

Ramsay's brows arched. "Doesn't every-one?"

For the first time that day, Gabriel really smiled. Yes, there was hope.

Chapter 26

Once in the carriage, the nets around Rory and Constance were removed and they were blindfolded with the head scarves they'd been wearing. They were jammed together on the hard seat, and there was comfort in that closeness. Rory found her cousin's hand and gripped hard. Constance squeezed back. At least they were together.

The jolting ride involved twisting streets and many turns, but wasn't very long. They made a last turn and jostled to a stop inside a walled area that smelled like a stable yard. She and Constance were pulled roughly out of the carriage and frog-marched indoors. Based on the distance they walked, the structure was large and complicated, possibly a series of linked buildings.

Eventually, a few guttural sentences were spoken and they were transferred into the custody of different captors. More walking, until finally they were halted in a room fragrant with rose petals. The head scarves were removed and one of their looming escorts bowed and said, "The new Frankish slaves, Valide."

Grateful for the Turkish lessons they'd had, Rory blinked and looked around. In front of them sat a sharp-featured and richly dressed old woman who was studying the new arrivals with distaste.

Rory knew that the highest-ranking woman in the Ottoman empire was the Valide Sultan, the mother of the reigning sultan. She had great power and presided over the royal harem. Was the same title applied to the mother of any great lord, or did Gürkan think himself so grand that he applied it to his own mother even though the title was incorrect? She guessed the latter.

Besides the Valide, the richly furnished room held four tall, powerful African men dressed in Turkish livery. They had to be eunuchs since they were in the harem. Two attended the Valide; the other two had brought the captives in.

The Valide said in badly accented French, "Your names?"

Eyes cast down demurely, her cousin said, "Constance, my lady."

Looking submissive was wise, so Rory did the same. "Aurora, my lady."

"Englishwomen, I'm told," the Valide said musingly. "The first English females in my harem. Other than that, nothing special. Take them to the hammam and clean them up; then have them examined for purity."

Rory said, "My lady, I am virgin, but my cousin is a widow."

The Valide snorted. "A pity." She waved a hand in dismissal.

Once more Rory and Constance were marched away by their expressionless guards. The hammam baths were at the opposite end of the large harem complex. Outside the entrance, they were turned over to a brisk middle-aged woman who led them into a gorgeous room with a high domed ceiling, a fountain in the center, and beautifully patterned tile.

Eyes wide, Rory gazed around her. She'd heard of the glory of Turkish baths, and this one lived up to the reputation. She might be a slave, but at least she'd finally be clean after weeks on shipboard with limited water.

The proprietress gestured for them to strip off their garments, then turned them over to several young female slaves, who scrubbed, steamed, and cleaned them head to toe. Then the two of them were laid out on marble tables and a burning paste was applied to their body hair, even in the most intimate places. Rory and Constance were horrified and in pain, but their attendants made gestures to indicate the procedure would be over soon. When the paste was washed off, their bodies were as hairless as infants. This was how Turkish men wanted their women to look? Apparently.

After that ordeal, they were led to a perfumed pool large enough to hold a dozen women without crowding. Their giggling attendants were thoughtful and thorough, clicking their tongues at the bruises Rory and her cousin had sustained during their abduction.

The attendants particularly enjoyed washing and brushing out the new arrivals' hair. Constance's soft, dark blond tresses were admired, but they adored Rory's bright gold locks. She suspected that her life on the Barbary Coast would have been simpler if her hair were merely brown.

After the new arrivals had been dried, the brisk older woman took them one at a time into a side room to check the state of their hymens. Rory gritted her teeth and accepted the humiliating examination. What would have happened if the examination had shown her to be less than "pure"? She suspected that could have been disastrous. She understood now why Gabriel had been adamant about limiting their intimacy.

Gabriel. She closed her eyes against stinging tears. She must not think too much about him or she would fall apart entirely.

After the examination, they were given light robes and returned to the quarters of the Valide. The old woman ordered, "Take clothes off!"

Constance flushed, so Rory whispered, "This will be over soon."

Knowing that Rory had endured naked exhibitions in front of potential owners, her cousin took a deep breath and complied. When they had stripped, the Valide rose and circled around them with a frown and an occasional poke. "Open mouth!"

Rory complied, feeling like a horse being examined at a fair. The Valide approved of their good teeth, and liked Constance's full figure more than Rory's slim build. Rory's hair was a plus, though. The Valide fingered it with interest and muttered, "Healthy."

Finally, the evaluation was over and they were dismissed. Outside the Valide's quarters, they were met by a petite and strikingly pretty European woman a year or two older than Rory. She had tobacco-brown hair and was exquisitely groomed, and she offered a friendly smile. Speaking in English with a charming French accent, she said, "I am Suzanne and was given the task of guiding you because I am also European."

"How fortunate your English is so good!" Constance said. "My name is Constance, and my French is not as good as your English."

Rory introduced herself also. "Thank you for guiding us. It's all so confusing!"

"It won't take you long to become accustomed to harem ways," Suzanne assured them as she led the way out to a vast open courtyard. "It's a very comfortable life. After I show you around and explain how things are done, I'll take you to your quarters so you can rest. It has surely been a tiring day for you."

"Suzanne, will it be possible to have the garments we wore when we were brought here restored to us?" Rory made her eyes look large and sad, which was easy. "The gowns were gifts to me and my cousin from my mother. They are all we have left since we will never see her again."

Suzanne clucked sympathetically. "They are not suitable to wear in the harem and you'll not want for fine clothing, but I'll see what I can do. Now come view the gardens, the schoolrooms for the children, the fountains, the dining rooms."

As they set off, Rory studied the harem

walls. They were at least a dozen feet tall and topped with metal spikes. "Has anyone ever escaped from here?"

"No. Why would a woman wish to leave?" Suzanne said as she led them through the vast courtyard, which was lush with palm trees and flowers. "Here she is safe and well provided for."

Rather than a large open space, trees and shrubs and low walls were used to divide the courtyard into many areas rather like outdoor rooms. Tiled benches and fountains invited lounging, and Rory saw a number of women doing just that. Some sipped coffee or tea, and one group was sharing a water pipe. Under another cluster of palms, a young woman played a stringed instrument and several others danced gracefully.

The harem inhabitants glanced up to study the newcomers, then returned to what they'd been doing. All were attractive, well dressed, and well groomed. Rory supposed that cultivating one's appearance was a major activity in the harem. "What do ladies of the harem do with their time?"

"Oh, many things! We talk, we play games, we feast, we visit with the children." A longing expression touched Suzanne's face. "Sometimes we leave the harem to picnic in the country or even to visit the bazaar. That is rare, but it's great fun. We're heavily guarded for protection, of course."

"Don't you get bored?" Rory asked.

That look of longing showed again. "Sometimes life is a bit slow," Suzanne admitted, "but we are safe and cared for. It's more than most women know."

Rory had the sense that the Frenchwoman was doing her best to accept her fate, but would prefer freedom. "This is indelicate, but how does Gürkan choose his bed-mates?"

Unoffended, Suzanne said, "My master likes to try new women when they arrive, but unless you become a favorite, you'll see little of him." She glanced at Rory apprais-ingly. "Since you are a virgin, you'll be given training before you are summoned to his bed. With your golden hair, you might be lucky enough to become a favorite."

The thought made Rory gag. Seeing her expression, Constance drew Suzanne's at-tention by asking, "Since I'm a widow, what might I expect?"

"He might never summon you, but I was told you are well skilled in the arts of love, so he might wish to see if that's true." She shrugged. "Favorites are summoned by him regularly, but there are some women who never visit him."

Constance's eyes widened a little at mention of her amatory skills. Rory guessed that Malek had been trying to make his captives sound more interesting to Gürkan. She asked Suzanne, "Are we free to go wherever we wish within the harem? I am often restless at night and would like to explore these beautiful gardens by moonlight."

Suzanne frowned. "After the last meal of the day, we retire to our quarters. Women caught outside their rooms later in the evening are punished. Harem guards patrol the courtyard through the night."

A young girl approached with a tray holding goblets of a pink fruity drink. Suzanne gestured for them to take one. The drink was pleasantly cool and sweet.

As Rory sipped the beverage, she wondered what the odds were that Gürkan would leave them alone. Given the effort involved in abducting them, she feared that he would feel compelled to rape them at least once.

She shuddered, thinking of the tender intimacy she'd shared with Gabriel. The thought of being touched in those now hairless private places by a monster like Gürkan made her ill.

There was a thought. Could she make herself throw up on him at the right time?

It was worth a try.

Her ever-active imagination spun vivid images of rescue and escape. Maybe an earthquake would shatter the walls of the palace and they could flee in the confusion. Or perhaps Gabriel could find a hot-air balloon and swoop in to rescue them.

She gritted her teeth. In her stories, she could do anything, but realistically, this was her new life. She must come to terms with it, or go mad.

As they circled back around the way they'd come, they heard the sound of a small child weeping behind an iron-barred door. Frowning, Constance said, "That poor child. Does it need cuddling?"

Suzanne sighed. "That is a sad case. A widow and her two children. Her husband was a relation of the master's and after he died, Gürkan took them in since they were destitute. But there was bad blood between the men, so the woman and her children are locked in private quarters until Gürkan decides what should be done. I have no idea what will become of them."

The crying subsided and a woman's soothing voice could be heard speaking in the Arabic dialect of Algiers. Rory came alert. Surely this must be Malek's wife, Damla, and their children! Later, she would come by and speak through the bars.

"Now let me show you your quarters," Suzanne said. "Because you are new and cousins, you will share a room. Likely that will change when your status is determined, but you will be comfortable here. If you need something, ask me or one of the eunuchs."

"Thank you," Constance said. "You've been so kind."

Suzanne smiled and said graciously, "When you become used to our ways, you'll be content, I'm sure. I will see you later."

She escorted them to the door of their quarters, then left. The room was not unlike the one they'd shared at Malek's, though the furnishings were more sumptuous and instead of having a small private courtyard, they had the freedom of the whole harem. But they were no longer sustained by the hope that Rory's parents would ransom them.

With an ache that pierced her heart, Rory sank down on one of the low beds. "Gabriel and Jason will be going mad."

Constance settled on the other bed, biting her lip. "I pray Jason wasn't hurt too badly. There was so much blood!"

"You know that head wounds bleed very freely. I'm sure he'll be all right," Rory said encouragingly.

"But we will never know," Constance said in a choked whisper before she buried her head in her hands. "I never really believed it would come to this!"

"Neither did I. It's still difficult to think that two wellborn Englishwomen can be deprived of life and freedom, yet here we are. We must make the best of our circumstances, or go mad." Rory stood and laid a comforting hand on her cousin's shoulder. "Get some rest. I'll explore more on my own."

"Looking for a way out? I don't think you'll find one." Constance stretched out on her bed and wrapped herself around an embroidered pillow, clutching it in a vain search for comfort. "Or do you want to investigate the Algerian woman and her children?"

"Both." Rory left the room and began wandering apparently aimlessly, as if she were exploring, but it didn't take long to work her way over to the locked chamber.

The child was no longer crying and this corner of the grounds was quiet. Shrubs and trees provided a screen, so Rory stepped up to the bars and said softly, "Damla?"

After a long moment, a dark-haired woman came to the door, her expression wary. "That is my name."

"Are you the wife of Malek Reis of Algiers?" Rory asked in French. "I hope you speak French or English — my Arabic isn't good enough for a complicated conversation."

Damla's face spasmed. "I am his widow," she replied in accented but fluent English. "My lord was to set sail to Stamboul several days after us. His ship was attacked and he and everyone aboard died."

"Well, he was alive this morning," Rory said briskly. "He left our ship early today to call on his cousin Gürkan."

Damla gasped and moved to the iron barred door. She was lovely, with great dark eyes and a face that suggested both softness and steel. "He is here in Stamboul?"

"Yes, Malek has been desperate to get you and the children back. Ever since he learned of your capture, all his time and energy have been devoted to bringing you home."

Damla sank to the ground and covered her face with her hands as she struggled to control her tears. "That evil Gürkan lied to me! I had thought I would know in my heart if my husband was dead, and I didn't feel he was gone. Tell me what has happened!"

"Gürkan set an impossibly high ransom for you, so Malek returned to the corsair trade in hopes of raising enough money to buy your freedom." Rory smiled ruefully. "Which is why I and my cousin are here. We are the most valuable captives he took, but he set a ransom price too high for my family to pay. So he gathered what money he could and took ship for Constantinople with me, my cousin, and a hold full of animals from his menagerie in hopes the sum would be enough to buy your freedom."

Damla bit her lip. "So because of us, you and your cousin are now slaves?"

"I'm afraid so," Rory said bleakly. "Since you are still here, Gürkan must be taking all and giving nothing back."

Damla looked ready to spit. "That would be like him!" Her expression crumpled. "If Malek came here to challenge the lion in his den, he will not leave this palace alive."

Rory felt like wringing Malek's neck herself. His obsessive determination had damaged so many people, not least herself and Constance. But that was not what Damla needed to hear. "Remember that whatever Malek has done, he has done for love of you and his children."

"If only he had succeeded," Damla whispered, her delicate hands gripping the iron bars of her prison.

Feeling deeply sad, Rory rose and said softly, "We'll talk again." Then she headed back to her own quarters.

She opened the door of their luxurious room, thinking of all the other rooms she'd occupied in her traveling days. A few were filthy and vermin infested, a few had been grand, and most had been pleasant enough.

But she was tired of travel, of continual adaptation. She wanted a home she could call her own, and she wanted it to be in England. Why couldn't she have figured that out when she'd been in a position to make it happen?

Because she had wanted to break free of the restrictions of her rank, see the world in all its diversity, and of course then she hadn't found a man she wanted to stay with. She smiled wryly. For all her adventurous imagination, she was a woman like any other, and more than anything, she wanted a lover, a companion, a mate who loved her in all her imperfections, and whom she could love back in equal measure. She'd found him, and now it was too late. . . .

She locked down her regrets and entered the room she shared with Constance. Her cousin was sitting cross-legged on her bed, which was much easier to do in a loose Turkish robe than in European clothing.

She looked up with a smile and gestured at the bundle on her lap. It had been wrapped in the long scarf Jason had given her, and inside were the clothes she'd been wearing when abducted earlier in the day. "Look! Suzanne was able to retrieve and return our belongings!" She pulled the scarf loose and draped it around her neck, petting the fabric as if it were Jason.

Rory's scarf-wrapped bundle was also on her bed. She dropped down and eagerly unwrapped it. "Everything, including our stays?"

"Everything," Constance said emphatically.

Rory pulled out her stays. Well made and lightly padded, they were comfortable to wear. And sewn into a narrow pocket between the breasts was a whalebone busk that she'd paid a bored sailor to whittle into a weapon during the long voyage to India. The sharpened end tucked into a matching piece of whalebone that acted as a scabbard.

She pulled the bone blade from its scabbard and contemplated it. "Remember when I came up with the idea for this to put in a book?"

"Yes, *The Warrior Maiden.*" Constance pulled the busk from her own stays. Because of her fuller figure, this busk was a little broader, its sharpened blade a little more dangerous. "I thought your idea was clever, but I wasn't sure it would work, so you had these made. And they convinced me."

Rory tested the razor-sharp point on her left middle finger. A dot of blood formed. "These were good at stabbing a piece of meat in the galley so I put the idea into the book. But I never thought I might actually use this as a weapon."

Constance slid the two pieces of her busk together so they looked like one long curve of whalebone. "I don't know if I'd be able to actually stab anyone with this."

Rory tried to imagine plunging that lethal bone dagger into another human, and her stomach turned. Then she thought of stabbing it into their evil captor, and her mouth hardened. "I might be able to use it on Gürkan. The man needs killing."

"He does," Constance agreed. "But I'm sure he has enormous, dangerous guards who won't let such weapons near him."

"True." Rory smiled as a wicked thought occurred to her. "Unless the busks can be used as part of a strange European hairstyle?"

Constance gave a smile of unholy amusement. "Trying that should keep us busy for a while."

Yes, and sometimes Rory's wild ideas proved useful. . . .

Chapter 27

Gabriel doubted that he made a convincing Turk, but in the robes and turban Ramsay provided, at least he didn't attract unwanted attention. Siçan lived in a seedy neighborhood not far from the docks. His compound consisted of several old buildings surrounded by a high wall that appeared shabby, but seemed very well constructed, with vicious-looking spikes around the top. A sharp-eyed guard let them through the heavy gate.

Inside, the main house all was spotless and luxurious. The Rat obviously did well out of his illicit activities. Siçan was a wiry middle-aged man with a gleam of wicked mischief in his eyes. The hand that had been cut off was replaced by a hook that would be useful for stabbing fruit or enemies. Gabriel assumed that the master thief took the hook off at night, or he risked killing himself in his sleep.

Siçan greeted Ramsay warmly and called for coffee. After a courteous exchange of greetings, Ramsay introduced Gabriel and Boran, speaking in English. "These gentlemen have a dire problem which must be solved very quickly, and only you might be able to help."

Siçan studied Gabriel and replied in fluent Cockney-accented English. "I trust you are a rich man, because my services do not come cheap. Tell me your problem."

"We need to secretly break into the palace of Gürkan and rescue two Englishwomen from the harem, and also Malek Reis of Algiers, if he is still alive," Gabriel said succinctly. "And it must be done tonight."

Siçan's brows arched in surprise. "Gürkan! One of the wickedest men in the empire. He deserves a slow and painful death. But why is your hurry so great?"

Gabriel tersely explained the situation, including Gürkan's threat to impound the ship and take everyone prisoner if they didn't leave by the middle of the next day. "I'm not sure if he has the authority to do that, but I'm sure he has the malice."

"With his position in the customs department, he could indeed." Siçan frowned. "Much detailed information about the inside of Gürkan's palace is needed."

Boran spoke up. "I served in his guard, sir. It was said in the guardroom that deep in the palace cellars is a secret exit to the ancient tunnels that lie under the old city. I do not know if that is true, nor where such an exit might be, but I know well the palace and grounds outside the harem. I also know the dungeons. There are several, and worst of all is the black hole, a shaft in the earth that is impossible to escape without help from above. If Malek Reis still lives, that will be where Gürkan has put him."

"I know the secret entrance because a black eunuch escaped from Gürkan and he is now in my employ. He does not know the overall palace as well as you, but he knows the routines of the harem." Siçan tapped his iron hook on the table, which showed the scars of similar tapping. "To break into the house is simple. Dealing with Gürkan's guards and rescuing your prisoners is more complicated."

He rang a bell and a scarred servant came in. Siçan rattled off a command in Turkish. Gabriel thought he was asking for two people to be brought to him. Reverting to English, Siçan said, "Black eunuchs are the only males allowed in the harem, so we need several, or men who can be disguised as such."

Gabriel said, "I want to be part of the rescue. If I cover my skin with ink and wear a turban, I should be able to pass if the light is poor. The ladies will trust me, and I'm an experienced fighter if that is needed."

Siçan studied him, still tapping the hook on the table. "The light would have to be poor, but I understand your desire to help. The ladies are dear to you?"

"Yes. One particularly so."

A large, powerful-looking African man and a small woman in a head scarf entered the room and bowed to Siçan. He explained, "Kerem is the harem guard who escaped from Gürkan. He knows how the harem is guarded." Siçan rattled off some questions and nodded at the reply. "Kerem will be glad to be part of this, but he doesn't want to kill any of the harem guards if it can be avoided. Some were friends."

Gabriel knew enough Turkish to reply directly. "There has been enough death. I want only to rescue Gürkan's captives."

Kerem nodded acceptance. Siçan turned to the woman and spoke to her at greater length, then translated. "Esma was a servant in the harem and knows many women who dwell there. She also knows where new slaves are most likely to be quartered." Esma spoke again.

Looking interested, Siçan translated, "There is a Frenchwoman, Suzanne, who was a favorite, but her status is threatened because she has born no child to Gürkan. He is not a good breeder, siring only several daughters, who flourished, and sickly boys, who died young. Esma says that Suzanne is concerned not only for her status, but for her very life. If she can be found, she might give us much aid."

Better and better, assuming Suzanne was willing to help. "What size should the raiding party be?" Gabriel asked. "There are many men on my ship who would gladly volunteer." He glanced at Boran. "Will you, Mülazım?"

Boran's teeth flashed again. "Very gladly indeed."

"Count me in," Ramsay said. "I wouldn't miss it."

Since Ramsay knew Turkish and the city, he'd be an asset, but Gabriel asked, "Will it cause a diplomatic incident if you're caught taking part in something like this mission?"

Ramsay shrugged. "It would, but I won't be caught."

Gabriel envied that confidence, and hoped it was contagious. "What will be the price of this raid, Siçan?"

The thief master considered. "Ten thousand British pounds paid in advance."

It was a very large amount of money, but Gabriel thought that sounded reasonable for a miracle, and the funds were available. He glanced at Ramsay, who gave a small nod.

Gabriel said, "I'll have to return to my ship to get the money, and also to talk to my officers. What more do you need from me, and when must I be ready for the raid?"

"Return here by three hours after sunset." Siçan turned his attention to Boran. "Are any of Malek Reis's soldiers African, and will they be willing to take part in this?"

"There are three," Boran said. "Powerful warriors, and they will be honored to be asked."

A few more details were discussed, and the meeting ended with a plan in place. Ramsay had to return to the embassy, so Gabriel and Boran walked the short distance to the *Zephyr*'s berth. Gabriel asked quietly, "Do you think this plan might succeed?"

"Inshallah," Boran said. "It might. There is much that could go wrong, but God willing, we might rescue your ladies."

Rory. He couldn't bear to think of that bright, free spirit imprisoned. He would pay any price, including his life, to free her and Constance.

When they arrived back at the ship, he found Landers up and about with a clean bandage around his skull. Gabriel gestured for him to come down to the captain's day room. When he explained the planned raid, Jason immediately said, "I want to go, too!"

"You can't," Gabriel said flatly. "The *Zephyr* must leave before noon tomorrow, and if we're lucky enough to rescue the ladies, sooner than that. Make sure we're fully provisioned and with feed and water for the animals since they'll be making the return journey. The ship must be ready to leave at a moment's notice."

When Jason looked ready to protest, Gabriel said sharply, "That's an order, Mr. Landers! If something happens to me, you're the captain and it's your responsibility to get everyone away safely."

Jason drew a slow breath. "Yes, sir. Most of the provisioning has been done, but I'll double-check that it's all in order." He got to his feet. "And by God, bring our ladies back to us!"

It didn't take long for Rory and Constance to arrange their modest possessions in their new quarters. Then they had some bloodthirsty amusement building hairstyles around their whalebone busks. Constance came up with the idea of placing a busk high at the back of the head, then French braiding hair over the structure before allowing their shining locks to fall down from the busk and over their shoulders.

Rory had found a pair of small hand mirrors among the beauty instruments that were apparently necessary for harem inhabitants. She used them to study the hairstyle. "I rather like this. It resembles something my great-grandmother might have worn. All it needs is a bird's nest for decoration."

Constance chuckled. "I'm not sure where we'd find a nest, but there are plenty of flowers out in the courtyard that could be added. Let's go out and look."

"A good idea." Rory was already feeling restless. How would she ever adapt to the confines of the harem?

She led the way outside, and she and Constance amused themselves with surveying the courtyard flowers and deciding which blossoms would best suit their hairstyles. They settled on small blue flowers for Rory and red ones for Constance.

They were about to return to their quarters when Suzanne approached them. Intrigued, the Frenchwoman asked, "Is that how European women are wearing their hair these days?"

Constance looked guilty, so Rory said breezily, "No, we were just playing as a way to fill time."

"Eating is also good for that," Suzanne said with a smile. "I was coming to summon you to the evening meal, which is a pleasant and time-consuming ritual."

"Good!" Constance said. "I'm starving."

"The food here is excellent," Suzanne assured them as she led the way to a spacious dining room that opened onto the opposite side of the courtyard. Women were already gathering and there was much talk and giggling.

Servants held brass trays over their heads and arranged the food on a center table. Harem women collected what they wanted, then sat on cushions by low tables with their friends. No eating utensils, only fingers used with astonishing grace. Rory guessed that was a skill they must learn.

As Suzanne had promised, the food was good, composed of lamb and vegetables and cheeses and bread, and a vast array of sweets. The Frenchwoman sat at a small table with the newcomers and explained the customs and dishes they didn't recognize.

The meal was far better than anything they'd had on shipboard. They would eat well, probably too well; many of the harem women were very large. Too much food and limited exercise were not a good combination. Rory now understood why she'd been considered skinny.

When the meal ended, servants delivered silver pitchers and basins for washing hands. As Rory dried her fingers with a towel embroidered with silver threads, an authoritative eunuch entered and spoke to Suzanne, then stood back with arms folded. The Frenchwoman asked a surprised question and received a curt reply.

Expression tight, Suzanne said, "You are both summoned to Gürkan's bedchamber later tonight. You must go with this man, the captain of the harem guard, to the Valide's chambers, where you will be prepared."

Rory felt as if she'd been kicked in the stomach, and Constance looked ready to faint. "He wants both of us at the same time?" Rory asked, appalled.

"Not just you two. Also the widow of his relative is being summoned."

Constance said in a shaky voice, "This isn't good, is it?"

"No," Suzanne said grimly. "Not good at all."

CHAPTER 28

Boran helped Gabriel carry the heavy gold to Siçan's house three hours after sunset. The group that gathered was sober and determined. Siçan produced robes that he said matched those of Gürkan's harem guards and lit lanterns to guide them through the darkness.

Kerem and Esma had drawn up a detailed floor plan of the house and the harem. Siçan pinned it to the wall and led the team through the planned actions. It was straightforward. Boran and another of Malek's men would go to the black hole deep in the cellars to discover whether Malek was there and alive. If he was, they'd free him and take him down to the exit that led to the underground tunnels.

Kerem, Malek's other two African soldiers, Ramsay, and Gabriel would accompany Esma into the harem and immobilize the real harem guards. Then Esma would see if she could find where the ladies were held. Failing that, she would try to find Suzanne. There would be no killing if it could be avoided, but the expressions of Malek's men said there would be no hesitation if killing was necessary.

If all went well, they'd collect the ladies and withdraw quietly, and the raid wouldn't be noticed until the next morning. By then, the *Zephyr* would be well away.

If things went wrong, by morning they might all be dead.

Gabriel and Ramsay had darkened their English complexions so they wouldn't stand out, then donned the uniforms. When all was in readiness, Siçan led them down two long stairways to the depths of his own cellars. As he opened a concealed doorway into dank darkness, he said, "One reason I bought this house was because it has two different exits into the old tunnels. If I'm ever attacked, my household can escape to a safer place."

Gabriel's nostrils flared as they filed into the old tunnel. The atmosphere was damp and smelly and unpleasant, and the path was rough in places, but Siçan led them unerringly through different turns and levels.

At one point, they traversed a causeway

over a vast underground lake where the ceiling was held up with giant stone pillars. This must be one of the cisterns Ramsay had mentioned. Siçan murmured, "People in the households above lower buckets here to get water. Sometimes they even catch fish."

They finally reached a door set into a darkly shadowed alcove that was so old, filthy, and battered that it was almost invisible even to someone who knew where to look. Siçan produced a massive iron key and unlocked the door, revealing thick brick walls and oppressive darkness. He stood aside and the raiders filed in one by one. The Rat Thief and one of his servants would remain at the door to guide the men home later.

As each raider passed him, Siçan murmured, "Until you return, *inshallah.*"

God willing.

Malek lay in damp and filth in absolute darkness, and wondered drearily how long it would take for him to starve to death so the rats could gnaw his bones as Gürkan had promised. A water skin had been lowered so he could drink.

He should have refused it so he'd die sooner, but his thirst-ridden body betrayed him and he'd drunk it all. He would try to be strong enough to spill the next water skin without drinking.

Half delirious with pain, he didn't think at first the hoarse whisper was real. "Malek Reis, Malek Reis! Are you there?" There was a burst of creative profanity. "Damn you for a foolish donkey, are you *there*?"

Stunned, he recognized the voice of Boran, second in command of his soldiers. Malek staggered dizzily to his feet and snarled, "Drop a rope with a loop in it and haul me from the depths of this hell, and I'll teach you to respect your master!"

There was an excited babble of voices. "Malek Reis! Sir! Do you need help?

"Just drop a damned rope!"

A couple of minutes later, a scratchy rope dropped down by him. As requested, there was a loop at the bottom large enough for Malek to put both his feet in. "Pull!"

The rope spun and he banged against the wall as he was hauled upward, but he didn't care. When Boran and another of Malek's men hauled him over the edge of the black hole, he found himself hugging them and weeping. The tongue lashing could wait till later.

Rory and Constance were escorted to the Valide's quarters, where servants perfumed and polished and gowned them in robes of heavy silk. Luckily, their hair was left alone; the maids preparing them for the night's ordeal seemed to find the style intriguing.

The two of them spoke little for there was nothing to say. They drank tea and silently worried until another woman was brought to the preparation chamber: Damla. Her eyes were huge and dark, and she seemed resigned to being ravished.

The three of them waited for hours as night fell and the harem became silent. Half mad with frustration, Rory wanted to scream and break things, but guessed that would only make her situation worse. So she plotted a story about maidens waiting to be summoned to their ruination, and how they murdered their captors and escaped.

What would the warrior maiden do? Rory thought about the sharpened whalebone busk and wondered if she would have the courage to use it.

Perhaps she might fight to save her life, but if she was merely ravished, it would surely be wisest to relax and endure. Even if she was brave and strong enough to slice Gürkan into small pieces, the cost would be her life, and she wasn't ready to die yet. As long as she was alive, there was hope for freedom.

Finally, a large harem guard with vicious eyes came and collected them with a barked command in Turkish. Damla looked frightened at the sight of him, and Rory wondered what crimes the man had already committed. His elaborate insignia and turban said that he was high in the harem hierarchy, perhaps the captain of the harem guards.

Damla drew a deep breath, then rose and meekly followed the man, so Rory and Constance did the same. A second harem guard fell in behind them and they were escorted into a narrow passageway that ran between the harem buildings and the wall that separated it from the rest of the palace.

The passage ended in a broad door covered with hammered silver. Their escort knocked, then opened the door when a voice called in Turkish, "Enter, Captain Daud!"

The door led into Gürkan's bedroom, a spacious, elaborately furnished chamber with a vast square bed, rich Turkish carpets layered about the floor, and hanging lights that cast eerie shadows. The air was thick with a heavy incense that made Rory gag.

A low table contained silver platters of meats and sweets, with an exquisitely made gold and enamel samovar gently steaming in the middle. All the decadent trappings of a rich, wicked man. When they entered, Gürkan rose from the giant cushion where he'd been lounging with a tall *nargileh,* a water pipe. The scent of tobacco mingled with the incense and made Rory long for cool, clean sea air.

The evil master of this vast household with the power of life and death over all within its walls, was a broad, powerful man now running to fat. He also had bruises and a black eye, and his nose was swollen. Rory hoped fervently that Malek had inflicted the injuries. There was a slight, unnerving resemblance to his cousin, but Gürkan's dark eyes glinted with cruelty above his shaggy beard. Malek could be ruthless if necessary, but he'd never been wantonly cruel.

Damla hissed when she saw him. Gürkan smiled nastily and approached the three women. All of them wore head scarves, and he began by peeling away Damla's. "So this is my cousin's boring little squab of a wife," he said in French. "Hard to imagine why he made such a fuss over losing you. In his place, I'd have been grateful to be rid of you."

Damla's expression was murderous, but she ducked her head and said nothing. Gürkan moved on to Constance, jerking off her head scarf. After scrutinizing her face, he sneered, "You must be the one with a whore's skills since you're certainly not beautiful enough to be the virgin."

He turned to Rory and yanked her head scarf from her face. She stood rigid, fighting the impulse to attack him. His hand cupped her cheek, then stroked down over her breasts. Her skin shrank from his touch. With sudden viciousness, he yanked on a lock of her golden hair.

"Damn you!" She jerked away and he laughed, catching her jaw with one powerful hand and squeezing it painfully. "So at least one of you can talk," he said in French. "You'll all be screaming soon enough."

He turned to Damla. "I will rape you first, taking your husband's honor. Then Daud here will skin you alive. He's very good with his knife, and he does so enjoy the opportunity to practice his skills. He can remove skin from muscle without killing you for a long time. I'll send for your children next."

Damla stared at him with horror while he continued, "While you scream and bleed, I'll take tea to restore myself, and then I'll proceed to the wanton widow. The golden virgin I shall leave for last."

He waved a dismissive hand at Daud.

"Watch and enjoy until I give her to you."

Daud made a deep animal sound in his throat, his gaze hungry. Gürkan grabbed Damla's arm and wrenched her down to the bed. She shrieked and fought him, but he was too large and only laughed at her resistance.

With a flash of absolute certainty, Rory knew he planned to murder them all this night, and Damla's children as well.

Rage blazed through her veins. She would not stand still to be slaughtered like a sheep!

She glanced at Constance and said quietly in English, "He wants to kill us all. Remember the *Warrior Maiden.*"

In that story, her heroine had fought for her life with a chair and other furnishings, and ultimately the bone knife hidden in her busk. What here could be used as a weapon?

The samovar. A metal tube filled with burning coals ran down through the center and had raised the water in the main chamber to the boiling point. This one was only a few feet away and small enough that Rory could lift it.

She looked at the samovar, then deliberately raised her gaze to Constance and flicked her eyes toward the water pipe, a tall brass and glass fixture. The device was a distant cousin of the samovar and also had charcoal and a tube so the tobacco smoke was drawn through water to cool and smooth the taste.

Constance nodded grimly. Their interchange took only an instant.

As Gürkan pinned Damla to the bed, Rory lunged for the table and grabbed the samovar, scorching her hands as she bashed Daud over the back of his head. As he pitched to the floor, she spun around, still swinging the heavy samovar. She rammed it into Gürkan's back, hurling scalding water and coals over him.

As soon as Rory moved, Constance leaped for the water pipe and swung it like a club, hitting Gürkan so hard that the glass bowl shattered and splashed more coals into his face. Stunned, he collapsed on the bed as Damla rolled away so she wouldn't be trapped under his body. He lurched to his feet and pulled a dagger from under his robe. Then he came at Rory with a guttural roar. At the same time, Daud staggered upright.

All five of the people in the room were moving, grabbing for weapons. Rory skittered backward and yanked the whalebone busk from her hair. She'd wondered if she would have the courage to kill. As she pulled the sharpened end from its scabbard, she realized that she was about to find out.

Constance swung the broken water pipe again and smashed it onto Gürkan's hand, the one holding the dagger. It spun away, and suddenly the odds in their favor were much, much better.

As terror transformed into rage, Rory drove in with her razor-sharp bone knife, and found that she was indeed a warrior maiden. . . .

Gabriel and Ramsay followed Kerem and the other two African soldiers into the harem. The soldiers were able to move without a sound, and were expert at silently taking down the real harem guards and gagging and tying them up.

Doors into individual women's quarters were set around the perimeter of the courtyard and some showed slivers of light at the bottom, but no one moved through the vast gardens and the space was eerily quiet. Esma had explained earlier that harem inhabitants must stay in their quarters after dinner on pain of whipping, or worse.

While the imposter harem guards spread out through the courtyard to watch for possible trouble, Esma led Gabriel, Ramsay, and two of Siçan's men to the room she thought two new arrivals would have been given.

Siçan had provided a skeleton key that he said should work on all the doors of the harem quarters. The ten thousand pounds he'd charged was a bargain. Heart in his throat, Gabriel unlocked the door and quietly opened it, raising the lamp high to dimly illuminate the room.

Empty. Neat piles of European clothing were on the beds so the room must be theirs, but of Rory and Constance there was no sign.

Looking worried, Esma led them around the edge of courtyard to an area of larger apartments. She stopped in a corner unit with no light showing and whispered, "Mistress Suzanne, if she has not been moved to lesser quarters."

Gabriel tapped softly but there was no answer. Warily, he unlocked the door and allowed Esma to enter first. The raiders followed, and Ramsay quietly closed the door behind them. The apartment was larger than the one Rory and Constance had been assigned, and they were in a sitting room with another door opening from it. Esma called softly, "Mistress Suzanne?"

"Who is there?" A frightened voice spoke from the bedroom in Turkish. In French,

Gabriel said, "We are English and have come to free the English ladies, my beloved and her cousin. They are not in their quarters. Do you know where they are, Mistress Suzanne?"

Swathed in a luxurious night robe, Suzanne emerged warily, her eyes darting around the intruders. Her expression cleared when she recognized Esma.

"The Englishwomen were summoned to Gürkan's quarters along with another woman who has been imprisoned here," she replied in English, her expression agonized. "Such a summons is most unusual, and . . . and very dangerous. Sometimes a sick madness comes over Gürkan. When that happens, he is capable of *anything.*"

Gabriel sucked in a breath, fighting to control his fear for Rory and Constance. "Can you guide us there?"

Suzanne studied him, her gaze stark. In a rush of words, she said, "I can lead you to his rooms, but in return, take me with you to freedom!"

Esma had been right about Suzanne's feelings concerning the harem. "Gladly, and I'll see you safely back to France if we all survive long enough. Lead on."

"Give me a moment to change." It took her more than a moment, but not much more. She returned in dark, unobtrusive daytime robes and a head scarf, gesturing for the party to follow her. The door to freedom had opened, and she had the courage to bolt through it without looking back.

She led them into the courtyard, around a corner, and then through a door that opened into a long, narrow passage running between the women's quarters and the high outer wall. It was a long walk since Gürkan's quarters were on the far side of the harem and his large suite of rooms was the gateway between the women's quarters and the rest of the palace.

They rounded another corner and saw a hammered silver door at the end of the passage, light visible under it. "Here," Suzanne said in a choked whisper. "Usually the captain of the guard waits here. Daud is a monster, and if Gürkan has invited him inside, there will be murder done tonight." She drew a shaky breath. "If there are screams, no one will come."

Praying they were in time, Gabriel quickened his pace to a near run; the rest of the group raced after him. When they were a dozen feet from the door, it was thrown violently open, banging into the passage wall, and three women bolted out.

The woman in the lead was Rory, and all three of them were drenched in blood.

Chapter 29

At first Rory didn't recognize the people running toward her and the other women, and for a horrific moment she thought it was Gürkan's men come to slaughter them. Then Gabriel's voice called out, "Rory!"

"Gabriel! Dear God, Gabriel!" she gasped and hurled herself into his arms, barely remembering in time not to stab him with her blood-stained busk. His skin had been darkened but his strength and warmth were unmistakable. "Thank heaven you've come!" she stammered. "G . . . Gürkan and his captain of the guard are dead!"

He glanced at the bloody busk before enfolding her shaking body in his arms. "What happened?"

"We k . . . killed them," she said shakily. "All three of us. We killed them!"

Constance was two steps behind her, and Gabriel put out one arm and gathered her in as well. "My brave girls! Now come, we must get out of here as swiftly and silently as possible."

Suzanne moved past them and hugged Damla. "Thank God you're all right, Damla!"

Damla was shaking with sobs, but after a moment she broke free of the hug and started purposefully down the passage. "My children!"

"We'll collect them on the way out," Suzanne promised. "I'm escaping with you."

A tall man with European features under skin darkened like Gabriel's offered Constance his arm. "Come along with me, my lady," he said in a crisp British accent. "We'll be free soon."

Constance took his arm, but said a little shakily, "I'm not a lady."

"No, you're a heroine," he said. "I'm Ramsay, by the way, from the British embassy."

"Such service for British subjects!" Rory said, beyond being surprised.

"It's all unofficial," Gabriel said as he wrapped a supportive arm around her shoulders. "Which is just as well."

A large African man who looked like a harem guard but wasn't dressed quite right touched a finger to his lips for silence, then led the group into the empty courtyard at a near run.

Damla's quarters required only a short detour, and inside they found Malek's son and daughter huddled together in one bed, tearstained and shaking with terror. They greeted their mother with such relief that she had to shush them. "Quietly, my darlings! We are now going to flee this dreadful place!"

Two of the men with Gabriel lifted the children, and the group crossed the courtyard at a fast trot. They were challenged once by a genuine harem guard who swore and drew his scimitar. "Kerem, you traitor!"

Before the guard could shout an alarm, their large African guide whipped out a dagger and hurled it into the other man's throat. As the man collapsed to the ground choking on blood, Kerem retrieved the dagger, wiped it on the fallen guard's tunic, and said tersely, "I knew this man. He was evil."

Rory flinched to see another swift death, but was willing to believe that Kerem had good reason. She clung to Gabriel as they exited the harem and followed a dingy passage to a long, steep flight of steps. Single file, they went down and down around the tight turns of the stairs, and she sensed that soon they were below ground level.

Gabriel put his arm around her shoulders again when they reached the bottom of the steps and started picking their way over a rough, cluttered stone floor. Rory was grateful for the support since she was still shaky. Quietly she asked, "Where are we going? How did you get in here?"

"There are ancient tunnels and sewers beneath the old city," he explained. "Ramsay is the embassy's special operations secretary, which probably means spy, and he's very familiar with the city and its secrets. He knew a man called Siçan the Tunnel Rat, who is a master of the underground ways and who led us here. Siçan is waiting at the exit from Gürkan's palace to guide us the rest of the way."

"How far is it to the *Zephyr*?"

"Not far. We have to leave the city before midday, but we'll be well away by then." A smile sounded in Gabriel's voice. "Ramsay is one of the men who cheated the firing squad with me in Portugal. We are skilled in improbable escapes."

Rory suppressed the urge to laugh hysterically. "I could not have written such an outrageous story!"

"Think of the material you'll have for future books!" Gabriel pointed out.

This time she did laugh. Quietly.

Siçan waited for them at the exit from the palace cellars. Gabriel was relieved, for he'd not have liked to find his way out of these ancient tunnels without help. He said succinctly, "Gürkan is dead."

The Rat gave a small whistle of surprise when the women and children emerged from the cellar exit. "Gürkan is dead and you have rescued your women, I see! Well done. My man took Malek and his men out, and now I'll guide you to your ship. The rescue is not complete until you are safely away."

"How badly was Malek hurt?"

"He'd been beaten, but he was well enough to run," Siçan said reassuringly.

"Alive!" Damla gasped. "My husband is *alive*!"

"So you are Malek's beloved!" Siçan said with interest. "And these must be the children. Allah be thanked for a good night's work! Now come."

Still scarcely believing that they'd succeeded and Rory was unharmed, Gabriel kept one arm around her as he followed Siçan. Ramsay was similarly supporting Constance. The others followed with Malek's men still carrying the children.

Siçan took them back by a different, longer route that brought them to the surface in a narrow alley very near the *Zephyr.* Gabriel's neck prickled as he listened for possible pursuit, but the sewers and cisterns were silent except for the drip of water and the rustle of rats and other vermin that sheltered in this underground maze.

One rat made the mistake of darting at Siçan, who moved with unbelievable swiftness to stab the beast with the metal hook on his right hand. It screamed, and Siçan gave a hard shake that reminded Gabriel of The Spook at work. Then he tossed the rat aside and they resumed their march.

Cool night air was a relief after the interminable journey and an ascent of more broken stairs. Turning to Siçan, Gabriel bent in a deep bow. "You have my most profound gratitude, Lord Rat. Truly Allah guided you this night."

The other man grinned, his crooked teeth bright against his beard. "It has been a pleasure, Captain. I have made a great deal of money, contributed to the death of an evil man, and have a splendid new story to entertain my friends and family. Go with Allah, unbeliever." He returned the bow, then led his people away.

Gabriel smiled back, and turned to take Rory's hand for the last leg of the journey. He quickly released her when she gasped with pain. "You're hurt?"

"I burned my hands when I grabbed a samovar to use as a weapon," she said tersely. "Nothing serious, but I'm not ready to hold hands, I fear."

Trying to imagine the battle that had taken place, he took her arm and led her toward the waterfront. When they were within sight of the *Zephyr,* Ramsay stopped. "It's time for me to go my own way, Hawkins. If you get to London, leave a message on my behalf at Hatchards bookstore. Now that the wars are over, maybe we Rogues Redeemed can meet in person and share lies and drinks."

Gabriel laughed and offered his hand. "I owe you everything, Ramsay. I'll give thanks for your unofficial methods of aid till the day I die."

Ramsay looked wryly amused. "No thanks necessary. I'm still working on redeeming myself."

Rory rose on her tiptoes and brushed a kiss on his cheek. "The work you've done tonight is surely enough to redeem any sinner's soul, Mr. Ramsay."

He caught his breath and touched his

fingers to his cheek. "The scales aren't yet balanced, Lady Aurora, but I'm honored to have helped you and the others to freedom."

As Ramsay disappeared into the darkness, Gabriel and Rory followed the rest of the group through the shadows to the ship's berth. The guards at the bottom of the gangway were grinning with pleasure as the raiders and escapees passed by them.

Gabriel and Rory were the last to ascend. Jason Landers was at the top of the gangway, and when he saw Constance, he grabbed her so hard that he swept her from her feet. She wept, her fingernails digging into his back. "Jason, *Jason!*"

Suzanne was standing in the middle of the deck looking bedraggled, confused, and exultant. Gabriel said to his second mate, "Mr. Lane, this French lady, Madame Suzanne, was vital in helping us complete our mission. Make sure she has everything she needs and take her to the cabin that the English ladies shared so she can rest."

Lane touched the brim of his hat. "Aye, aye, Captain. Madame Suzanne, will you come with me so I can get you settled?"

The Frenchwoman bit her lip. "It has been five years since I've had a choice about anything," she said in a shaking voice.

"Now you have the freedom of the ship,

Madame Suzanne," Gabriel said. "Rest well with all our thanks."

"And my thanks to you for doing the impossible," she said in a low voice as Lane led her away.

Gabriel said, "It's time to cast off, Mr. Landers. Where is Malek?"

"Below in his cabin. He was beaten badly, but doesn't seem to have taken any permanent harm." Releasing Constance, Landers started giving orders to set sail.

Gabriel smiled at Damla. "Come, my lady. Your husband awaits you. Constance, you come, too."

Eyes shining, Damla took both children by the hand and followed Gabriel down into the captain's quarters. Having heard the commotion above decks, a battered and bandaged Malek was limping from his cabin when he saw Damla and his children dashing toward him.

He froze, looking ready to faint. "Merciful Allah! Are you ghosts? Gürkan said that he'd had you strangled!"

"Why would he kill us when he could still use us to torture you?" Damla's voice was calm, but silent tears glinted on her checks as she fell into her husband's embrace.

The children hurled themselves around their father's legs, almost knocking him over in a radiant four-way hug. Malek sank to the deck, crushing his family to him as gulping sobs racked his battered body.

Feeling the reunion was too private to observe, Gabriel led the Englishwomen into his starboard cabin. "I'm staying on deck until we're in the Bosphorus, but you two must rest, and my bed is big enough for both of you." He also privately thought the two of them shouldn't be alone just yet after all they'd been through. "Rory, you know where the key to the brandy cabinet is kept."

"Don't expect to find much left in the bottle," she said with brittle humor.

He pulled Rory into another embrace, hating to let go of her. Clearly feeling the same way, she wrapped her arms around his waist and buried her face against his shoulder. "I can never thank you enough, my captain. I was sure I was doomed."

He smiled teasingly. "I retrieved you as much for my benefit as for yours, my lady bright. Who would be the light and joy of my life if you were still locked in a harem?"

"There is more darkness in me than you knew." She opened her blistered hand to reveal a sharp, bloodstained bone dagger. "In the past, my darkness was in my stories. Tonight, it erupted into my life."

He raised her battered hand and kissed

her fingertips. "That is not darkness but strength, and it won you your freedom."

As Rory blinked back tears, Constance gently took her arm. "Let us drink brandy, wash away blood, and share nightmares, cousin."

Rory managed a watery smile. "As always, your ideas are excellent."

Gabriel watched them disappear into his cabin. Later he wanted to hear the whole story, but for now, he needed to sail the *Zephyr* as far and fast as her sails and good seamanship could take her.

Exhausted but feeling a vast sense of peace, he returned to the main deck. He could feel the *Zephyr* quivering as anchors were raised and sails unfurled. Tide and wind were in their favor, and there was enough moonlight for the ship to edge cautiously out into the main channel. By dawn, they should be out of the Golden Horn and into the Bosphorus.

There were a number of threads to be untangled for the *Zephyr's* passengers, but now, *inshallah,* Gabriel and his friends would have the time and freedom to set the courses for their futures.

Constance lit the lamps in the bedroom, then removed her bloodstained outer robe, revealing the clean layers of silk below. "Where is the brandy kept?"

"In that cabinet there." Rory removed her own outer robe, then sank wearily onto the edge of the bed. "I burned my hands when I grabbed the samovar. There should be salve and bandages in a drawer below the brandy."

Constance clucked her tongue at the sight of her cousin's blistered hands. "I'm glad the water pipe wasn't as hot! Sit still and I'll dress those burns. They don't look too serious, but I'm sure they hurt."

Rory sat passively as Constance cleaned her hands, spread salve over the burns, and wrapped light bandages over the palms. After Constance gave her a glass of watered brandy, she said, "If I ever write another story, it will be about lambs and kittens and daisies. Real adventure is much nastier than I realized."

"Believe me, I understand the impulse to write only sweet stories! I'm envisioning a whole series of books about good-natured pigmy goats." Constance poured brandy for herself, then piled pillows against the headboard and leaned back. "But if not for your imagination and storytelling skills, I doubt we'd still be alive. Think of all the daring escapes our characters have had. As you and I discussed how to save them, we were doing a kind of rehearsal for how we might react to real dangers."

Rory shaped the rest of the pillows and leaned back as she sipped her brandy. "What makes you say that?" she asked, puzzled. "I've never written anything so horrible as we experienced tonight."

"No, but together we developed the habit of thinking about danger and how to deal with it." Constance took a thoughtful sip of her brandy. "I felt like a paralyzed rabbit when Gürkan started threatening us. There was nothing in my mind but fear. Then you said he was going to kill us and mentioned *The Warrior Maiden.* Even more important, you refused to tamely surrender to greater strength. You *acted.* That broke through my paralysis so I could act, too."

"Those two big bullying men didn't expect us to fight back effectively, which was why we took them by surprise," Rory agreed. "It all happened so quickly!"

"You inspired Damla as well. She's the one who got Daud's sword away from him before he could use it."

"Hearing Gürkan threaten her children turned her into a blood-thirsty dervish." Rory glanced at the scarlet-stained busks, which Constance had deposited on a bedside table. "They certainly didn't expect us to be carrying bone knives."

"That's another example of how your imagination saved us. I was doubtful when you suggested that Lady Alana could have carved the busk of her stays into a knife." Constance gripped her brandy tumbler. "If you hadn't said that we must see if it worked, we wouldn't have had our weapons to hand when we needed them."

"I suppose that's why soldiers are drilled so much. So they know what to do when danger threatens." Rory swallowed the rest of her brandy and covered a yawn. "I think I've relaxed enough to sleep. I'm not looking forward to the nightmares, though."

"We'll face them together just as we faced those monsters," Constance promised. "I'll leave one of the lamps burning. I don't want to wake up in darkness."

"Nor do I," Rory murmured as she stretched out and rolled over on her side. She blinked. "Where did The Spook come from? I'd swear he wasn't here when we arrived."

"He has the magical ability to travel through solid doors, I think." Constance scratched the cat's head before dowsing all but one of the lanterns.

She curled up next to Rory and slowly

relaxed to the gentle roll of the ship cutting through quiet seas. By the time the bodies of Gürkan and Daud were discovered, they should be well away.

Constance and Rory had often shared beds in their travels, and after the ghastly events of the night, it was a relief to be with her cousin and best friend. It was also a relief to have a long, warm cat settle between them and purr.

Thank God and the brave men who'd rescued them, they were *safe*!

CHAPTER 30

Constance awoke as dawn lightened the cabin windows. She'd always been an early riser, and she felt surprisingly rested considering that she'd had only a few hours of sleep. Rory was still sleeping soundly, The Spook lying along her side. Rory had always been more of an owl, reading and writing well into the night. The tension lines had smoothed out on her face, and she looked younger and more relaxed.

Constance imagined they'd both have nightmares about the previous night's horrors for years to come, but already the bloody violence seemed distant. Not quite real. For that, she was grateful.

Feeling restless, she slipped from the bed. She wanted to go down into the hold and visit with the animals that were returning home to Algiers.

Well, why not? She considered her costume, which was several layers of Turkish robes in shades of blue. She couldn't retrieve any of her own clothing from the cabin she'd shared with Rory because Suzanne was there. But the Turkish robes covered her far more thoroughly than most European gowns so she shouldn't shock anyone too much.

Amazingly, she still had the head scarf Jason had given her since she'd been allowed to keep it when being prepared for Gürkan. She tied it around her waist like a sash and left the cabin. She liked the ship's quiet at this hour. Soon, the cook would be busy in the galley preparing breakfast and the ship's bells would be ringing for the change of watch, but for now the ship was hers.

The *Zephyr* was sailing smoothly west. *Home.* They must go to Algiers first to deliver Malek, his family, and his men, but in a few weeks they'd be back in England. Though there would be major changes in her life, at least she'd be in a country where she spoke the language and understood the customs.

She smelled the familiar scents of the menagerie as she descended the companionway to the hold. The miniature hippos were sleeping, the tips of their noses above water for breathing. She greeted the small horses and donkeys and ostriches. Even the lion just blinked at her sleepily.

Inevitably, she ended up at the enclosure that held the pygmy goats. They tumbled over each other to reach her, giving happy little bleats. With a contented sigh, she settled down in the straw with her back to the wall and cuddled the small warm bodies. "Blackie, I'm going to make you the hero of a series of children's books."

Oblivious to the honor, he tried to chew her sash. As she gently tugged it from his mouth, a familiar voice said laughingly, "Is this a girl-and-goat party only, or may I join you?"

"Jason!" She half turned in the straw, smiling at him as he entered the enclosure and latched it behind him. When she'd seen him briefly on her return to the ship, he'd been wearing a hat, but now he was bareheaded and bandaged. "How is your head? I was terrified when Gürkan's men attacked you. I . . . I was afraid you were dead."

"Americans have hard heads," he said reassuringly as he slid down next to her and looped his arm around her shoulders. "I bled all over the place and was out for a while, but there was no real harm. How are you feeling? You endured much worse than I did."

She shuddered. "I'm doing my best to

convince myself that Gürkan and his harem never happened. It's hard to believe that it all took place in less than a day."

"Credit goes to the captain for putting together a rescue so quickly. I wouldn't have believed it possible. I wanted to go with him on the raid, but he flat-out ordered me to stay on the ship to take her away if necessary." His arm tightened around her. "Do you want to tell me about what happened to you, or would you rather not?"

She realized that she did want to tell him, so she burrowed under his arm and briefly outlined what had happened from the time they were kidnapped until their safe return.

He gave a soft whistle when she was finished. "Thank God you all worked together so effectively!"

"Credit for *that* goes to Rory. She had the courage to strike back, and she inspired Damla and me to do so as well." Constance drew a deep breath. "Now I'm trying to get used to the idea that I have a future."

"I hope you'll spend it with me." He kissed her forehead. "Marry me, Constance?"

Her heart leaped, then returned nervously to its usual place. "Are you sure that's what you want? We talked about it, but that was just daydreaming about a future that didn't seem possible."

"It wasn't daydreaming for me," he said seriously, his gaze catching hers. "I was praying every night that you and Lady Aurora would be on this return journey. This may be too soon to ask you after all that has happened, but the offer is open until you're ready to give me an answer."

She bit her lip as tears stung her eyes. The time they'd spent together on the outward journey had seemed magical. Not quite real. But the solid warmth of his arm, the deep honesty in his eyes, was very true. She must be no less honest. "Are you *sure,* Jason?" she asked uncertainly. "Don't make a huge mistake because of what we did and said before Constantinople. You don't owe me anything."

Voice soft, he said, "I'm not making a mistake. I think you'll be happy if you marry me. I know *I'll* be happy."

She sighed. "You're a lovely romantic, Jason. But don't forget that I'm illegitimate, a foreigner to your country, and I have no fortune. I'll bring you nothing but myself."

"Coming to America would be a huge change for you," he agreed. "But you don't need a dowry. My family has a fine business and one day I'll be running the Landers shipyard. They'll adore you, and my mother will be glad not to have to deal with a rival mother-in-law. As for being illegitimate . . ." He shrugged. "It's a new land, and a new start for you, and a new name. Your English past won't matter, only your future as Mrs. Jason Landers. If you'll have me."

She swallowed hard, and spoke of an even deeper impediment. "It would be so hard to leave Rory. She's done so much for me. I don't know who I'd be without her. She . . . she's the only person who has ever loved me."

"That may have been true once, but no longer," he said intensely. "I love you, Constance Hollings. I love your sweetness and intelligence and laughter." He grinned. "And I love your beautiful, luscious body, but maybe it's ungentlemanly to mention that."

Hope began bubbling through her. But now was the time to ask the difficult questions. "You can say that as often as you want, Mr. Landers! But how can you not be in love with Rory? She's so beautiful and witty and brave."

"Love is mysterious," he said thoughtfully. "She's a splendid, attractive, and admirable woman, but it's you I saw and thought, 'So she's the one I've been looking for.' And you're the one I have trouble keeping my hands off. In fact . . ." The arm around her shoulders began inching lower and now his hand cupped her breast.

She laughed and clasped her hand over his, moving it over her heart. "I like that you can't keep your hands off me!"

He leaned into a kiss, and the two of them subsided into the straw together. The kiss was long and thorough and lasted until Jason lifted his head and said, "There are two goats standing on my back and one of them is tugging at the bandage."

Chuckling, she pushed herself upright again. He sat up also, displacing the goats.

Constance scratched behind Blackie's ears. "I'm so glad the menagerie is returning safely home. I was afraid my goats would end up as stew if Gürkan had them."

"Not much meat on them," Jason pointed out. "They're much better as pets."

"Do you think Malek might give these four to me? Rory said he had other miniature goats, and I've become so fond of these fellows."

Jason grinned and brushed hay from her hair. "I think that, today, Malek Reis is so happy that he'll grant any requests made of him."

Constance thought of something else she might ask Malek, but the idea vanished when Jason kissed her again. The whole world vanished. Even the goats.

Despite his fatigue and faith in his crew, Gabriel spent the rest of the night on deck, guiding his ship to safety. Since they were heading west, the rising sun was behind them when morning came, the rays creating a golden highway toward home.

He was about to retire and was thinking about where he could find a bed when he saw Malek and his family coming up the companionway from the captain's quarters. He'd seen Damla's face during the escape from the harem and knew her for a dark-eyed beauty, but this morning her lower face was demurely covered by her head scarf, as was that of her small daughter.

Both children were looking around with interest. Guessing that Gabriel wanted to speak with Malek, she gave him a respectful nod, then took the hands of her children and led them forward.

Malek looked like a different man from the driven, angry one who had forced the *Zephyr* and all her passengers on their grim voyage east. Face relaxed, he approached Gabriel and offered his hand. "I owe you many apologies, Hawkins. You have reason to hate me, but I have no regrets because you succeeded beyond my wildest dreams."

Wryly amused, Gabriel shook the other man's hand. "It's been an interesting several months. Now the bill has come due."

Malek fell into step beside him as they began strolling along the port railing. "Your ladies are free, and also the crew of their ship. How much did Siçan's help cost?"

"Ten thousand pounds. A bargain, I thought. The remaining money should be returned to Lady Aurora's mother."

"That is only fair," Malek agreed.

"Are you through with the corsair trade?"

"Yes, I'd not been a corsair for years until Damla was captured." He smiled. "She certainly would not approve if I became a pirate again. From now on, I'm merely a merchant who is known for dealing honestly with his customers."

"Who will inherit Gürkan's fortune and household?"

"His nephew Mustafa. He is an agha in the Ottoman army, a just and honorable man. I don't envy him having to untangle the chaos Gürkan left behind."

"Will Mustafa attempt to take revenge on you and your family?"

Malek laughed. "He's is more likely to send me golden gifts as a thank you. There will be no consequences." His voice turned wistful. "I only wish that I'd been the man to kill Gürkan."

"The women were up to the task." Gabriel covered his mouth for a yawn. "But for now, I'm going off duty. It's been a long day and a half."

"Sleep well, Hawkins. You've earned your rest." Malek glanced around the deck to locate his family, then headed purposefully toward them when he saw they were in the bow enjoying the wind and sea spray.

Gabriel should probably find a hammock below decks, but he couldn't resist going down to his cabin for a quiet look at his sleeping heroines. When he opened the door, he saw that Constance was gone and Rory was sleeping alone, her bright gold hair cascading around her shoulders and half over her face.

Since Constance wasn't there, he gave in to temptation and quietly removed his coat and boots. Then he lay down beside Rory, not wanting to wake her. He laid a gentle arm across her waist. Peace . . .

CHAPTER 31

Gabriel. She'd been having a nightmare about the harem and Gürkan's evil when she felt the weight of his body depressing the mattress. She inhaled his familiar male scent, admired the strong bones of his handsome face, caressed his tangled hair and unshaven jaw. Gabriel, her hero and friend.

Rolling into his arms, she clung to him, frantic with relief and need. "I was so afraid I'd never see you again!"

"I felt the same about you." He drew her into a full embrace, and she molded herself against him, wanting to melt into his bones and never let go. Then she raised her face into a kiss, feeling the accelerating beat of her heart, a spark of desire deep inside her that was swiftly building into raw fire.

Gabriel's mouth was hungry, and she felt matching fire in him. Recklessly, she rolled him over so she was on top, her legs bracketing his as she tore at his clothing. He'd removed his coat and boots, and in one fierce yank, she ripped his shirt down the front so she could glory in his powerful chest and shoulders. So male, so beautiful, so *present.*

After a moment of pure female indulgence, she tugged his shirt free of his trousers and began fumbling with the buttons of his fall. "This time, we don't stop," she said huskily.

When he started to reply, she stopped his words with lips and tongue. She could feel the moment when his control snapped and desire took over. Even more than she, he'd had to exercise discipline throughout this voyage, and at the end, he'd conjured a rescue for her and the other women out of thin air.

Now the need to maintain control was gone, and it was obvious he wanted this culmination as much as she did. He breathed, "You're sure?"

"Utterly sure." She slid her hand under his clothing and across his flat belly. When she clasped his hard, hot length, he groaned and every muscle in his body turned rigid. She reveled in the knowledge that she could affect him so intensely.

The drugging kiss continued as his broad hands caressed her curves from neck to waist to backside. The filmy layers of the Turkish robes were easily tugged up to her waist so his powerful fingers could knead her bare flesh. Skin to skin, with no barriers between them.

"*Now,* my lady bright!" he said huskily. In one swift motion, Gabriel reversed their positions so he was over her, between her legs, his skilled fingers sleeking and teasing her most sensitive places. She bit into the crumpled lines of his ruined shirt to prevent herself from crying out.

During their secret nights in the last weeks of the voyage, they'd learned each other's bodies, how to touch, how to tease, how much pressure was just enough. He used that knowledge to drive her half out of her mind with yearning.

"We've waited long enough!" she gasped as her body began throbbing out of control. "No longer!"

He moved forward into her, and for just a moment there was a sharp stab of discomfort. Then they were fully joined, his hot pulse beating within her as he held still while she adjusted to his weight and heft. This, *this,* was what she had yearned for from the time they'd met! This joining and giving and taking. These moments of intense oneness.

She ground against him, wanting more, and they began to move together in a fierce rhythm of uncontrollable need. This, this, *this* — until she shattered around him, her body convulsing with violent sensations she'd never experienced but recognized with primal feminine understanding. She loved the deep sound torn from his throat as the seeds of life spilled from his powerful body into her yearning womb. Man and woman, together, complete.

As they gasped for breath, raging passion faded gracefully into peace and tenderness. He rolled onto one side, pulling her close. "I can't quite believe that happened," he said unsteadily. "I thought I'd lie down and hold you and we'd rest together. I believed a chaste kiss was part of the plan. If I'd known what would happen, I'd have locked the door at least!"

She laughed quietly, triumphant and happy. "We both needed that. I was very desirous of ridding myself of my virginity, which has caused me nothing but trouble in these last months."

He stroked her damp hair back from her brow. "Indeed. But you must know that I'm enough of a traditionalist that I hope you'll marry me. The sooner the better."

She hesitated as uncertainty tainted her

happiness. She knew the consequences of making love, and for a crazed interval she hadn't cared. But now reason reasserted itself. "Are you sure you want to marry a woman as thoroughly scandalous and difficult as me? I might drive you mad."

"Only in the best possible ways." He smiled as he combed her hair with his fingertips, gently loosening knots. "As soon as I saw the miniature of you in your mother's locket, I was doomed. I knew I should turn down her request for any number of reasons, but I couldn't bear to think of a bright spirit like the girl in that locket condemned to the deadly life of a harem. I never dreamed there could be anything more between us than my mission, hopefully a successful one."

He brushed a kiss on her temple, his lips warm against her pulse. "But now that I know you, the thought of losing you cracks my heart into jagged pieces."

"You are more of a romantic than you let the world see." She lifted his hand and kissed his palm before pressing it to her cheek. "When I first saw you in Malek's garden, I thought *'this man, now.'* You looked like someone who could be trusted to the ends of the earth, and you are. But I don't deserve someone as strong and sane and kind as you!"

"I believe it's the other way around," he said with a deep chuckle. "You're the daughter of an earl, high born and much loved. I'm a disowned and dishonored sailor. I've earned a modest fortune, but nothing compared to the way you were raised. Not to mention that I'm rather a boring fellow most of the time."

"That I'll never believe! You're the only man I've ever been able to imagine having in my life," she said with a smile. "But I'll admit I wouldn't like it if you spent most of your life at sea and only came home for occasional visits." She bit her lip as she thought of dangers of sea and storms and pirates. "In the months between your visits, my horrid imagination would conjure up all the ghastly things that might happen to you."

"I wouldn't like that, either." He wrapped a strong arm around her waist and pulled her against him, skin intimately pressed to skin. "I want you close all the time. Yes, I love the sea, but I also love the land. I've saved some money and I've been thinking of buying a small estate and spending most of my time there. I hoped The Spook would join me since it would be lonely, but I'd much rather have both of you."

The Spook had materialized on the bed again so she scratched his head. He leaned into her hand with a deep purr. "I think The Spook is ready to retire to the land with us. Will you give up the sea entirely?"

"No, I'll keep the *Zephyr* and hire a captain to sail her. I might acquire another ship or two. We'd live comfortably and you could write your books and be as splendidly eccentric as you wish. Constance could live with us if you both want that, but I suspect Jason Landers has other plans for her future." He smiled at her with deep affection. "If I sail anywhere, my lady bright, you'll go with me. So shall we marry?"

Uncertainty dissolved. How could she ever have questioned the rightness of sharing Gabriel's bed and his life? "Yes, my captain! With great gladness. Do you think the imam could be persuaded to marry us right away? Since you saved his life, he might be willing to overlook our unbeliever status."

"Hajji Asad is a tolerant fellow, and I think he'd be cooperative even if I hadn't saved him from the fishes. Constance and Jason might be interested in engaging his services also," Gabriel said thoughtfully. "We'd want to have a Christian ceremony back in England, I think, just to reassure your family. But any man of God will do for me now. If he'll perform the honors, I'll feel most gratefully wed."

She sighed. "I'll miss Constance dreadfully, but the time has come for us to go separate ways. We'll write masses of letters and collaborate on our stories, but having an ocean between us will be hard to adjust to."

"The two of you are family and always will be." He stroked his hand down her bare torso. "I've heard how Turkish women have all body hair removed. Was the process painful?"

She made a face. "I might put that into a book, but I will *not* do it again myself! I must look like a plucked chicken."

He laughed and leaned forward to kiss a bare, intimate part of her body. "A most enchanting plucked chicken. Your golden hair will grow back." Gabriel's playful expression changed. "Damnation, there's something I forgot to tell you that might change your mind about marriage."

"Unless you have another wife, I can't imagine what that would be," she said lightly.

"No other wives. But Hawkins is my middle name. I dropped my family name after my grandfather disowned me. I was christened Gabriel Hawkins Vance."

Lady Aurora Vance. That sounded fine to her. Then her brows furrowed. "Vance. Is your grandfather Admiral Lord Vance, the fierce indomitable hero of sea battles beyond counting?"

"That's him." Gabriel's smile was twisted. "You can see why I was such a shocking disappointment."

"Nonsense, the fact that he's a famous admiral changes nothing," she said briskly. "As a young officer, you did what was right. Forcing you from the Royal Navy was their loss, not yours. And no decent parent or grandparent would throw you away as your grandfather did. The honorable admiral should be *ashamed* of himself!"

"That is not in his nature, but I appreciate your partisanship, Rory." He smiled and squeezed her hand. "Now I think I'd better lock that door, and then we can get some proper rest."

"Lock the door," she said demurely as she petted The Spook, who had materialized on her pillow, "and we'll see what happens after."

He laughed as he rose to turn the lock, then stripped off the rest of his clothing. She loved that she could make him laugh like that. And she loved, loved, *loved* looking at his beautiful masculine body, which would soon be hers as she was his.

Hajji Asad was pleased to be asked to officiate at the double wedding held on the *Zephyr's* main deck. As he said, marriage customs varied across many lands and peoples, but Muslims and Christians worshipped the same God, and honored marriage as a sacred commitment.

The imam worked with Malek and Gabriel to combine some of the words and phrases from both forms of service. Malek offered to give the two brides away, which was appreciated for its irony, but was firmly refused. Rory and Constance were giving themselves away, thank you very much. So instead Malek dowered Constance with four pigmy goats.

Suzanne used scraps of bright fabric to make two pretty nosegays for the brides to carry. The ship's carpenter raised pieces of siding to create a third cabin in the captain's quarters, this one for Constance and Jason. It was small but private, and it contained a cobbled-together bed wide enough for two.

Malek's children were assigned a tiny cabin to share, and Meryem and Kadir squabbled about who would get the top bunk. Damla ordered them to take turns. Immune to orders from humans, The Spook spent most nights on Gabriel and Rory's bed.

The day of the wedding was sunny, with a light breeze that caused ribbons and veils to flutter gaily. Two sailors who were skilled with fiddle and pennywhistle played solemn music as Constance and Rory walked together up the companionway from the captain's quarters, holding hands. Then they separated and moved to the sides of their waiting grooms.

Gabriel had never seen a more beautiful sight than Rory's radiant face. Now that she had made her choice, there were no more doubts, only joyful certainty. She'd chosen him, and he knew she would never look elsewhere. Neither would he, because there wasn't another woman in the world who was her equal.

Voice serene and reverent, Hajji Asad began the service. Some phrases were in Arabic, others in English, but there was no mistaking the vows till death did they part. Gabriel particularly liked the Muslim custom of kissing the bride three times on the cheek and once on the forehead at the end. "Till death do us part," he whispered.

Eyes shining, Rory whispered back, "Amen, my captain!"

Then, to the surprise of everyone but the

imam, Malek and Damla renewed their vows, attended by their children. After the terrible disruption they'd endured, Gabriel thought it fitting.

Then everyone feasted long and well on the best food the galley could produce, the musicians changed the music to celebration — and everyone danced to the sounds of the silver seas.

Chapter 32

January 1815, London

After the *Devon Lady's* captain and crew had been delivered to Dover, the ship's home port, the *Zephyr* sailed on to London. They docked on a crisp, sunny winter morning, port formalities were taken care of, and then it was time to go home.

Rory was almost jumping up and down with excitement as the two carriages Gabriel had ordered arrived at the *Zephyr's* berth. The small one was for Suzanne, who chose to go to relatives in London rather than confront the uncertainties of a France recovering from decades of war. She gave hugs and thanks to her new friends, then glided down the gangway to the waiting carriage, her head high and the gown and cloak she'd sewn on the voyage home as elegant as that of any Parisian lady.

The larger carriage had been ordered by Gabriel to take him and Rory and Constance and Jason to Lawrence House. Rory wrapped the cloak she'd made around her shoulders and skipped down the gangway, one hand skimming the rope railing. "I can't wait to see my parents! With Parliament in session, they'll surely be in town."

She stepped onto the dock, then turned and took a firm grasp on Gabriel's arm when he joined her. "They'll approve of the fact that I'm now a proper married woman. It will be the first thing I've done in years that they approve of!"

Gabriel laughed and pulled her under his arm. "I think that mostly they'll just be very happy to have you home, safe and sound, my lady bright."

Constance, who was on Rory's other side with Jason next to her, said nervously, "I'm not at all sure they'll be happy to have you bringing me along as a previously unknown relative from the wrong side of the blanket."

"They'll be surprised but pleased," Rory predicted. "You are a Lawrence, and it's only right that you be accepted as such."

Jason grinned. "She's a Landers now and there is no question of her acceptance. But I agree with Rory, my love. You should take this chance to meet your relations. We'll be leaving for Maryland in a few days and you won't be back for some time to come."

Rory and Constance exchanged a wistful glance. "But you will be back," Rory said. "And we'll visit you. There's an advantage to both of us marrying sea captains!"

When the carriage deposited the two couples by Lawrence House in Mayfair, Gabriel helped Rory from the carriage, saying, "Aristocratic London being what it is, it won't surprise you to know that Vance House is only about two blocks away."

His lady wife said blithely, "Perhaps we can pay a visit there after we meet with my family."

"Let's have one family crisis at a time!" he said, alarmed.

She gave him a "we'll see" look, then scampered up the steps. "It's been almost four years since I saw my parents. So much has happened!"

Gabriel followed at a slightly more sedate place, with Constance and Jason a step behind. Constance held tightly to her husband's arm. Even if Lord and Lady Lawrence were less welcoming than Rory predicted, Jason was at Constance's side and that was really all that mattered.

Rory banged the door knocker like an impatient child. She'd wanted to surprise her parents, so she hadn't sent a message ahead. Gabriel smiled, thinking how much he loved her enthusiasm and passion for life. Her passion in general.

After several long minutes, the door was opened by a stiff-looking butler. "Greetings, Hastings," Rory said blithely. "Are my parents at home?"

Stiffness vanished as the butler gasped, "Lady Aurora!" His voice rose to a shout. *"Lady Aurora is home!"*

Pandemonium broke out and the vestibule of the house rapidly filled with people. If there had ever been any doubt about how well Rory was loved, it was instantly dispelled. Gabriel, Constance, and Jason stood out of the way while the reunion took place. Lady Lawrence shrieked and fell into her daughter's arms, and the earl was only a few steps behind. Gabriel thought it just as well that none of Rory's brothers and sisters were present, or the hugging might have turned lethal.

As the noise abated, Lady Lawrence blotted her eyes with a monogrammed handkerchief and finally noticed her daughter's companions. "Captain Hawkins, you succeeded in bringing my baby home! God bless you, sir!"

She kissed him with an enthusiasm that strongly suggested whom Rory had inherited her exuberance from.

He bowed. "The pleasure was all mine, Lady Lawrence. I hope you won't mind that I exceeded my commission and married your daughter."

The countess gasped and the earl stared. "Well, you have been busy, Aurora!" said Lady Lawrence. "Come into the drawing room where we can talk and you can introduce your other companions. Hasting, send refreshments in."

One hand on the back of Rory's waist, Gabriel followed her into the gracious room that opened from the vestibule on the right. As their hostess invited them to take seats, Lord Lawrence targeted Gabriel. "I look forward to becoming better acquainted, Captain Hawkins," he said sternly.

"As do I, my lord. But my full name is Hawkins Vance, so your daughter is Lady Aurora Vance."

The earl frowned. "Vance. Vance? Are you related to Admiral Lord Vance?"

"He's my grandfather." Gabriel smiled cheerfully. "But he's disowned me, so you won't have to deal with him."

The earl blinked. "We'll talk later, Captain Vance."

"Don't worry, Papa." Rory settled onto a sofa in a flurry of skirts and pulled Gabriel down beside her. "My husband is the bravest and most honorable of men. You'll like him, and not only because he's taking me off your hands."

"He must be a brave man," her father said wryly, but his gaze on his daughter was very fond.

Completely at ease, Rory gestured to the sofa set at right angles to her own, where Constance and Jason were sitting together. "Mama, Papa, this is my writing partner, traveling companion, and best friend, Constance Hollings Landers, and her husband Captain Jason Landers. He's an American and was Gabriel's first mate."

The earl offered his hand. "An American, you say? A good thing that the Treaty of Ghent was signed on Christmas Eve and our countries are no longer at war, Captain."

"I couldn't agree more," Jason said as he stood to shake hands.

A cart with cakes, sandwiches, and tea appeared with startling speed, pushed by the wide-eyed butler himself. Lady Lawrence thanked and dismissed him and lifted the silver teapot to begin pouring tea. "It's a pleasure to meet you, Mr. and Mrs. Landers."

Then she stopped with the pot in midair

as her gaze rested on Constance. "My dear, you look more like Rory than any of her sisters do."

"It's not an accident, Mama," Rory said calmly. "She's my first cousin. Papa's niece."

After a frozen moment, the earl said, "Let me guess. You're the daughter of my wastrel youngest brother, Frederick?"

"Yes," Constance said in an almost inaudible voice. "Rory said you'd want to meet me, but truly, I'm not here to cause trouble. My husband and I will be sailing for America in a few days."

"My dear girl!" Lady Lawrence rose and crossed the room to give her a swift hug. "Of course, we want to meet you! The only question is why we didn't know about you years ago!"

"Indeed," her husband agreed. "Did Freddie make proper arrangements for your upbringing? He wasn't a bad fellow, but he could be dreadfully careless."

"I doubt that Uncle Frederick did anything beyond mention Constance's existence to Grandmother Lawrence," Rory said tartly. "You know how she hated scandal. Constance's mother died in childbirth, so Grandmother placed the baby with a foster family, leaving a small stipend for her keep until she was eighteen, and told no one else of Constance's existence. My cousin has not been treated well by the Lawrences."

Blushing violently, Constance said, "Indeed, I expect nothing! I was blessed with the gift of Rory's friendship. That is more than enough."

"Nonetheless, the family owes you a dowry and recognition," Lord Lawrence said gravely. "My mother died two years ago, and I regret that she kept her silence about you to the end. But blood is blood and you're clearly a Lawrence. I shall arrange a belated dowry for you, along with my most sincere apologies."

"That is not necessary!" Constance gasped.

"Yes. It is." Clearly, the earl had made up his mind, and that was that.

Gabriel was liking Rory's parents. If she got her exuberance from her mother, surely her fair-mindedness came from her father.

Lady Lawrence returned to her chair. "Aurora, you said Mrs. Landers is your writing partner?"

"Yes, we wrote several outrageous romantic adventure stories together," Rory said. "Aunt Diana in India liked them and said she'd send the stories to a publisher she knew in London. She'd use the pseudonym

Countess Alexander, but give your names as the business contacts. Did anything ever come of that? Is the publisher interested?"

Her mother laughed delightedly. "Your books are the toast of London! Two were published while you were returning from India and being captured by corsairs, and the third is scheduled. I believe that Diana sent six stories, so the public is waiting breathlessly."

"I made sure the contracts were fair," Lord Lawrence said. "Can't trust publishers — they're a low breed."

"But this one knows good stories when he sees them." Lady Lawrence's voice dropped to a whisper. "I couldn't put the books down, though I'm very glad they were published under a false name. I'd never have heard the end of it from the ladies of London if it was known the author of *The Warrior Maiden* is my daughter!"

"Daughter and niece. We worked together, Mama." Rory leaped to her feet and caught her cousin's hands. "We did it, Constance! We did it! We're famous authors!"

"Surely that's *infamous* authors," Constance said with a laugh. "That's a grand incentive for us to keep writing even though we'll have to do it long distance." Releasing Rory's hands, she returned to her seat by

Jason. "I wonder if the publisher would be interested in my children's stories. They're going to feature miniature goats," she added for the edification of her newly acquired aunt and uncle.

"I don't know about that," Lord Lawrence said. "But there's quite a tidy sum waiting for the two of you at Barclays bank. Romantic rubbish sells very well."

"Show some respect, Papa!" Rory said sternly. "You may not consider our stories great literature, but they are not easy to write."

"They're certainly popular with your mother and sister and friends," he admitted. "Though I'm not entirely sure why."

"Because the heroine always gets what she wants," Constance said, then blushed and ducked her head when everyone looked at her.

"Enough of business," Lady Lawrence decreed. "It's time for tea and cakes and for you to tell us everything that happened. As long as it isn't too frightening."

Rory squeezed Gabriel's hand, and he guessed that she was mentally editing the events into a less alarming story. Their adventures in Barbary were described with a lighthearted flourish over the refreshments.

When she finished, Rory swallowed the

last of her tea, then rose to her feet. "After all that talking, I need some fresh air. Come, Gabriel, let's go for a short walk." When her mother started to protest, Rory said reassuringly, "We won't be gone long."

Wary of her motives, Gabriel rose and followed her into the vestibule. As she collected her hooded cloak and he donned his hat, he said, "You want me to call on my grandfather, don't you?"

"Yes," she said, her voice turning grave now that she wasn't performing for her family. "You don't have to, of course, but will there ever be a better time?"

He thought about that as he took her arm and escorted her outside, turning left so they could walk the short blocks to Vance House. "I suspect you're right," he said slowly after they'd turned the first corner. "His anger and disapproval have haunted me since I was a boy. I'll never be entirely free of them, but I'm starting a new phase of my life." He drew her closer. "I'm a married man with a wife and a cat and no longer only a sailor." He smiled down at Rory. "To be honest, I'd like him to see how lucky I've been."

Her smile affirmed that he was doing the right thing. It was time to face the past so he could move into his future. "He may not be in residence, you know."

"Perhaps not," she agreed. "But if he isn't, the next time you choose to beard the old lion in his den will be easier."

Marrying a writer meant that his wife always had something to say. Sometimes that was a mixed blessing.

In far too few minutes, they reached Vance House. The door knocker was up so perhaps his grandparents were in. The brass knocker was shaped like a sailing ship. He gave several crisp raps.

The butler answered the door more quickly than the Lawrence butler had, and he was unfamiliar. Taking the initiative, Gabriel said, "Are Admiral and Lady Vance in? If so, please tell them that Captain Gabriel Hawkins and his wife are calling."

The authority in his voice got them admitted into the small front hall even though they didn't have calling cards. "Wait here, Captain."

Moments later, the butler returned and bowed. "This way, please."

They were led to the small sitting room, as Gabriel had expected. He'd spent a good part of his childhood in this house. When they entered the room, his gaze went immediately to the small, silver-haired woman by the fire. "Grandmother!"

She looked startled, then joyous as she rose and moved across the room, her arms open. "My dear boy, what a sight for tired old eyes you are!" She was warm and soft in his arms, and he realized this moment was worth having his grandfather berate him.

A brusque throat-clearing made him look up, and he saw that his grandfather was sitting in the shadows on the other side of the fireplace. The admiral looked as if twenty years had passed, not a dozen, and Gabriel saw a telltale sagging of the left side of the old man's face. A stroke.

He bowed respectfully. "Sir. I've just arrived in London and wished to present my wife to you. Lady Aurora Lawrence, the youngest daughter of Earl Lawrence."

His grandmother turned to beam at Rory. "And what a lovely wife she is, Gabriel!"

The admiral snorted. "This would be the one they call Roaring Rory Lawrence?"

Gabriel took her hand. "Indeed, sir, it is."

The admiral stood, looking less tall and more fragile than he had in the past. "I suppose that only a scandalous girl would accept you."

"Sir!" Gabriel snapped. "You may say what you wish about me, you may call me a scoundrel if you please, but you will *not* insult my wife."

The admiral gave a creaky laugh. "As quick tempered as you always were. I'll admit she's a handsome wench."

Rory smiled sweetly. "And capable of killing a man twice my size with a sharpened whalebone busk from my stays."

The admiral looked at her in shock, as if unable to determine whether she was joking. Deciding to ignore her comment, he returned his attention to Gabriel.

He was leaning on a cane. For the first time, Gabriel had the visceral realization that his grandfather was human, and aging. Not an angry, implacable god of war. The knowledge dissolved much of his own anger.

He said quietly, "I didn't come here to fight with you, sir. Only to see my grandmother and introduce my wife. We'll leave now and not bother you again. Though I do hope to see more of you, Grandmother."

"Don't go," his grandfather said abruptly. "Walk with me in the garden."

Wondering why, Gabriel said politely, "As you wish, sir."

He opened the door at the back of the sitting room. The garden steps now had wooden railings on both sides. More proof of his grandfather's advancing years.

The garden ran long and narrow between brick walls. At this winter season, it was largely dormant, but the paths and pruned bushes were neat.

As they walked down the central brick pathway, the admiral asked brusquely, "What have you been doing these years?"

"Sailing. Blockade running. A bit of smuggling to people I felt needed the supplies. Nothing you'd be proud to hear about. I acquired my present ship when escaping from Barbary slavery." Gabriel's voice took on an edge. "Though I knew you despised me, it was still a surprise that you wouldn't ransom me out of exile. I'm told the price was quite modest."

"I was too angry," his grandfather said in a throaty whisper. "You were such a promising young man, the best Vance of your generation. I couldn't bear that you threw that away to save the life of a young man who was a nobody."

"A nobody to you, perhaps, but he was my friend. I have no regrets for what I did." Gabriel smiled. "Rory believes I'm brave and honorable, and will defy anyone to say otherwise, even you. Her opinion matters more to me than anyone else's."

"She seems a spirited wench. Did she really kill a man twice her size with a bone knife?" the admiral asked with interest.

"Yes. She's quite amazingly intrepid."

"A good match for you then." They reached the end of the garden path, where a bench was set in front of the wall. The admiral folded down onto the bench, so Gabriel did the same, still not quite sure what this discussion was about.

The admiral clasped his hands on the golden head of his cane, which was shaped like a seagull. "You're heir to the barony now," he said brusquely. "You'll be the third Baron Vance."

Gabriel's jaw dropped. "What of my cousins Edmund and Peter? They were both in line to inherit before me."

His grandfather gave a dry little sigh. "They served with honor in the Royal Navy. And died of it."

Gabriel was silent for long moments as he remembered playing with his cousins, offspring of the admiral's oldest son. Both of the admiral's sons, including Gabriel's father, had died in the service. "I'm very sorry to hear that. They were good fellows."

"They were, and they were good officers." The admiral gave that sigh again. "But you were the most like me. The most independent. The most pigheaded. The most likely to defeat the French if facing overwhelming odds."

Hiding his amazement, Gabriel said, "I've won some sea battles. But none where the fate of Britain was at stake."

"If you'd stayed in the Royal Navy, you might have fought at Trafalgar."

"Lord Nelson managed nicely without me, though he didn't survive the battle." The damned fool man wouldn't have died if he hadn't been wearing all his medals, making a perfect target for a French sharpshooter. Gabriel preferred life to grand gestures. "The past is done with. I'm happy with my life even if you aren't. But I hope that I won't be banned from your house till you die."

His grandfather gave a rusty chuckle. "You're the heir, can't ban you now." After a long silence, he said, in an almost inaudible whisper, "I've missed you."

Could Gabriel say the same of the admiral? No, the old man's anger had always been with him. There was never a chance to miss him. But today Gabriel's view of the past had changed. "There's no need to miss me in the future, sir. And if you find me a disappointment, I guarantee Rory can charm any man out of the sullens."

His grandfather laughed outright. "That

puts me in my place." With effort, he rose from the bench. "Time to go in. I feel the cold in my bones these days."

With wonder, Gabriel realized that he and his formidable grandfather had made peace. There was even a wary fondness between them. He would not have believed it possible.

They returned to the sitting room to find his grandmother and Rory chatting happily away. When his wife looked up at him, he gave her a small nod and a smile.

She responded with her own radiant smile. Rising, she said, "We've overstayed the limits of a proper call, Lady Vance, but I'm so happy to have met you. I hope you don't mind if I call again soon."

"Not at all," his grandmother said, looking younger than when her visitors had arrived. "Good-bye, my dear girl." She kissed Rory, then Gabriel. "You chose well, my lad."

He grinned down at her. "I know."

He said no more until they were outside. "Have I mentioned lately how much I love you?"

"Not since last night," Rory said. "I'm glad to hear that hasn't changed after the events of today."

"You were right to persuade me to come."

He looped an arm around her shoulders. "My cousins have died, and someday you'll be Lady Vance. A mere baroness, but it's the best I can offer you."

"It will more than suffice, my love." She stopped and turned to him, her gaze mischievous. "Can we book a room in a hotel tonight?"

"If you wish," he replied, puzzled. "But don't you wish to stay at Lawrence House?"

She leaned in and whispered wickedly, "I'm not sure I have the courage to ravish you with my parents just a room or two away!"

Laughing, he swept her up in his arms and kissed her for all of Mayfair to see. "I look forward to being ravished, my lady bright!" He leaned his forehead against hers, vastly content as he added softly, "And I rejoice in knowing that I'm the luckiest man in Britain."

"I'm glad you think so," Rory said with matching softness. "But I am surely the luckiest woman."

AUTHOR'S NOTE

I remember as a child singing the "Marines' Hymn" and being puzzled by "from the halls of Montezuma to the shores of Tripoli." Montezuma I got, that being nearby Mexico, but what's this Tripoli business? That's North Africa!

Much later, I found that line referred to the Barbary Wars in the early nineteenth century. (The first was 1801-1805, the second in 1815.) The school history lesson was that the Barbary states of North Africa were pirates who captured American and European ships, held the crewmembers for ransom or sold them into slavery, and demanded tribute as protection money from nations that wanted their shipping to be left alone.

I do not find pirates romantic. They were greedy and sometimes murderous criminals who preyed on the vulnerable. Barbary pirates were the scourge of the Mediterranean from the sixteenth to the nineteenth centuries, and sailed as far as Iceland and even South America. The town of Baltimore in County Cork, Ireland, was famously sacked and virtually the whole population was captured and sold into slavery in 1631.

In the early nineteenth century, when *Once a Scoundrel* is set, many of the larger European nations found it easier to pay tribute to the Barbary states, particularly those countries that were busy fighting the continent-wide Napoleonic wars. The United States, on the far side of the Atlantic, preferred to stay neutral and maintain a healthy shipping trade with European countries.

This did not work out well for the U.S.; Britain was blockading France and didn't want irresponsible colonials selling their goods in Europe. This was a primary cause of the War of 1812 between Britain and the United States.

Barbary pirates were another matter. It wasn't just national pride that made the United States go to war, nor was it the chip-on-the-shoulder testiness of a fragile new country that felt it was being disrespected. The plain fact was that the demands for tribute were so insanely high that the country couldn't come close to affording to buy the pirates off. Hence, the United States went to war.

An excellent and highly readable account of the Barbary Wars is in *Thomas Jefferson and the Tripoli Pirates,* by Brian Kilmeade and Don Yaeger. I recommend it.

It may sound unlikely that a European ship was forced to carry men and a menagerie to Constantinople, but in fact the *USS George Washington* was compelled to do exactly that. Besides having to transport over two hundred extra men, greatly overloading the ship, Kilmeade and Yaeger said there were "4 horses, 25 cattle, and 150 sheep, in addition to 4 lions, 4 tigers, 4 antelopes, and 12 parrots." And the ship had to orient toward Mecca for prayers. Gabriel and the *Zephyr* got off lightly!

Fantasies of harems and polygamy were wildly popular in the West and inspired lush paintings and lascivious writings, and those institutions did exist. But the Koran specifies that multiple wives must be treated with strict equality in economic, emotional, and sexual terms. Which would be both expensive and exhausting! In real life, the clear majority of Muslim marriages were (and are) monogamous. Hence, Malek's devotion to his wife is as true and real as any romance — and I do love a good romance!

ABOUT THE AUTHOR

Mary Jo Putney is a *New York Times* and *USA Today* bestselling author who has written more than 50 novels and novellas. A ten-time finalist for the Romance Writers of America RITA, she has won the honor twice and is on the RWA Honor Roll for bestselling authors. She has been awarded two Romantic Times Career Achievement Awards, four NJRW Golden Leaf awards, plus the NJRW career achievement award for historical romance. Though most of her books have been historical romance, she has also published contemporary romances, historical fantasy, and young adult paranormal historicals.

The employees of Thorndike Press hope you have enjoyed this Large Print book. All our Thorndike, Wheeler, and Kennebec Large Print titles are designed for easy reading, and all our books are made to last. Other Thorndike Press Large Print books are available at your library, through selected bookstores, or directly from us.

For information about titles, please call:
(800) 223-1244

or visit our website at:
gale.com/thorndike

To share your comments, please write:
Publisher
Thorndike Press
10 Water St., Suite 310
Waterville, ME 04901